LIARS, INC.

LIARS, INC.

PAULA STOKES

An Imprint of HarperCollins*Publishers*

HarperTeen is an imprint of HarperCollins Publishers.

Liars, Inc.

www.epicreads.com

Library of Congress Cataloging-in-Publication Data
Stokes, Paula.
    Liars, Inc. / Paula Stokes.
        pages   cm
    Summary: Seventeen-year-old Max, his girlfriend Parvati, and best
friend Pres form Liars, Inc., expecting that forging notes and lying for their
peers will lead to easy cash, but when Pres asks Max to cover for him, it may
be a fatal mistake.
    ISBN 978-0-06-232328-6
    [1. Mystery and detective stories.   2. Conduct of life—Fiction.   3. Missing
persons—Fiction.   4. Dating (Social customs)—Fiction.   5. Adoption—
Fiction.]   I. Title.
PZ7.S8752Li   2015   2014022689
[Fic]—dc23   CIP
                                                                            AC

Typography by Erin Fitzsimmons
15 16 17 18 19 CG/RRDH 10 9 8 7 6 5 4 3 2 1
❖
First Edition

—to DK
for Einstein, for Odd, and for
being so nice to my mom

THE MIDDLE
IS
THE BEGINNING
OF
THE END

December 6th

I DON'T MAKE TO-DO LISTS, but if I did, today's would have gone something like this: 1. get drunk, 2. get laid, 3. go surfing (not necessarily in that order). Noticeably absent from the list: get arrested. And yet here I am, spending my eighteenth birthday with my back against the wall of the Colonel's hunting cabin, two FBI agents prowling the dark with their guns drawn, both trying to get me to confess to the murder of my friend Preston DeWitt.

"It's all right, Max," one of them says. "We just want to talk." It's the nice agent, McGhee.

"How'd you guys find me?" I ask, stalling for time. I push my long bangs out of my eyes with the hand that isn't clutching a gun. To my left, I can just barely make out a razor-thin beam of gray light creeping in under the back door. I debate making a run for it, but it's too far away. By the time I get there and undo the bolt, both agents will be on top of me.

"Colonel Amos tipped us off," Gonzalez says. That's the other agent. He's kind of a dick. "Your little girlfriend ain't as smart as she thinks she is."

My girlfriend, Parvati. The Colonel's daughter. I knew hiding out here was a bad idea.

"Where's Preston?" McGhee again.

"I don't know."

"Did you kill him?" Gonzalez sounds like he's already made up his mind.

"No. Of course not."

The blackness ripples in front of me. One of the agents is moving. I can hear him inching his way across the floor. Slowly, methodically, like I'm a rabid raccoon and he's a guy from animal control.

"Don't come any closer." I wave the handgun back and forth in front of me. "I don't want to shoot anybody."

They probably don't think I'll do it. They're right. I've never shot a gun before. I'm not even sure if I know how. But if there's one thing I learned from spending a year on the streets, it's that people are afraid of weapons.

"Everything is going to be okay, Max." Soothing voice. Another quiet scuff. They're closing in. I have to do something. I point the gun at the ceiling and pull the trigger. Nothing happens. Apparently I *don't* know how. I swear under my breath. Then I remember what Parvati told me. *You just slide the lever and pull the trigger.* I fumble with the little lever on the side of the gun and feel the bullet enter the chamber. I shoot at the ceiling again. Fire erupts from the muzzle. The light fixture explodes and glittering shards of glass rain down on my shoulders. The gun shudders violently, but I manage not to drop it.

The agents mutter four-letter words as they duck and cover. It's all the distraction I need. With my ears still ringing, I lunge for the back door. As soon as I open it they'll be able to see me, but all I have to do is make it to the woods. I can lose them in the trees.

As I throw open the door, I hear shouts. Hoping the feds won't shoot me in the back, I cover the distance between the cabin and the edge of the tree line in just a few strides. It's as black in the forest as it was in the house, but I'm not afraid of the dark or what hides within its shadows. To me, Mother Nature isn't nearly as scary as human nature.

I plunge through the shrubbery, branches clawing at my face and arms. I hear McGhee and Gonzalez behind me, crashing through the brush like angry bears. Lengthening my stride, I propel myself forward. I know these woods. I know where I'm going. The river. These guys aren't superhero TV FBI agents. They won't go over the cliff.

But I will.

I've done it loads of times. Never while being chased, but still, it's easy. Run. Push off. Fall. Sink. Emerge.

Breathe.

The moon shucks off a veil of clouds, illuminating the widening path in front of me. I can see where the trail deadends at a sheer drop-off. Water roars, just out of sight. My tennis shoes crunch gravel as I accelerate. Blood pounds in my ears. Where's Preston DeWitt? I don't know. That's the truth. Not the whole truth, because it's too late for that. Even if I told the feds everything, they wouldn't believe me.

My left foot lands at the edge of the cliff. I push off with all my might, rocketing my body out toward the middle of the river, far away from the jagged rocks below. As I plummet through the crisp night air, I think about whether things might have been different if I had just told the truth from the beginning.

THE BEGINNING

ONE

October 21st

About six weeks earlier . . .

THE TRUTH IS, IT ALL started the day I tried to get detention. I tended to be late a lot and occasionally fell asleep in class, so I usually got it without much effort. Not that week, though. It was Friday, fourth period, when my girlfriend, Parvati Amos, strutted by my desk in a shiny black-and-red dress that looked like a sexy superhero costume.

"I didn't see your name on the list for tomorrow," she murmured, just loud enough for me to hear. Parvati was an office assistant during third period. Between that and writing for the school newspaper, the girl knew everything about everyone.

"Working on it." I had already tried being late to algebra and swearing in Spanish class. For some reason, all my teachers were in a charitable mood that week. Or else they were just too lazy to fill out the paperwork for a detention.

Parvati leaned in as she slid into the chair behind me, just close enough for me to catch a whiff of her vanilla perfume. "Work harder." She was wearing a scarf made out of a bright orange-and-red fabric with gold embroidery. I wondered if she'd taken scissors to one of her fancy saris. She liked pushing the limits with her parents.

I glanced around the room, as if the solution to my problem might lie between the row of pastel file cabinets and the bulletin board featuring cartoon drawings of famous figures from American literature. If I didn't get assigned Saturday hours, my parents would assign me an even crueler punishment—babysitting my three younger sisters. Not only would I end up covered in glitter pen and strained peas, I'd miss my weekly rendezvous with Parvati.

Her dad had forbidden her to see me, but we quickly figured out a way around that. Every Saturday I went to detention and she went to newspaper club. What our parents didn't know was that these activities only took two hours, instead of four. That gave Parvati and me two uninterrupted hours of alone time every weekend. Two hours that I didn't want to miss.

The tinny chorus of Boyz Be Bad's unfortunate hit, "Doll

Baby," interrupted my train of thought.

My English teacher, Ms. Erickson, glared at the class over the tops of her pointy glasses. "Whose cell phone is that? Please bring it to my desk."

"It's mine," I blurted out. Around the room, I heard snickers and giggles. There was no way I, Max Cantrell, boy voted most likely to drop out of school and become a roadie for the all-girl hard-core band Kittens of Mass Destruction, had a Boyz Be Bad ringtone. But Ms. Erickson didn't know that.

I slid out of my seat and started making my way to the front. My eyes skimmed across the rows of students, trying to figure out who it was that owed me big-time.

"Max. Now." Erickson gave me the evil eye. She held out her hand, wiggled her crimson fingernails.

"Coming," I muttered, shuffling the rest of the way up to her desk. I slipped my cell phone out of the center pocket of my hoodie, double-checked to make sure it was turned off, and slid it in the general direction of Erickson's outstretched talons.

She grabbed my phone and made a big show of depositing it into the top drawer of her desk. "You can come get it after school," she said. "You can pick up your detention slip then as well."

Score. I gave her what I hoped was a look of apathy tinged

with frustration and then headed back to my desk.

Parvati tapped me on the shoulder. "Smooth," she whispered.

I peeked back at her. "You have no idea."

She winked. "Oh, but I do."

Resting my head on my desk, I let Erickson's nasal voice fade into the background. I played with the shark's tooth pendant I wore on a leather cord around my neck, poking the sharp point into the fleshy pad of my fingertip. The necklace was a gift from my real dad. It wasn't really my style, but it was all I had left from him and I only took it off to shower and surf. He had been an oceanography professor at UCLA and found the tooth when he was scuba diving during a research trip.

Hands went up around me—Erickson must have asked a question. I focused my eyes on the sleeve of my shirt. She called on Parvati, who rattled off the definition of "irony." What was ironic was that I had to get in trouble to have the thing I wanted most in the world—time with my girlfriend.

I didn't blame her parents for wanting her to stay away from me. She was smart and rich and pretty, and I was none of those things. We both joked that she had only started dating me to piss them off, but sometimes I wondered if it was true. I was decent-looking, tall and thin, with messy brown hair that managed to look cool even right when I rolled out of bed, but I wasn't the kind of guy that girls drew hearts around in the yearbook.

Parvati was gorgeous, though, with skin the color of almonds and eyes so dark that her irises receded into her pupils. She had hacked her waist-length, inky black hair to just above her shoulders at the end of the summer. Sometimes I pretended to miss it—I mean, long hair is totally hot—but the shorter cut fit her feisty personality. She refused to be the half-Indian Barbie her mother wanted her to be.

I imagined burying my face in what was left of her hair, tracing her pillowy lips with my fingers, inhaling the scent of her vanilla perfume. My brain wanted to take things further. Parvati and I hadn't had sex in almost a month, since the Colonel caught us in the family hot tub, called me a despicable little shit, and told me if I ever came back he would kill me. Slowly.

The bell rang and I sat up with a start. Lunch. Parvati was deep in conversation with the girl sitting next to her. "Newspaper stuff," she mouthed, scribbling something in the sticker-covered mini-notebook she carried everywhere with her.

"I'll save you a chair," I said. It was our little joke. Half the school would have killed for our seats in the cafeteria, but no one ever took them. You needed an invitation to sit with the Vista Palisades All-Stars, at the long table right in the middle of the caf. We sat there because we were friends with the school MVP, the football team's star running back—Preston DeWitt.

I grabbed my books and headed for the hallway. I had barely made it out the door when I felt a hand clamp down on my arm. I looked down. Red fingernails. I turned, expecting to see Ms. Erickson, thinking maybe somehow she had figured out I lied about my phone. But it was Cassie Rhodes, first-team all-American breaststroke champion. (At least that's what her T-shirt said.)

I pulled loose from Cassie's formidable grip and gave her a look. I didn't think she'd ever spoken to me before.

"Max, right?" she said.

"Yeah. So?" I looked down at her arm again. She had the muscles of a marine. I knew swimming was good exercise, but damn.

"How much do you want?"

I glanced up, thinking maybe I could figure out what she was talking about by her expression. No luck. "What do you mean?"

"For taking my detention."

Oh. That. I imagined Parvati and me parked at the beach overlook, our hands all over each other. If Cassie only knew.

She pulled a twenty-dollar bill out of her purse and slipped it into my fingers. "I would have missed our semifinal meet.

You totally saved us. I never would have guessed you were a girls' swimming fan."

"Yeah, well, go team, you know?" I slid the folded bill into the pocket of my hoodie. "Thanks." I hadn't given a surfing lesson since September, so money was tight. Besides, Cassie could afford it.

She leaned over and gave me a half hug. She smelled like a whole freaking garden of flowers. I hoped Parvati wasn't lingering nearby watching this. She could be a little jealous sometimes.

"Talk to you later." I sneezed. Pretty sure I'm allergic to flowers.

"For sure." Cassie flashed a smile that could've been the "after" picture in a tooth whitening commercial. The fluorescent lights reflected off her shiny lip gloss, the whole effect nearly blinding me.

I turned away and strolled down to the cafeteria, thinking about the best way to spend twenty bucks. Grabbing the least toxic-looking things from the hot lunch line—a chicken sandwich, a basket of limp french fries, and a chocolate chip cookie—I headed toward my seat.

Parvati and Preston were already at the table. So were a few guys from the football team, some guy from the tennis team who'd won a couple matches at Junior Wimbledon, and pom-pom captain, Astrid Covington, and her friends. None of them even looked up when I sat down. They were used to having me there, Preston's outcast playmate. They probably thought I was his drug dealer or something.

I actually met him the way I meet most people—through surfing. He'd signed up for a lesson at my parents' boardwalk shop. When he showed up on the beach, wearing high-end surfing clothes and carrying a thousand-dollar board, I planned on hating him. Obviously he was just another rich kid padding his extracurricular résumé. He'd take one lesson, check surfing off his badass to-do list, and then run back to the country club.

But Preston was legit. We stayed out for five hours on our first day. He went from struggling to pop up on his board to going after his own waves. A few lessons later, Pres was almost as good as me, and we'd hung out together ever since.

"So you and Swimfan. What was that about?" Parvati's voice was light, but her eyes were slitty. She had obviously seen me with Cassie.

Preston sat at the head of the table where he could see everyone and be part of the All-Stars' conversations when he so desired. "Yeah, what *was* that about, Maximus?" He swiped at his phone with one finger and then angled it in my direction. Pres had an obsession with recording people. At school. At parties. In the football locker room. He definitely had some boundary issues. "The lovers are fighting," he intoned. "Let's hear what the guilty party has to say."

"Get that thing out of my face." I grabbed for Preston's phone. He didn't even know what had happened. He was just trying to stir up shit as usual. With his shiny blond hair and green V-neck sweater, he looked more like a golf pro than a shit-disturber, but looks could be deceiving.

"Is this your first fight?" He turned the phone toward Parvati. "You guys might want this moment captured for posterity."

Parvati faked like she was going to karate chop Pres in the throat. Still grinning, he slipped his phone back into his pocket.

She turned back to me. "Let me guess. That was Cassie's phone playing Boyz Be Crap."

"Yep. Apparently the fate of the Vista Palisades girls' swim team has now been secured, since yours truly took her detention."

"Ah," Parvati said, nodding. "What's the opposite of collateral damage?"

"Collateral benefits?" Preston suggested. He was half listening to us and half listening to one of the football players talk about next week's game.

I pulled the twenty out of my pocket and snapped it open in front of them. "Speaking of benefits."

"No way. She paid you?" Parvati's eyes widened. "Who

knew lying could be so lucrative?"

"Lawyers," Preston said.

Parvati smirked. Her mom was a defense attorney. "And politicians," she shot back. Preston's dad was a U.S. senator.

Sometimes hanging out with them felt like being miscast in a prime-time teen drama—one where everyone else was rich. My parents, Darla and Ben, owned a souvenir shop called The Triple S. Sun, sand, and surf. Mostly we sold hermit crabs and five-dollar T-shirts.

I peeled the bun from the top of my chicken sandwich and squirted a couple packets of mayonnaise on top of a translucent tomato slice that had seen better days. Even smothered in goo, the sandwich still managed to be dry enough to make me gag.

Parvati's eyes scanned the caf, a pen poised over the mininotebook balanced on her lap. She wrote a gossip column for the *Vista Palisades High Gazette* and was always jotting down seemingly random observations.

"Maybe you should join the twenty-first century," Preston said. "Use a tablet or a laptop like a legit reporter."

"I have a laptop," she said, "but the battery is fried." She scribbled something down and then looked up, her gaze locking on to something over my shoulder. Before I could even ask what she was looking at, I felt fingers tap me on the arm.

"Max?"

I craned my neck to see who was talking. Amy Westerfield stood behind me in her silver-and-blue cheerleading uniform, awkwardly transferring her weight from one foot to the other.

Parvati stared at Amy like she was an endangered species that wanted to eat out of my hand.

"Yeah?" I said, expecting another grateful thank-you for preventing a swimming catastrophe of epic proportions.

Amy leaned over close to me, resting her forearms on the table. She dropped her voice to a whisper. "I have a proposition for you."

TWO

THE DAY WAS TURNING MORE surreal by the minute. On a normal day, no girl besides Parvati even spoke to me, and now I'd been approached by school royalty twice in an hour. "Oh?" I said, taking extra care not to let my gaze drop below the neckline of Amy's cheerleading outfit.

She fished around in her purse, pulled out a permission slip for the senior civics field trip to Coronado Naval Base, and slapped it down in front of me. "My parents wouldn't sign this. I'm grounded and they don't want me to have a whole day away from school with Quinn. Ten bucks if you help me out."

Quinn was Amy's meathead jock boyfriend. Even though I had nothing in common with either of them, I knew how bad it sucked to be banned from your significant other.

"Why not just sign it yourself?" I asked.

"Because I'd get caught. And suspended. And kicked off the squad. And grounded for a jillion years." She pulled a pen from her purse.

"What makes you think I can do a better job than you?" My eyes flicked across the table at Parvati. She was chewing on one of my french fries, watching the proceedings with what seemed like mild interest.

Amy shrugged. "Because you don't write in big, bubbly letters?"

"Fine." I grabbed the pen from her hand. "What's your dad's name?"

Parvati slapped her hand on top of mine. "Twenty bucks," she said.

"*Fifty* bucks," Preston said with a languid smile.

"Preston!" Amy looked a little offended.

"What?" He adjusted the gold band of a watch that cost more than my car. "I'm a businessman."

A mass of wrinkles formed across Amy's normally smooth bronze forehead. "I don't have that kind of cash on me."

"No worries. Max here'll take an IOU," Preston said. "If you don't pay he'll just have an attack of conscience and confess his little deed."

"I will?" I looked back and forth between Preston and Parvati.

"You will," Parvati assured me. She arched a thick black eyebrow at Amy. "Name?"

"Tom. Tom Westerfield." Amy's tan skin was starting to turn blotchy and red in places. I wondered if she was that nervous about forging a permission slip or if she was just mad at being taken for fifty bucks.

She coached me on the signature and I practiced a couple times on a napkin. When she nodded her approval I scrawled the name on the form and handed it back to her.

"Thanks, Max," she chirped, slipping the permission slip back inside her purse. "It'll totally be worth it." A couple of other girls in blue and silver waved at her from across the cafeteria, and she practically skipped over to their table.

The bell rang, and most of the guys from the football team got up as a group. They all had fifth-period gym. "You coming?" Our center, a guy named Nate, looked straight through me to Preston.

"Catch up with you guys in a minute," Pres said.

Nate grunted and turned to follow the others. They lumbered off like a herd of buffalo.

"Let me know if any of your football buddies need their permission slips signed," I told him. "I'm seeing serious business opportunities here."

"Sounds fun. Almost like old times, eh, Parv?" Preston said. "Like our shenanigans at Bristol Academy. Too bad you weren't there too, Max. Parvati and I ruled that school." He smiled to himself. "Good times, good times."

Parvati gave him a dark look. "Yeah, except those 'good times' got us expelled, and these little fibs have the potential to make us cold, hard cash. She gestured around the table with one hand. "Liars, Inc. All of your duplicitous needs serviced by Max et al."

"Et al.?" I glanced back and forth between the two of them.

"Us, obviously." Parvati's skin was glowing the way it did after a major hookup session.

"You two are both loaded," I protested. "And college bound. Why would you want to help with an unethical and possibly illegal business?"

"My parents have been stingy lately," Preston said. "And as you know, I have expensive vices."

He was referring to his gambling habit. He bet on everything: online poker, college basketball, women's tennis. Once he told me he won fifty bucks on the outcome of a minor military skirmish in the Middle East.

"It'd be a good training exercise for me," Parvati added.

I snorted. Her main goal in life was to work for the CIA, and if there was one thing she did not need any training in, it was how to lie. When the Colonel caught us in the hot tub, she turned on the tears in five seconds, telling her dad that nothing had happened, that we were just kissing. And the hilarious thing is, he seemed to believe it, even though our clothes were strewn across the deck.

"Fine," I said. "If you two want in, then you're in charge of drumming up more clientele."

"Word of mouth seems to be working so far," Parvati said. "What is that? Seventy bucks in an hour? Not bad."

"I'll spread the word a little," Preston added. "Liars, Inc., huh? Could be just what we need to liven up our senior year." He slid his chair back from the table. Parvati and I followed his lead. The three of us dumped our trays.

Pres thumped his right fist twice against his chest. "Be good, you two." He headed toward the gym.

Parvati and I turned down the main hallway where all of the seniors had their lockers. "So I'll see you tomorrow around ten," she said with a wink.

"Meet you by my car. Same as usual."

"We'll talk more about our new business venture." Her voice lowered to a growl and her eyes practically smoldered, like the idea of running a mini–crime empire with Preston and me really turned her on.

"Okay." I wasn't convinced that anything was really going to come of it, but I'd talk about the new Boyz Be Bad album or the vegan-friendly cafeteria choices if it was going to make her keep looking at me like that.

THREE

October 22nd

PARVATI WAS LEANING UP AGAINST the side of my beat-up Ford Escort by the time I got out of detention. Her wheels were a lot nicer, an almost-new VW Jetta with air-conditioning that actually worked, but it was too conspicuous. For some reason—probably just to see if her parents would do it—she had requested a purple paint job for her last birthday. Now the whole school referred to her car as the Grape.

"Max time." She glanced around to see if anyone was watching before giving me a peck on the cheek. "My favorite time in the whole world."

I unlocked the door for her and we both tossed our backpacks into the backseat.

"So," she started, as I pulled away from the curb, "Preston and I had a little brainstorming session last night about what other *services* we could offer our fellow classmates."

The muscles in my neck tightened. "You went over to Preston's house?"

"No, on the phone, silly," Parvati said. "Don't be jealous. I'm all yours."

I believed her, but I was still jealous. Pres and Parvati were friends before I knew either one of them. They had both attended the same ritzy private school until they managed to get expelled together as juniors. Neither of them ever told me exactly what they did to get kicked out. Pres claimed substance-induced amnesia, and Parvati vaguely explained it as "stealing a bunch of stupid stuff from different classrooms, rare books from English, chemicals from chem lab, that sort of thing." Apparently this was a dare game they played with their friends: one group would steal a bunch of crazy shit, and another group would have to put it back without getting caught.

Each time I asked her about the story, the details got more vague, and part of me always imagined this string of thefts culminating with Parvati and Preston having wild sex on the headmaster's desk. Both of them assured me this was not the case, but I still couldn't shake the idea completely.

I pulled my car out into the street and headed toward the

beach. "What'd you two come up with?"

Parvati ticked things off on the pads of her fingers. "Lying. Forging permission slips. Calling in sick for people. Switching tests. Creating alibis."

"Alibis?" I raised an eyebrow. "Wow, we really *are* starting a life of crime."

"Not for crimes," she said. "More like cover stories. Maybe someone is grounded but wants to sneak out to a party, or maybe a guy wants to take his girlfriend to that crappy Seabreeze Motel for the night. We can pretend to have group projects to work on or make up overnight field trips, that kind of thing."

I nodded. "I guess the next question is, what are we going to do with all the money we're going to make?"

"Nights at the Seabreeze?" She laughed, but I knew she'd be down for it if I was, even though it was way below her standards.

"Is there any chance we could sneak up to your dad's cabin?" I asked. The Colonel's cabin was on the outskirts of the Angeles National Forest, a remote wooded area an hour north of here. Parvati and I had driven up there occasionally this past summer so we could be alone, but her dad loaned the place out to his military buddies during hunting season, so it was only safe at certain times of the year.

"It's still deer season." Slouching down, she rested her

head on my shoulder and sighed. "Trust me. You're not the only one going crazy." She reached across the center console and curled her hand around my thigh, her fingers toying with one of the fraying strands of my jeans. Her light touch was all it took to get me excited. The car swerved slightly as the wheel twisted a little in my hands. I swallowed hard.

Right on cue, we arrived at the Ravens' Cliff Overlook parking area. The lot was empty except for a pea-green Volkswagen bus covered in rainbow dancing bears and surf stickers. It belonged to the Jacobsen brothers, Vista P's resident clan of surfing demigods. Pres and I liked to surf, but the Jacobsens were *surfers*: shoeless, sand-covered, hand-wiggling, "chaka brah" surfers. If the ocean was right, you never saw them at school before lunchtime.

I shut off the engine and looked toward the water. In the distance, the dark blue of the Pacific met the lighter blue of the sky. A seagull swooped low, dive-bombing the waves in search of a fish. I turned toward Parvati. It was always a little awkward, those few seconds before we started hooking up. "How was newspaper?" I asked, not caring remotely about the answer.

"Scintillating," she said, wiggling her way out of a black cardigan sweater. Underneath, she was wearing a form-fitting T-shirt with the word "Succubus" printed across her chest and a pair of gray leggings.

My eyes followed the curve of her thighs. Skintight pants had a way of burning through the awkwardness. I leaned over and nuzzled my lips against her collarbone. "I find you pretty scintillating."

"Oh yeah?" She reached down with one hand and reclined her seat, extending her neck to give me better access. "Any particular parts?"

I tugged at the collar of her T-shirt. "Maybe." My hand inched the shirt downward, my lips trailing after it.

She squirmed as if I was tickling her. "You're bad." She lifted my mouth to hers, biting my lower lip softly as she snaked her arms around the back of my neck. My fingers reached up under her T-shirt, fumbling with the clasp of her bra. She kissed me harder. The windows got foggy. An hour and a half passed in an instant and my phone alarm chimed.

I sighed. "It's time to go back." We couldn't be late. If we were, Colonel Dad would probably scramble a squadron of recon jets to find her. Her parents had threatened to send her to Blue Pointe Prep, a military school on the East Coast, if she got in trouble again. Being caught with me would be enough for them to make the call.

Parvati nodded, raising her seat back up. She reached beneath her shirt to hook her bra. "I know this sucks, Max.

I'll work on my parents, all right? Worst-case scenario, Mom and Dad said they'd shell out for a private room at USC if I behave until then and declare myself prelaw."

"Great, so ten months from now you and I might get to be alone together." I started the car and backed out of the parking place. "I thought you were going to major in Arabic or something."

She leaned over to check her reflection in the rearview mirror. She finger-combed her shiny hair. "You can be prelaw and major in Arabic," she said. "I'll play along for a while."

I turned onto the road that led toward school. "More playing along," I muttered.

Like the way she had convinced her parents that she and I were over by going to homecoming with Preston. Pres had called to make sure I was okay with the idea. He didn't actually want to go to the dance any more than I did, but as the Vista Palisades football captain he was expected to show up. Parvati had actually wanted to go, which surprised me, but I guess even the coolest chicks get sucked in by stupid shit like high school dances. It had turned out to be no big deal and we all got drunk later on at Preston's after-party, but she set up her "date" without even telling me, and I still got pissed when I thought about it. She never even apologized.

"Sorry" wasn't part of her vocabulary. She thought apologies were for the weak.

Parvati ruffled my messy brown hair, pushing my bangs back from my eyes. "Speaking of playing along, my parents said I could go to Preston's party next week." She blinked her long eyelashes innocently.

Of course they would say that—they loved Preston. Colonel Dad had no idea Pres and Parvati got expelled together from Bristol Academy. Senator DeWitt had donated a truckload of cash so Preston could finish out the semester and then announced that Pres was switching to Vista P for his senior year to play for a bigger football district. Parvati's dad would probably shit a hand grenade if he knew the truth.

"What party?" I asked. "I thought he couldn't have parties anymore." Senator DeWitt apparently had a shot at being appointed to the Presidential Cabinet next year, and he'd started cracking down on any activities that might be detrimental to his political career. He didn't want any scandals.

"The one I made up so we can hang out." Parvati winked. "I told my parents it was a Halloween party. Maybe Pres will let us *haunt* one of the spare bedrooms for an hour."

"Yeah, maybe." It wasn't like Parvati and I would be the first high school kids to get it on at Pres's house, but it felt a little sketchy. What was he supposed to do while we got naked?

"Oh, come on, Max." Parvati forced the corners of my mouth upward with her spangly blue fingernails. She leaned over and ran her teeth along my earlobe, sending a shot of chills down my spine and into my lap. "I promise to make it worth your while."

"Well, when you put it like that," I said, my face relaxing, "how can I refuse?"

FOUR

October 28th

PRESTON OPENED THE DOOR WEARING ripped jeans and a T-shirt emblazoned with a pot-smoking zombie. A half-empty bottle of Irish whiskey dangled from his left hand. "Welcome to the party," he said in a slightly slurred voice. He made air quotes around the word "party."

"Nice hair," I replied. From the neck up, he looked like he was ready for basic training. He must have spent the time between football practice and now at the salon, getting what I jokingly referred to as his weekly trim.

"Fuck you, Max Factor. My helmet wouldn't fit right if I let my hair get all long and girlie like yours."

He disappeared into the cavernous living room, and I followed him through it and down to the basement, where a movie was playing on the big-screen TV. Parvati was stretched out on the sofa in a black dress and knee-high socks patterned with glow-in-the-dark skulls. She sat up when she saw me. "I'm so glad you're here," she purred, but her voiced hitched slightly and the words sounded forced.

"Me too. Now she'll quit talking so much." Pres took a slug from the bottle of whiskey and then started fooling around on his computer. I flopped down on the sofa and started fooling around with Parvati.

As she crawled into my lap, I smelled alcohol on her breath. I wondered how long she'd been here, how long she and Pres had been drinking together. She glued her lips to the place where my neck met my shoulder and proceeded to suck hard enough to leave a mark. She pulled her head back for a second and admired her handiwork. Then she pressed her mouth to my skin again.

"I should be charging you for this," Preston said. "You can be Liars, Inc.'s first official customer."

"My parents aren't the ones threatening to send me to military school," I said. "It's her alibi. Charge *her.*"

Parvati came up for air long enough to mumble something about putting it on her tab.

Preston picked up a yellow squirt gun and managed to hit the back of her head from across the room. "Seriously. Cool off, Pervy. I sit on that sofa sometimes. At least wait until the maid goes home so you can use a guest bedroom."

Parvati wiped away a spray of water that was trickling down her neck. "What kind of weirdo just happens to have a loaded squirt gun lying around the house?"

"A weirdo with badly behaved pets," Preston said, aiming the gun at his mom's Himalayan cat, who was curled up on an empty bookshelf and minding its own business. The cat jumped when the spray hit it, hissing, nearly falling to the floor. It gave Preston a baleful look with its smooshed-in face before abandoning the shelf and padding its way up the stairs.

A girl screamed at us from the big-screen TV. We all turned to watch as a man wearing a black sweatshirt with the hood pulled low swung at her with an axe. The silvery tip lodged in her forehead and blood spattered onto the camera lens. The scene cut away to another room in the house where the dead girl's friends were giggling and doing each other's hair.

"That's what she gets for saying Woody in the Hoodie three times while looking in the mirror," Parvati said. "If you're going to be stupid, you deserve what you get." Her voice sounded off again.

Preston gave her a look but didn't say anything. He took a long drink from the bottle of whiskey and then turned back to his computer.

I glanced back and forth between him and Parvati. "Are

you two all right? You're acting weird."

They both started to speak at the same time, but then the maid yelled from the top of the stairs. "Preston. Enchiladas in fridge, okay? You just heat. You need more help before I go?"

"No. We're good, Esmeralda. *Gracias*," he hollered back, without looking away from the computer screen.

"Man, you'd starve if it wasn't for her," I said.

He grunted in agreement. "I know. You should invite me over to your house to eat. I want to kick back around the kitchen table and have a nice family dinner."

I snorted. "If you call Hamburger Helper a nice family dinner." I never invited Pres or Parvati over. I wasn't embarrassed by where I lived, but I figured they'd rather hang out in their own bigger, quieter houses.

"At least your parents make an effort." Preston tipped back the bottle of whiskey again.

Parvati yanked me up from the overstuffed sofa. "I believe I owe you a life-changing time."

"What's your hurry?" I lowered my voice. "I just got here." I wasn't sure if I felt bad about taking advantage of Pres or if I was going into panic mode at the thought of getting to be with Parvati again. I hadn't found the time to take precautionary measures today and didn't like the thought of lasting only five seconds, especially in Preston's house.

She turned to Preston and fluttered her thick black eye-lashes in his direction. "We'll be back, all right?"

"Can I record you guys?" He turned toward us and held up his phone.

Parvati threw a yellow sofa pillow in his direction, and he took aim with the squirt gun again. "You're a freak," she said, using a second pillow as a shield.

He rolled his eyes and turned his phone around so that he was filming himself. "Sadly, it appears there will be no footage of this epic union." He pocketed his phone and fiddled with the gold band of his watch. "Go on. I wouldn't want to be the guy who stands in the way of true lust."

Parvati's eyes narrowed. "For all *you* know, it could be true love."

I coughed. Even though we'd been dating for four months, I didn't think Parvati and I were anywhere near the L word. Not that I wasn't crazy about her. Love just always seemed like something for people who were older. Stable. People who had their shit together.

Preston grabbed the TV remote off a glass end table. "You're not capable of love, Pervy."

"You wish you knew what I was capable of." She scoffed.

I couldn't help but feel like a second conversation was taking place in the dead space between their words. I looked back and forth again, wondering if they'd had a fight.

Pres flicked a button and axe-wielding Woodie became pulsing music videos. He punched the volume up a few notches, and his features melted into his usual relaxed grin. "Use the guest room on the main floor. And don't say I never gave you anything."

Parvati practically skipped up the stairs and down the hall. I followed behind her, creeping around each corner as if I might run into Senator DeWitt or Esmeralda at any moment. The guest bedroom was at the back corner of the house, its wooden door pulled tightly shut. I froze up for a moment, half convinced Parvati's father would be hiding in the bedroom with a squadron of air force commandos.

"Come on." She pushed the door open. The room wasn't much bigger than the rooms at the Seabreeze, but it was nicer, with muted blue walls and pastel paintings of flowers and lakes. The bed was wide, with a fluffy gray comforter. Parvati collapsed backward into the center of the mattress, pulling me down with her. Threading her fingers through the belt loops of my jeans, she pulled my body up against hers, her mouth finding the tender spot she'd been sucking on earlier. "Max time," she murmured. "My favorite time in the whole world."

I rolled her over so that she was on top of me. Her skin glowed. Her eyes were dark tunnels, made even deeper by the thick eyeliner goo she was wearing. "Are you guys fighting?"

I asked. "Things seemed kind of tense downstairs."

"It's fine." She brushed her lips against mine. "I think he's pissed about something online. Probably lost more money."

"Are you sure? Because I always felt like he was into you—"

"Preston is only into Preston," she said. "And I'm only into you."

I loved the way she said it. So matter-of-fact. But I didn't want Pres to be pissed at us. I didn't exactly have a lot of friends. "I don't know, Parv—" My voice cracked in the middle of her name.

"Oh, that's so cute. You're nervous." Her fingertips expertly undid the button of my jeans and whatever I'd been planning to say died on my lips. "I'll relax you," she said. Pushing my shirt up to my armpits, she kissed her way downward from my chest.

My muscles went weak. I sank deep into the soft mattress, like it was an ocean and the current was pulling me under. My breath caught in my throat. I was drowning, in a good way. Nerve cells fired across my body, little fireworks that made my arms and legs twitch. Parvati slowly worked her way back up, landing soft kisses on my abs and chest until we were eye to eye and I was staring into those dark hollows again. She tugged her slippery dress over her head, and the heat of her body made my heart stutter. Blood pulsed hot in my veins. I muttered something, a combination of words that didn't make sense together.

She laughed her tinkly little laugh. I grabbed a condom from my wallet, and we quickly lost the rest of our clothes.

Parvati took the foil package from my hand and opened it. "I got this." I watched her for a moment, my eyes taking in every inch of her bare skin. Then I pulled her tight against me. Her thick hair fell around my face like a tiny cave. The room disappeared as we started to move together.

Time passed. Slowly. Quickly. I had no idea. Wave after wave crashed down on me. I just kept moving. Faster and faster until everything blinked hot. I exhaled forcefully and Parvati collapsed on top of me a few seconds later, her body slick with sweat.

We lay there, motionless, for several minutes. "God, you are so amazing." I buried my face in her hair.

"You too," she said, lifting up so that I could see her face. Her eyes were shining; her mouth curled into a wild smile. "Still feel tense?"

"Maybe a little." I grinned. "Why? Are you up for a replay?"

She dragged one fingernail down the middle of my breastbone. "Pres said his mom won't be home until after midnight."

"Oh yeah?" Fake or not, this was going down on the books as Preston's best party ever.

About twenty minutes later, Parvati and I got dressed and then laughed at our failed attempt to remake the bed. The comforter hung crookedly over one side and was lumpy where I had tried to tuck it underneath the row of feather pillows.

She shook her head. "I hope Pres has Esmeralda on speed dial. It'll take someone trained in the fine art of bed-making to fix this."

"I know, right?" I said. "Let's go find him and see if he'll share those enchiladas. I've kind of worked up an appetite."

Preston was still downstairs, the television now muted. He was typing out an email, his fingers rattling the keys with machine-gun-like ferocity. When he saw us, he minimized the screen. "I trust you guys didn't break anything?" He scanned both of us up and down. "Nobody needs medical attention?"

"The pillows might need a little fluffing," Parvati said.

Preston snickered. He slouched back in his chair, relaxed, like he'd fixed whatever was bothering him. Or maybe he was just drunk enough not to care anymore.

"I owe you one, Pres," I mumbled, slicking my still-damp bangs back behind one ear.

He smirked. "Wait until you get the bill."

It made me think about Liars, Inc. again. About alibis. I wasn't the only guy in school who struggled to be alone with his girlfriend. Would I have paid for the opportunity Preston just gave us? Hell yeah. Suddenly the idea of coming up with cover stories for classmates in the same situation made a whole lot of sense. After all, it wasn't like we'd be hurting anybody.

FIVE

SO WE DID IT. WITH Preston's and Parvati's help, it took only a few days to spread the word about Liars, Inc. across the entire junior and senior classes. They were an unbeatable team when it came to publicity work. Because of her office assistant and newspaper connections, Parvati knew the head of every clique. As the new football captain and host of the school's biggest homecoming party, Preston knew just about everybody. I handled the leftovers—detention regulars, special-edders, a handful of juvenile delinquents from the alternative wing. PR wasn't really my gig. I was the man who got his hands dirty.

By the beginning of December, I had set up two alibis and was "under contract" to sign a number of semester failing notices. Parvati was developing a specialty for calling kids in sick. She had the perfect fake-mom voice, altering it to be a fake aunt or fake grandmother as the situation called for. Preston was more of a marketing and promotions guy, but he had a regular customer from his calculus class who paid in advance to trade quiz papers, since "he couldn't get a grasp on differential equations," whatever the hell that meant.

Liars, Inc. was on pace to make over two thousand bucks before Christmas, and I knew exactly what I was going to spend my windfall on: an awesome present for Parvati. She had bought me a new surfboard for our three-month anniversary, and I wanted to surprise her with something equally amazing. If I had any money left over, I'd pick up something for Pres too. Then again, what could you buy for the guy who had everything?

"How do you feel about camping?" Preston asked, startling me out of my reverie. We were in the cafeteria. The whole area was decorated with garlands and paper snowflakes, even though Vista Palisades never got any snow.

The usual crowd of jocks and pom-pom girls turned toward Preston when he spoke, but they went back to their own conversations just as quickly when they realized he was talking to me. Across the room, Parvati was chatting up a table of sophomore tennis players, probably spreading the word about Liars, Inc. As I watched her, I wondered if things were getting out of hand. Sophomores were young and dumb, and the more people who knew about us, the better the chance that a teacher would find out.

"You want to go camping?" I asked dubiously, dipping a trio of limp french fries into a puddle of ketchup. I was pretty sure Preston never did anything that might take him outside the cell service grid. Especially lately. I hoped he wasn't gambling away his inheritance as we spoke.

Pres looked up from his lap. "No, but what if we *say* I did?"

I blotted my mouth with a greasy napkin. "Huh? I don't follow." I could still see Parvati, leaning over the table, her barely-there miniskirt exposing several feet of tawny skin. How did girls know exactly how far they could bend over without flashing the really good stuff?

"I'm saying I need my own cover story."

That got my attention. "For what? Your parents are never home."

Preston dragged a single fry through his ketchup, leaving a bloody trail across the bottom of his cardboard tray. "Dad's back from D.C. for the holidays. And I want to go to Vegas this weekend."

I coughed into my hand. "Do you really think Vegas is a good idea?"

Pres stared down at his fry with distaste. "I'm not going to gamble, Max. I can do that anywhere. I want to go see a girl."

"What girl?" I wanted to believe him, but it seemed unlikely that the poster child for Gamblers Anonymous would just happen to meet a girl who lived in the gambling capital of the world.

"Who cares what girl?" Then, seeing my look, he added, "I met her online, if you must know."

I laughed out loud. "Dude. You came in here and basically took over the school. You could get any girl you want." Dropping my voice, I continued, "Including Astrid Covington. Why are you hitting on desperate internet chicks?"

Preston glanced down the table at Astrid, who was busy giving her pom-pom minions a lecture on the importance of eyebrow plucking. "Astrid is made of plastic," he said. "And anyway, it wasn't like that. I met this girl playing online poker, not whoring around a dating app. She seems cool, so I want to meet her."

"Are you even sure she's a chick? Maybe you've been playing poker with some dirty old man."

"I've talked to her on the phone, Maximus. It's no big deal."

I craned my neck to get a glimpse of the phone in his lap. "I know you got a picture on there. Let me see her." Just then I heard Parvati's distinctive bell-like laugh over the dull roar of cafeteria conversations. I turned in the direction of the noise. She had finished talking to the sophomores and was standing in line at the cash register with her usual tray of wilted spinach and soy milk. The guy in front of her said something and Parvati laughed again.

Preston followed my gaze. "She really has you whipped, doesn't she?" he asked abruptly.

"What? I—" It had been over a month since the fake party at Preston's house, but things between Pres and Parvati still seemed a little tense. I didn't want to say anything that would make the weirdness worse. I watched her bat her eyelashes at the elderly cashier, who in turn flushed red and dropped the change all over the counter. "It's not like that . . ." I trailed off, because it kind of was. We both knew it.

A smile quirked at Preston's lips. "Do you think she's all in *lurve* with you too?"

"No idea." I knew she was into me, but Parvati wasn't exactly romantic. "Why? Did she say something?"

"No." The fluorescent light reflected off Pres's polo shirt, making his blue eyes look almost gray. "But even if she did, it's not like you could believe her."

"Come on. She doesn't lie to us." *Just everybody else.*

Preston slipped his phone into his pocket. "You don't think so?"

Damn it. I bet he *did* have a thing for Parvati. Maybe she called him out on it the night of his "party," so he hooked up with some online girl to feel better. That would explain everything. Parvati and I never should have had sex at his

47

house. *Maybe you never should have started dating her, if you thought he liked her first.*

No. Not fair. He knew her first. He had his chance.

I sucked down a gulp of soda. "So what's this mystery woman's name?" I asked, eager to change the subject.

"Violet."

"Sounds hot." I raised an eyebrow. "She's not some lonely stripper, is she?"

Preston grinned. "God, I hope so." He cast a look back over his shoulder. Parvati was grabbing napkins from the condiments station. "So you'll do it?" he asked quickly. "Just between us? I figure the fewer people who know, the safer it'll be." His jaw tightened. "Sometimes I feel like you're the only one I can really trust."

I nodded, but it wasn't like Parvati would rat him out. Pres just didn't want her to think he'd gone all rebound with some fugly internet girl.

"I'll tell my parents we're going to camp out at the beach this Saturday," he continued. "I'll meet you there and even help you set up the tent if you want. Once it's dark I'll sneak off."

"Wow, that's really going all out," I said. "Do you want to bring the boards and actually catch a few waves before you go?"

"Nah, we'll have enough stuff as it is. Besides, the water

gets cold at night, and the current can be a bitch." His face tightened as he said this, as if he was remembering some past fight he'd had with the ocean.

I had only seen him struggle once: during his second surfing lesson. Against my advice, he went after something a little too epic, wiped out, and almost drowned.

I was on the beach at the time. I saw the surfboard shoot out from beneath Pres's feet and watched him plummet into the water. He was no dummy—he made for the shore immediately. But he couldn't escape the series of waves that crashed over him, slamming his body around like a washing machine and pushing him toward the ocean floor.

I left my board on the beach and raced into the surf, swimming deep beneath the surface to avoid the churning waves. I managed to get a grip on one of Pres's ankles and pull him out of the impact zone, but not without nearly getting in trouble myself. Panic had apparently set in, and Preston fought me as I tried to rescue him. We're lucky he didn't drown us both.

Later, as we knelt in the wet sand, gasping for breath and coughing up seawater, I realized he'd split my lip out in the surf.

"Sorry, Max." He pulled his rash guard over his head and held it to my mouth to stanch the bleeding. "I've never felt like that before—I guess I lost it a little."

"Felt like what?"

"Like I was really going to die." Preston looked back at the ocean for a moment, at the two pieces of his broken board still bobbing on the waves. Then he turned toward the parking area. "I owe you one."

"No worries. Life-saving is included in the lesson fee," I joked.

We never talked about that day again, but it felt like the moment I stopped being Preston's surf instructor and started being his friend.

SIX

December 3rd

WHEN THE WEEKEND ROLLED AROUND, I did my usual detention and then met up with Parvati and took her to the overlook.

"What are you doing tonight?" she asked as I pulled the car into the lot.

I paused for a second, not wanting to lie to her, but not wanting to betray Pres's trust either. "Camping," I said finally, parking close enough to the edge of the cliff that we could look out over the churning water. "On the beach. I'm meeting up with Pres."

"Cool." She nestled her head under my chin. She smelled different. Like cinnamon. Maybe she was using a new shampoo. "Ouch." She pulled her face away and I could see the beginnings of a shark's tooth indent on her cheek.

I tugged the pendant over my head and tossed it into the center console. "Sorry." I stroked her cheek with one hand, but she didn't respond. I was kind of surprised she hadn't started groping me yet. If there was one thing I could normally count on, it was that Parvati would make the first move. "You okay?"

"Why? Because I haven't pounced on you?"

Did I mention she was a mind reader? Just one more CIA-worthy skill.

She tilted her head up so she could look at me. "Maybe I'm bored." Her lips twitched. I knew she was messing with me.

"You saying you're not into me anymore?" I gave her my best pathetic look. "I figured it was too good to last."

She smiled—not the slanted lips she gave people at school, a real smile that made her eyes get a little crinkly. "Do you know why I like you, Max Cantrell?"

"Because your dad hates me?"

She laughed out loud. "No, that's why I *used* to like you. Now it's because you're just *you*. You're not fake." She brushed her lips against mine. "And you like *me*, not some bullshit fake me you need me to become." Her voice tightened. "Nothing is ever good enough for my parents. Last week, they threatened to ground me because I got a C on a calc test. I swear I'd lose my mind if it weren't for you." She exhaled deeply. It was like watching a balloon deflate.

"Well, no worries, because I'm not going anywhere." I petted her soft hair, and she leaned her cheek against my chest again. I wanted to say something more, make her feel better, but in a lot of ways I couldn't relate to her life. Darla and Ben probably wanted me to go to college, but they'd never pressured me about it. Lately, they didn't seem to expect much at all, aside from the occasional babysitting shift.

"It's like sometimes I forget how to be happy," Parvati said.

Now *that* I understood perfectly. Except mine was more like I was afraid to be happy. Life had a way of coming in and screwing shit up whenever things started going good. My mother had died in childbirth, but I remembered being happy with my dad when I was younger. He was the one who had taught me to surf. We took trips all up and down the West Coast together. But then he had a heart attack. Age forty-one.

He had never even been sick.

As the paramedics bent over him in our living room, I prayed for the first time in my life.

It didn't do any good.

There weren't any relatives who could take care of me, so the state gave me to foster parents who lived in Los Angeles. They were nice, and eventually I was happy again. Right up until the night I heard them talking about how they were going to give me back. I didn't want to end up placed with some other family who would play with me until they got bored and then return me to the store like a defective video game, so I ran away.

For almost a year, I alternated between living under bridges and living on the beach, begging for change and eating from Dumpsters. Eventually, someone reported me and I got caught. The cops handed me back to child services, who took me to a nearby children's center. That's how the Cantrells found me. They were there the day the social worker dropped me off.

Darla and Ben seemed cool from the start, but I never really let myself get close to them, just in case. Sometimes it amazed me that I let myself care so much about Parvati. She owned me, and I was okay with that. I was still trying to figure out how I'd gotten so lucky.

"Do you know why I like *you*?" I asked her.

She turned to me and arched her eyebrows suggestively. "I can think of a few reasons."

"Well, there's that." I grinned. "And the fact that you're the hottest chick I know. But mostly I like how you're different from other girls. You don't even try to fit in."

Her smile faltered. "I used to try. It was painful." She paused. "My mom has told me stories about how ostracized she felt when she started dating my dad, because no one close to her could understand why she would do it. I feel like that too sometimes, not because of you, but because I don't want the same things as most girls I know." She shrugged. "I guess I'm just weird like that."

"You are weird in the best possible way." I kissed the top of her forehead. "And I think it's cool that you don't like all that boring girly stuff."

She snuggled in close to me again. "I like *some* girly stuff. I just don't expect you to like it too."

"I swear it's like you have some manual of exactly what to say."

"Likewise," she said.

We sat curled together for the rest of our time, listening to the water pound against the rocks, listening to each other breathe. I didn't even miss hooking up that day. It was a new kind of closeness for us.

After I brought Parvati back to her car, I headed home, still thinking about the way her hair smelled and the heat of her body next to mine. I spun the Escort around the corner and onto my street a little too fast, nearly slamming into a gray SUV that was going the opposite way. I whipped the steering wheel to the left and hit the brakes hard. The SUV glided past. I expected the driver to honk or give me the finger, but the figure behind the tinted glass didn't even glance in my direction.

Inside the house, Darla awaited me with her usual resigned look. Her hair was pulling loose from her ponytail and she had something green and oozy dribbled down the front of her flowered shirt. At her feet, my eight-month-old, newly adopted twin baby sisters, Ji Hyun and Jo Lee, were busy trying to untie her shoelaces. My other sister, Amanda, was engrossed in an episode of some gory cop TV show.

"I have to go help Ben at the store, Max," Darla said. "Will you watch the gang for a few hours?"

Darla always said that the bond was strong in our family because destiny had brought us all together. Every time someone asked her about the adoptions, she told the same story. She and Ben had been observing another boy at the group home when the social worker dropped me off. I was tangle-haired and covered with sand. I refused to speak to anyone. Darla was immediately drawn to me, and she and Ben came back a few days later for a visit. The social worker told them I was angry and suffering from PTSD, that I'd been living on the beach, that I would be "a problem child." I didn't say one word to anyone during the whole session, but the Cantrells didn't care. They just asked for the adoption paperwork to be started, and a couple of weeks later they took me home as a foster kid while they waited for everything to be processed. Apparently, it was similar with Amanda and the twins. It was fate, Darla always said. She didn't choose any of us. Life chose us for her.

It sounded nice, but if you ask me, Darla just liked fixer-uppers. Ben was a decent-looking guy with a laid-back attitude, but he was still a high school dropout with a tacky souvenir shop. I was a slacker with no clue what to do after graduation. Amanda had cystic fibrosis and spent a couple of hours each night strapped into a percussion vest. The twins? Other than being slightly demonic at times? They probably had heart defects or some special Asian illness Darla hadn't told us about yet.

"I'm supposed to be going camping with Preston," I said. "Isn't Mandy old enough to watch Ji and Jo?"

"I'm only eleven," my sister informed me, as if I had forgotten. "Watching the twins is a big responsibility." She was no doubt parroting something she had overheard my parents say.

"I really need you here. Just until six thirty, okay?" Darla said. "Thanks, Max," she added, grabbing for a navy sweater that was tossed over the back of the sofa.

"Like I had a choice," I mumbled, but she was already gone.

Ji Hyun tugged at the cuff of my jeans with smudgy green fingers. She babbled something that might have been Korean or might have been a mixture of Klingon and gibberish.

I reached down and unclamped her fingers from my jeans. I gave her the closest thing I could find—a rolled-up newspaper still in its plastic wrapper—and she curled her chubby hands around it. "I'm only eleven," I mimicked Amanda, as I plunked down next to her on the sofa. "And yet you're old enough to watch mutilated corpses on television."

"Hey. *Focus on Forensics* is educational."

I watched for a minute as they showed a dead body trapped beneath the surface of a frozen lake, one ghost-pale hand splayed out against the ice as if the victim was reaching out for help. "Sure it is."

Jo Lee pulled a tiny vial out from under the sofa and held it up in the air with a squeal. Amanda looked down and squawked in protest. "Max, Jo Lee has my nail polish."

"I care," I said.

"She's going to try and eat it," Amanda said in a singsongy voice.

"No, she isn't. She is not that stup—" I reached down and pulled the bottle of pink sparkly polish out of Jo's grubby fingers just before she could put it in her mouth. She started to wail at the top of her lungs. Immediately Ji started screaming too. God, they were the most lethal tag team ever. For a second I thought about the other kid, the one Ben and Darla almost adopted before they fell for my broken-down, ten-year-old, problem-child ass. He probably never had to babysit. "That kid dodged a bullet," I muttered. The twins screamed even louder.

I wrestled the remote control out of Amanda's hand and turned up the volume. I flipped through the channels and feigned interest in a hockey game. I didn't really like watching sports, but I loved torturing Amanda.

"Maaax," she whined. "This is boring."

"Why don't you go play tea party with Ji and Jo," I suggested. "Preferably in the street."

Amanda's face crumpled, and for a second I thought she was going to cry. I felt like the world's biggest dick. Sometimes I forgot my sister was just a kid and talked to her the same way I did to Pres and Parvati.

"Jeez. Only kidding, Mandy." I flipped the TV back to where she'd had it.

Her lips turned back up so quickly that I wondered if I'd just gotten played. "I know," she said. "Cool. This is the one where they find that girl everyone thought ran away to join a harem."

"That's a girl?" The soggy blob being hoisted from the water didn't even look human.

"Yeah. You remember the Prom Queen Killer, don't you? Supposedly she was his first victim."

"Doesn't this stuff give you nightmares?" I hoped the twins weren't going to grow up to be serial killers from seeing shit like this.

"Nope," Amanda said.

I pulled my phone out of the side pocket of my cargo pants and sent Preston a quick text telling him I wouldn't be able to meet him until after six thirty. I wanted to text Parvati too, but her parents were known to monitor her cell phone, and she'd catch hell if they saw a text from me.

It was right before seven when I pulled my car into the overlook parking lot. The lot was empty except for the Jacobsens' van and Preston's BMW.

"Hey." I slid out of my car. "Sorry I'm late. I had to babysit." I rolled my eyes.

"No worries." Preston smiled slightly as he slammed his car door behind him. "I wish I had some siblings I could corrupt."

I started to reply but then caught sight of his backseat. His whole car was packed full of camping gear. "Wow. You actually packed all that? You're really taking this alibi seriously."

"I didn't want my mom to find my tent and sleeping bag in case she goes snooping around in my room," Pres said. "Besides, I figured you might want to use my stuff. I know your little two-man piece of crap leaks."

I looked up at the night sky. Stars stared down at me, winking in a weird sort of synchronization. The moon hung low and heavy, a hair away from being full. "Is it supposed to rain?"

Preston had turned his back to me and was looking out at the ocean. "No, but you know how fast things can change around here."

I followed his gaze, watching the waves crest and break against the rocks. He seemed unusually pensive. Maybe he was just nervous. "You sure you know this girl well enough to go visit her?"

"Probably not." He turned and walked along the edge of the cliff, stepping carefully past unstable places and loose rolling rocks that might give way under his feet. "You ever feel like you don't know anyone?" He looked out at the water again. "Or like no one knows *you*?"

I inched closer, trying to decide if I could grab him if he started to fall. "What are you talking about?"

"I figured you'd understand, being adopted and all. You grew up with random strangers. How fucked up is that?" Preston held out his arms as if he could fly, like he was daring the wind to sweep him off the edge of the cliff. I leaned back, away from the drop-off. Below us, the tide had come all the way in and the ocean slammed viciously against the rocks. "Pres, come on," I said. "You're making me nervous."

"Don't be such a girl." His tone was light, but I sensed a weird undertone of hostility that had swirled up from out of nowhere.

"Is this about your dad?" We had just elected a Republican

president, and Senator DeWitt was the front-runner to be appointed Secretary of Labor. DeWitt had originally gotten rich as CEO of DeWitt Firearms, and his pro-gun viewpoint didn't sit well with many of California's hippie pacifists, so now his political opponents were jumping at the opportunity to rip him to shreds. Pres didn't seem to be upset by the internet headlines that had started cropping up, but maybe he just hid it well. It had to be hard seeing his family name dragged through the mud, especially when many of the accusations about his dad were probably true.

"What he does doesn't reflect on you," I said. "You're not the same person."

Preston stared downward, past the crags in the rock face where the ravens nested, earning the cliff its name. "I don't know who I am." The black water churned and sprayed.

"Dude, you're kind of freaking me out."

Preston turned away from the cliff. When he saw my expression, his face relaxed, his lips turning up into a slow smile. "Sorry, Maximus. I didn't mean to get all heavy. I think I just need a break from everything."

I forced a smile in return. I hoped this Violet chick was cool, that she and Preston really hit it off. Part of that was selfish, like maybe if he had a girlfriend too then everything would go back to normal with him and Parvati. I had never really been that interested in making friends, but now that

I had some, I didn't want to choose between them. "I've got stuff for barbecuing. You want to head down to the beach and have a hot dog or four before you head off?"

Preston shook his head. "Nah, I don't want to run into the Jacobsens. I lost on the UCLA game, and Jonas will be looking to collect. Besides, it should only be four hours to Vegas. I'm hoping to get there by eleven or so."

"Does this chick live with her mom?" I asked.

"She's a little bit older. Has her own place."

I nodded, again wondering if Violet was a stripper or a showgirl. Preston's parents would absolutely die. "Why didn't you go last night?"

"Dad wanted to parade me around at some holiday brunch thing today," Preston said. "Besides, this way if Vio turns out to be crazy I don't have to make excuses for not staying a second night. I'll be home late tomorrow, in time for school on Monday."

He popped the locks to the BMW and pulled out his designer tent. It was beige with blue cloth trim and had a detachable rain fly and gear overhang. "Here," he said.

I glanced up at the sky. "I don't think I'll need it."

"Take it just in case."

I shrugged but went ahead and loaded Preston's tent and sleeping bag into my trunk. "You really did think of everything, didn't you?"

"You can't be too prepared," he said. "You want help carrying stuff down to the beach?"

"Nah, I got it covered."

"All right. Be safe." Preston thumped his fist twice against his chest and then hopped back in his BMW, waving as he peeled out of the parking lot in a cloud of gravel dust.

I watched him leave and then grabbed my frame pack out of the backseat. I debated for a second, but then I bungee-corded my own sleeping bag and tent to the bottom of the pack. Pres's stuff was nicer, but I had never pitched his tent before. I camped all the time with my own gear and could easily set up my tent in the dark. Weaving my way back and forth down a series of switchbacks, I made it to the beach just as the tide started going out.

I hiked through the shallow surf until I found an area of dry sand and dropped my gear near one of the fire pits that lined the beach. I threaded the flexible rods through the rigging of my tent and staked it deep into the sand. Then I searched the beach until I found a handful of dry driftwood pieces. I arranged them into a wobbly pyramid. At the base I shook a small pile of Aztec Dust, an easy-to-light kindling that my parents carried at the shop. Using my body to block the wind, I struck a waterproof match and lowered it gently onto the kindling. The match went out. It took a couple more tries, but eventually the kindling flared up and the nearest piece of driftwood caught fire. When the whole pyramid was safely ablaze, I jabbed a stick through one of the hot dogs and held it over the flames.

I downed half the package and threw the leftover hot dogs out on the beach for the birds to eat. Then I crawled inside the tent and nestled down in my sleeping bag. My rain fly had gotten lost last summer, so there was nothing but sheer nylon above my head. The night had turned clear; not even the whisper of a cloud lingered in the sky.

I thought about Preston's comments about really knowing people. Something had to be going on with his family. Hopefully this Violet chick could mellow him out the way Parvati did me. Again, I wished I could text her. No, screw that. I wished she could be next to me, looking up at the same night sky. She would love this: the wind off the water, the occasional shriek of a gull or a raven outside the tent, the sky glittering like diamonds on black velvet.

I closed my eyes and imagined her curled against me, my lips relaxing into a smile. I had no idea what she saw in me most of the time, but maybe weird girls just have weird taste. Or maybe she was my cosmic reward for surviving my crap childhood and emerging as a mostly decent guy.

SEVEN

December 4th

SUN FILTERED THROUGH THE NYLON the next morning. The breeze blew snarls of seaweed up against the side of my tent. I unzipped the flap just far enough to peek through. High tide was coming again. I must have slept a long time. I checked my phone; it was almost 10:00 a.m.

Yawning, I rubbed my eyes and then rolled up my sleeping bag. Crawling out of the tent, I turned my face to avoid being pelted with clouds of sand that the wind had loosened. I pulled up the stakes and stuffed my tent inside its nylon carrying bag. As I headed up to my car for my board, I rattled off a quick text message to Preston. He didn't answer. Knowing him, he had probably just gone to sleep.

I tossed my camping gear in the trunk and unhooked my

surfboard from the top of my car. As I made my way back down to the beach, I could see the Jacobsen brothers out at the lineup where the waves were breaking. The twins, Jasper and Jared, were seniors with me. Their older brother, Jonas, worked at a seafood restaurant just down the street from my parents' shop. He was also Vista P's unofficial bookie. Jasper waved as I started to paddle out, which was surprising. I didn't think any of the brothers liked me. I was a sellout who made money teaching tourists to surf. The Jacobsens thought of the ocean as their private play area. They didn't want to share their waves with outsiders.

Giving the brothers a wide berth, I sat on my board and let my feet dangle into the water, watching each of the Jacobsens ride a wave into the shore. By the time Jared cruised to a stop in the shallow surf, Jonas was already paddling back to the lineup.

"You gonna ride?" he hollered over at me. "Or are you just here to fangirl for us?"

"Funny." I dropped down to my belly and felt the water pitch and roll beneath me. I heard the wave before I felt it. The roaring filled my ears and I paddled as fast as I could, popping up into a crouch at just the right moment.

I leaned into the wind, cutting left and then right across the shoulder of the wave as the water carried me to the shore. Jared and Jasper were on the beach, watching my approach.

"Not bad," Jared said. "Where's your douchebag friend Preston today?"

Did I mention the Jacobsens were the only kids at Vista Palisades who didn't like Preston? That's because a few years ago Senator DeWitt helped green-light a deal for Covington Construction to build a small resort on the last pristine strip of Vista Palisades Beach. The hotel couldn't deny access to the public, but its existence meant more people in the water and more trash on the sand. It did kind of suck, but it wasn't like Preston had personally brokered the deal.

"He's not a douchebag," I said.

"Sure he's not." Jared snorted. He turned toward the ocean. "Race you back out there."

I followed Jared and Jasper into the foam, paddling after them as they headed out to where Jonas bobbed leisurely in the water. The four of us fell into a sort of rhythm, each taking our turn as the waves rolled in, riding left or right so as not to drop in on each other. The sun slowly moved across the sky.

When the sets started to turn choppy, I returned to the beach and went for a walk at the water's edge. Pres and I were supposed to be together all day, so I didn't want to return home too early. It was probably a mistake to let the Jacobsens see me without him, but it wasn't like they'd tell his parents.

68

Later, I packed up the rest of my gear and started for the trail. The Jacobsens were busy cooking something over one of the fire pits. "Hey, brah," Jonas called after me. "You want a tofu burger?"

"No thanks," I said. Those things barely even counted as food.

"Well, if you ever want to ride again, you know where to find us."

"Cool. I'll see you around." I ran a hand through my hair. Sand rained down on my shoulders. I wasn't good at approaching people, making friends, whatever. But you could surf without talking, and Preston would be going off to college somewhere next year. It made sense for me to get to know the local guys.

I sent Pres another text to tell him I was heading home. Still no answer. Either he had let his phone battery die or he and Violet were having too much fun to be bothered.

Back at the car, I clipped my board to the roof. There was a gray SUV that I had never seen at the overlook before parked in the corner spot. It reminded me of the car I had almost hit across the street from my house. The sun was reflecting off the windshield. I shaded my eyes with one hand, but I couldn't tell if there was anyone inside.

The engine sputtered a little as I started my car. The latest from Kittens of Mass Destruction, "Burst into Flames," was on the radio. I cranked up the volume as I turned out of the parking lot and headed for home.

I didn't realize how starving I was until I pulled into my driveway ten minutes later. I left the gear in the car and took the porch steps in a single leap. My whole family was at the table, throwing back bacon-wrapped chicken nuggets and green beans. Amanda was going through a vegetarian phase, something probably inspired by Parvati, so Darla had cooked her a veggie burger in addition to the beans.

I grabbed a clean plate from the dishwasher and helped myself to the chicken nuggets. "You know those veggie burgers are glued together with horse's hooves," I said.

"They are not." Amanda rolled her eyes at me.

Normally I would have screwed with her some more—I mean, come on, an eleven-year-old vegetarian?—but the long day of surfing had worn me out.

"Hey, Max," she said. "Where's your shark's tooth?"

I reached up to where it usually hung, right at the top of my breastbone, but the pendant wasn't there. Had I forgotten to take it off before I went in the water? I couldn't remember. Hopefully it was tangled up with my tent or sleeping bag. If it had come off while I was surfing, it was gone for good.

My phone buzzed and I fished it out of my pocket. It was a number I didn't recognize. Darla gave me a disappointed look as I answered, but she didn't say anything.

"Max?" The voice was familiar, but I couldn't place it.

"Yeah?" I said. "Who is this?"

"It's Quinn, from school . . . from the football team?" He said it like maybe I knew seven or eight guys named Quinn. "I need your help with something."

"Yeah, just a second." I pushed my chair back from the table. "I'll be back. I need to take this in my room."

Darla's face drooped even further.

"Sorry." Holding the phone with my neck, I grabbed my plate of chicken nuggets. "School project stuff."

Once I was safely inside my room with the door shut, I flopped down on my bed. "Okay. What's up?"

Quinn didn't answer right away. I could hear him talking to a girl in the background—probably Amy.

"Hey," I said sharply. "You there?"

"I'm here," Quinn said. "Preston was supposed to write me a note that says I have a doctor's appointment tomorrow so I can leave school after second hour. But he's not answering his phone. Do you know how to reach him?"

"He's actually . . . busy tonight," I said. "But he's supposed to be back later. Maybe try him around midnight?" I took a quick bite of a chicken nugget.

"I can't get out of the house that late."

I swallowed before replying. "So then just get it from him tomorrow morning at school."

"Yeah, but what if he forgot or he's absent or something?" Quinn lowered his voice. "Is there any way *you* could write it? I can come pick it up." He paused. "Amy and I have lunch reservations downtown tomorrow. It's our one-year anniversary, and she wanted to go to Troff. I tried to get a dinner reservation, but that place is booked for months."

I made a face. Troff was one of those places that put feta cheese and seaweed on a burger and charged forty bucks for it. Thank God Parvati wasn't into fancy restaurants like that.

"Fine. But I don't have any parental-looking letterhead or anything. Pres probably made something on the computer."

"I'll snag some of my dad's legal stationery from his study," Quinn said.

"Okay." I gave him directions to my house. "Come on by and I'll take care of you."

I waited outside on the porch. I wasn't sure what Quinn drove, but I had a feeling I'd know it when I saw it. Sure enough, about ten minutes later a black Lincoln Navigator slowed to a stop in front of my house.

Quinn started to get out of the car. I strode across the grass and met him at the curb. "Let's go somewhere," I said, "so Dar—so my mom doesn't wonder what we're doing out here."

Quinn shrugged but let me in the back of the Navigator. Amy smiled at me from the passenger seat. I nodded to her as

Quinn pulled away from the curb. We turned into the parking lot of a Burger Barn a few blocks away, and he parked the car in a corner spot. He cut off the engine and coached me on his dad's signature until I had it close enough.

Quinn pocketed the piece of off-white stationery after I signed it and then removed a crisp fifty-dollar bill from his wallet. "Thanks again," he said.

"You're a lifesaver," Amy added. She tossed her reddish-brown hair back behind her shoulders.

"Pleasure doing business with you." I slipped the money in my pocket. "Have a nice lunch."

Quinn fired up the engine and I tapped him on the shoulder. "It's cool. I'll just walk home." I hopped out of the Navigator before he could reply.

"You sure?" Quinn asked through his open window.

"Yeah. It's a nice night." With a little wave, I loped toward the sidewalk. As I turned and headed for home, I wondered where Preston was, if he had the windows down on the Beamer as he headed back to Vista P. I debated if I should keep his share of Quinn's money since I had to cover his ass, not that he would care one way or the other. I was pretty sure Pres was only doing Liars, Inc. for the potential thrills.

EIGHT

December 5th

THE NEXT DAY I AWOKE to someone gently shaking my shoulder.

"Max." I opened one eye. Darla was standing over me, her hair hanging down in tangled clumps. She smelled like baby wipes as usual. My eyes flicked over to my alarm clock. Jesus Christ, it was only five forty-five. I didn't need to be up for an hour.

"What?" I asked, not bothering to cover up the hostility.

"It's Preston."

Okay. Now I was awake. Had he gotten stuck in Vegas? Had he done something stupid and gotten arrested?

The side of my mouth was wet with drool. I wiped at it with

the sleeve of my T-shirt. "What about him?" I rubbed my eyes.

"You saw him yesterday, right?" Darla's voice sounded uncertain, the way it did when she was having trouble telling the twins apart.

"Yeah." *Hopefully.* I was going to have one hell of a time explaining how Preston and I were surfing together if it turned out he spent the night in a Las Vegas jail.

"Claudia DeWitt is on the phone. She wants to talk to you. Apparently, Preston never came home."

NINE

AND THAT'S HOW I ENDED up in one of those rooms like you
see on TV. An interrogation room. Plain metal table, folding
chairs, two-way mirror cut into the upper half of one wall.
The air reeked of chlorine, which made me wonder what
kind of mess they'd needed bleach to clean up. I plunked
down in a chair at the far end of the table, leaving as much
space between me and the detectives as possible. No, not
detectives. FBI agents. Apparently when the kid of a senator
goes missing they bring in the top dogs.

The taller one went by Gonzalez, but he had pale skin
and green eyes and couldn't have looked less Latino if he'd
tried. He was skinny and square-faced, with hair that stuck
straight up in places. He paced back and forth, muttering to

himself and doing nervous things with his hands.

Gonzo's partner had introduced himself out in the lobby, but I had already forgotten his name. He was bigger, with shoulders like a linebacker and a belly that had seen a few too many cheeseburgers.

"So take us through your camping trip with Preston, from the beginning." The big guy's voice was low, gravelly, like he should be outside chain-smoking instead of sitting here busting my balls. Man, Preston was going to owe me big-time whenever he crawled back into town. I could only imagine what sort of debauchery he had gotten up to in Vegas that made him decide coming home was optional.

Big Guy loosened his tie and apologized for the room temperature, which was somewhere between sweltering and broiling. I leaned in to catch the name on his ID badge. Special Agent James McGhee.

"When did you and Preston DeWitt arrive at the—" He mopped his forehead with the cuff of his dress shirt as he glanced down at his notepad. "Ravens' Cliff Overlook?"

"Well, I had to babysit until six thirty," I said slowly, staring at the sweat stains underneath his armpits. "So it was about seven when we met up."

McGhee jotted something down on his notepad. I couldn't read it from where I was sitting. "And then what?"

I glanced around. Were Ben and Darla watching from

the other side of the two-way mirror? They had insisted on coming in the room with me, but the agents assured them I "was in no trouble" and "not under suspicion of anything" and "would feel more comfortable speaking freely without parents around." It had made sense at the time, but now the walls felt like they were closing in. The second hand on the clock seemed to accelerate before my eyes, ticking faster and faster—like a bomb eager to detonate.

"And then we pitched the tent, built a fire, and sat around bullshitting until we got tired and went to sleep," I said.

"Bullshitting," Gonzalez repeated, as if I'd slipped up and given something away. He slid into the chair across from me, tapping one foot repeatedly under the table. "Did that involve drinking?"

"Maybe. Big deal." It hadn't actually, but one thing I learned when I was homeless was that you had to give authority figures a little bit of what they were expecting. Otherwise they wouldn't believe anything you said, even the stuff that was true. Plenty of adults had seen me wandering the beach by myself and pegged me as a homeless kid. I always admitted it and told them my mom was standing in line to get us a bed at the shelter and had sent me looking for something to eat. That kept do-gooder types from calling social services, and it usually scored me a few bucks or some free food too.

McGhee nodded to himself and waited for me to say more.

I didn't.

That would have been the time for the whole truth—Liars, Inc., the alibi, Violet, Las Vegas—but I couldn't do it. For one, both agents were looking at me like I was some delinquent who accidentally killed his best friend in an alcohol-induced rage and dumped the body in the ocean. I didn't know how much they knew about my past, but if they'd already made up their minds that I was guilty of something, explaining that I headed up a shady business selling lies to my class-mates probably wouldn't have persuaded them to cut me a break. Not to mention, if I'd told them about Liars, Inc., they would have shown up at school and started interrogating the students. And then discovered that Parvati was involved.

My parents would have sighed and looked disappointed if they found out I was forging permission slips and providing cover stories. Her parents would have sent her to military school several thousand miles away.

What I should have done was just confess to the alibi. Tell them my buddy wanted to go hook up with a girl and needed someone to cover. I could have done that without ever mention-ing Liars, Inc. or Parvati. But when you put someone in a small stuffy room that's eighty-five degrees and reeks of bleach, they stop thinking clearly. I panicked. Everything became black or white. Lie or tell the truth. Keep to the alibi and assume Preston was fine or confess the whole fucking deal.

"So you make a fire, have a little booze. Then what?" Gonzalez prompted.

"Then we went to sleep."

"Alone?" McGhee asked.

"Huh? We were in the same tent, if that's what you mean."

"He means was it just you two or were there girls there too?" Gonzalez said, his hands twitching.

"Just us."

"What happened when you woke up?" McGhee asked.

"I went surfing," I said.

McGhee raised an eyebrow. "And Preston?"

Shit. My first screwup.

"I mean, *we* went surfing."

"Did anyone see you guys?"

"I don't know." I faked a cough. "Can I get some water?"

McGhee gave Gonzalez a look. "Grab a pitcher for all of us, would you?"

Gonzalez swore under his breath but rose up from the table. He stormed through the wooden door, letting it slam behind him.

"Sorry about him," McGhee said. "He's tightly wound."

And there it was. The whole good cop–bad cop routine. "No shit," I said.

"What did you and Preston do after you went surfing?"

I didn't know if it was the tiny break or just the absence of

Gonzalez that calmed me down, but I sensed an opening to squeeze in a little bit of the truth and took it. "He split early, actually. Said he wasn't feeling well."

"About what time was that?"

I shrugged. "Didn't look at my phone. Maybe nineish."

Gonzalez came back with a pitcher of water and three glossy paper cups. I accepted my drink with a polite thank-you and then guzzled down half of it in one swallow.

"Max was just telling me that Preston left the beach early on Sunday. Apparently he wasn't feeling good."

Gonzalez made a face like I had just taken a dump in my pants. "Oh yeah? A little too hung over to surf?"

It didn't sound like a real question, so I didn't answer him.

"Do you know if he went straight home?" McGhee asked.

I sipped my water. "I figured. But he didn't say."

McGhee nodded to himself again. "Did you and Preston take a walk along the top of the cliff on Saturday night?"

"Yeah," I said. "He was fooling around by the edge. Pretending to fly, stuff like that."

"Did you guys argue?" McGhee asked.

"What? No." Preston and I never argued. I had known him over a year and couldn't remember a single fight. "Why would you ask that?"

"Just following up on a tip. Probably irrelevant." He flipped his notebook closed. "I think that's all the questions we've got for now, Max. But if you think of anything else, please give me a call." He slid a business card across the table.

I slipped it into my wallet behind my health insurance card, back in the section of stuff I almost never looked at. "Thanks," I said.

Gonzalez stopped twitching long enough to give me one more glare. I stood up, unsure if I was just supposed to leave or if I had to wait for one of the agents to walk me back out to the front.

"Isn't it kind of early to assume something bad happened?" I asked. "I thought you had to wait forty-eight hours just to file a missing persons report."

"That's actually a myth perpetuated by TV shows," McGhee said. "There's no required waiting period in California. And it's been over forty-eight hours since either of his parents saw him. *You're* the only one who has seen him in the last couple of days."

I nodded. I wished I hadn't brought it up.

"We don't know anything for certain," McGhee continued. "But we need to consider the possibility that Preston's disappearance is politically motivated until we can rule that out."

"What? Like . . . terrorism or something? Don't you think that's a little unlikely?"

"A high-profile senator's son disappearing right after an

election? We're just trying to stay ahead of the curve," McGhee said. "Which reminds me. We'd appreciate it if you didn't talk to anyone about what we've discussed this morning."

I nodded. "Am I done? Do you know where my parents went?"

"I'll show you where they are." McGhee pushed his chair back and stood up.

I followed him out of the room and back down the hallway, past the desk sergeant and out into the police station lobby. Darla was chewing on her lower lip as she paced back and forth across the scuffed floor. Ben sat in the chair nearest to the door, his canvas sneakers crossed at the ankles. He was flipping through a sports magazine and swilling down a cup of coffee. Man, talk about opposites attracting.

"Max." Darla headed over to me, arms wide, like I'd just woken up from a coma.

"Jeez, Darla." I wriggled out of her grasp. "I was only gone for twenty minutes."

"I know. It's just the thought of your friend missing . . ." She trailed off.

"Have you ever met him?"

"Not officially, but I've seen you two surfing," she said. "Just because you don't bring your friends around doesn't mean I don't care about them. I can't even think about what I would do if it were you."

I resisted the urge to tell her she could always replace me with another broken child. Maybe upgrade to a nice amputee, or a blind kid. "I'm sure he's fine," I said. "He probably just needed to get away from all the political stuff going on at his house."

"You think so?" McGhee asked. His voice made me jump. I didn't realize he had stopped at the desk for a moment and could still hear me. "Did he ever say anything about taking off?"

"He said something about Vegas not too long ago," I hedged. Maybe I could dole out the truth in tiny pieces that, once assembled, would make a picture that resembled a reality in which I hadn't done anything wrong.

Darla put an arm around me. She cleared her throat meaningfully, and Ben looked up. "We all done here?" he asked. Reluctantly, he returned his magazine to the basket in the corner. The three of us headed for the door.

"One more thing, Max," McGhee said. "Did you and Preston both park at the overlook?"

"Yeah," I said, without much thought. "Why?"

He flipped his notepad open again and made a quick notation with his chewed-up pencil. "Just a routine question."

TEN

I MADE IT TO SCHOOL just in time for lunch. After tossing my backpack in my locker, I checked in at the attendance office and then headed for the cafeteria. I passed a group of freshmen arguing loudly about football, two boys in college sweatshirts pushing and shoving across the table as they made a friendly wager.

It made me think of Preston, how he hadn't wanted to surf because he was avoiding Jonas Jacobsen. I scanned the caf. Jonas's brother Jared stood in the salad line, fiddling with his puka shell bracelet while the cashier made change. He took his tray to the condiment station and then headed toward the lobby. It looked like he was going to eat outside. I used to do that too, before Preston transferred to Vista Palisades.

I followed Jared through the glass doors and out into the sunlight. "Hey," I said, plunking down on the front steps next to him. As usual, his nose was peeling a little, new pink skin emerging from beneath his perpetual tan. The wind whipped his blond dreadlocks around his mouth, obscuring part of his expression.

"What's up, Cantrell?" His eyes flicked around the parking lot and then back to me. He picked up a shrink-wrapped vegan cookie and popped the package open.

"How much money does Preston owe your brother?"

Jared set the cookie down on his tray next to a wilted spinach salad. He shook his dreads back from his face. "What makes you think DeWitt is doing business with Jonas?" he asked slowly.

"He told me he was avoiding your brother because of the UCLA game."

Jared blinked twice. "I don't know what to say, brah. As far as I know, DeWitt hasn't *invested* with Jonas in months. Maybe he found better odds elsewhere." He shrugged and turned away, his tan fingers snapping the hard cookie into pieces.

"But that doesn't make sense," I said, more to myself than

to him. "Why would Preston tell me that if it wasn't true?"

Jared swallowed hard, watching as the breeze stole a few pieces of spinach from his tray and sent them dancing toward the parking lot. "I guess you don't know your friend as well as you thought you did."

"Guess not," I mumbled. I went back inside and glanced around for Parvati. She wasn't in our usual spot. It looked weird, those empty seats at the end of the long table, like a seesaw with only one rider. And something else was off too. There were usually about twelve kids at the table, sometimes more if Astrid or Preston felt like inviting someone else over. But today there were only six. A couple of the football players were missing. Astrid glanced up and caught me staring. She held my gaze for a few seconds, her tan face slightly reproachful, as if it were my fault that the All-Stars had lost half their members.

"Max." Parvati snuck up on me from behind. "What's going on? Where have you been all morning? Where's Pres?"

I skipped past the first two questions. "I don't know. Did you eat?"

"I've been collecting fees for Liars, Inc.," she said with a grin. She opened the pouch of her tiny silk purse to show me a wad of twenties. "I was going to grab a protein bar from my locker and then work on something for the newspaper. It's not like I want to eat with *them* by myself."

"Yeah. Me neither." I could still feel Astrid's eyes on me as I turned away. Parvati and I headed down the main hall to where all the seniors had their lockers.

"A hundred of this is yours, by the way," she said.

I barely heard her. I spun my combination lock and opened my locker. Then I pulled my phone out of my pocket. No texts. No missed calls. "You haven't heard from Preston today, have you?"

She shook her head. "No, but some kid named David caught me after second hour and was freaking out about his calculus exam. I had to refund him his money. Pres was supposed to swap tests with him today."

"Yeah. So weird." I rattled off a quick text: *Dude. Where the hell are you? Everyone is freaking out.*

"Are you all right?" A mass of wrinkles formed across her forehead. "You're acting kind of strange."

I glanced down at my phone again, even though I knew Preston hadn't responded in the last five seconds. "I need to talk to you in private."

"Ooh, secrets." Parvati smiled. "I know where we can go." She kicked my locker closed with one of her boots and led me through the halls past the gym to the Olympic-sized indoor lap pool. One girl was swimming in the far lane. It looked like first-team all-American breaststroke champion Cassie Rhodes.

"Seriously?" I asked. "You want to talk here?"

"It's not like *she's* going to hear us." Parvati took my hand as we started circling the pool, carefully navigating the wet spots. "Tell me what's going on."

"I set up an alibi for Preston," I admitted. "He wanted to go to Vegas this weekend." I paused for a second. Parvati was still moving forward but she had her head turned, staring at me. "He never came home. I've tried calling him like a million times."

Cassie Rhodes broke the crystal surface of the water. She pushed her wet hair back from her face and then used the side of the pool to propel her body out of the deep end. With trails of water streaming from her arms and legs, she padded barefoot across the painted concrete to the low diving board where she had left her towel. Parvati waited until Cassie had toweled off and disappeared into the locker room before continuing.

"Vegas?" she asked. "How come I didn't know about this?"

"Pres wanted it to be top secret," I said. "He went to hook up with some girl."

Parvati used one hand to brush imaginary dirt off the lowest level of bleachers. She sat down, just the faintest sheen of sweat glistening on her forehead. I sat next to her.

"What girl?" she asked.

"Violet something."

Parvati made a face. "Are you sure she's real?"

"I never heard him talk about her before," I said. "He said he met her playing online poker, and that she seemed cool and invited him to go hang out."

"So then what's the big deal if he's a little late coming home? Senator Dad making a federal case out of it?"

"Literally. I got questioned by the FBI this morning."

Parvati whistled under her breath. "That's heavy. Did you tell them where he was?"

"Not really. I didn't want anyone to get in trouble for lying. I basically told them he left the beach early and I didn't know where he went."

The ends of her hair bobbed up and down as she nodded. "Maybe his phone is dead or he's just having too much fun to call anyone back. I'm sure he's fine. He's Preston, you know? Pretty street-smart for a spoiled little rich kid."

As usual, she made me feel better. "Like someone else I know." I nudged her in the ribs.

Parvati made a mock offended face. "Hey. I come from humble origins. The daughter of an immigrant and a hardworking military man." Her eyes sparkled. "Hopefully Pres will be back today and everyone can quit overreacting. It would suck if he bailed on your birthday."

I had almost forgotten that the next day was my birthday. I shrugged. "It's no big deal. I don't have any major plans." Or any plans, for that matter.

"I wish I could spend it with you." Parvati glanced up at the clock on the wall. "You know, Coach Raymond will be in here to set up for the freshmen any second."

"So?"

"So this." She tilted her neck up and pulled my head down to hers. Our lips met. I wrapped my arms around her back, threading my fingers together. She teased the inside of my mouth with her tongue and I almost slid right off the bleachers.

I broke away. "Enough. Or I'm going to have to take a cold shower before next period."

"That's kind of sexy." She winked.

"Really?"

"No." Parvati took my hand with a smile, just as Coach Raymond appeared from the locker room in a plain black racing suit with a pair of canary-yellow gym shorts over it.

It was definitely time to go. Teachers in swimwear— generally an epic fail.

Parvati and I walked back to our lockers together and then

I headed to fifth period. My acting teacher paced back and forth as she talked about the play *Arsenic and Old Lace*. It sounded halfway interesting, but I couldn't focus on pretend mysteries when a real-life one was brewing right under my nose.

ELEVEN

December 6th

THE NEXT MORNING I HAD two messages. One was a happy birthday text from Parvati. The other was a voicemail from my two favorite FBI agents. They had a few routine follow-up questions. Could I please call them at my earliest convenience so they could stop by my house?

Earliest convenience? How about never?

Darla frowned when I told her about the message. She was busy trying to put impossibly tiny sneakers on one of the twins. "Your dad and I both have to open the shop today," she said. "I know you're eighteen now, but I don't like the idea of you dealing with those guys alone."

"I'll be okay." I kept my voice casual, like it was no big deal.

She dodged a kick from Ji Hyun. "If you're sure," she said

dubiously. "I'll call the school when we get to work and let them know you're going to be late."

Ben appeared from the kitchen wearing black surf shorts and a T-shirt from last year's Malibu Open. He was holding a cup of coffee in one hand and a doughnut in the other. "Christ, Darla. It's his birthday. Just let him stay home."

"Could I?" I hadn't slept well, and crashing on the couch all day sounded like an excellent idea.

"I guess it'd be all right," Darla said. "And then we can all go out to eat tonight, okay? Unless you've got plans with your friends."

Not likely, since one of my friends was MIA and the other wasn't allowed to hang out with me. "Dinner sounds good," I said.

Darla looked forlornly at the tiny pink sneaker in her hand. Sprawled on her back on the sofa, Ji Hyun squealed and kicked her legs as if she thought being dressed by force was a really fun game. Nearby, Jo Lee sat on the floor trying to fit one of her own sparkly sneaks into her mouth. I pinned Ji's legs against the sofa's threadbare fabric one at a time, and she pouted as Darla wrestled the sneakers onto her tiny feet.

"I think she might need a bigger size already." Darla shook her head. "I can't believe how quickly kids grow up."

Ji Hyun kicked at the sofa and started wailing. Immediately, her twin sister joined in.

"Not quick enough for me." Ben winked at Darla to show her he was kidding. He chugged down the rest of his coffee and set the mug on top of the TV. With half a doughnut dangling from his mouth, he picked up Jo Lee and spun her around in a circle. Immediately, she quit crying and made a little cooing sound.

Amanda peeked out from the entrance to the kitchen. "Happy birthday, Max." She held out a box wrapped in snowman wrapping paper.

I ruffled her hair. "You didn't have to get me anything, Mandy."

"I made it," she said proudly.

"Seriously?" That could be good or bad. I ripped through the paper and prepared to gush over whatever was inside the box. Folding back a few squares of toilet paper that she had used as tissue paper, I uncovered a coffee mug painted with brightly colored surfboards and coated with a shiny varnish. It was actually pretty awesome.

"You made this?" I asked.

"Well, I painted it," she clarified.

"It totally rocks." I leaned down to give her a hug.

"How come you're not dressed yet?" Amanda asked. "You get to skip school because it's your birthday?"

"Yeah." I smiled.

"Are you still going to give me a ride home?"

"Of course." Darla didn't baby Amanda because of her cystic

fibrosis, but she hated the thought of her having to ride home on the crowded, dirty bus, so I always picked her up.

Her eyes narrowed. "Do I get to skip school when it's *my* birthday?"

"You can on your *eighteenth* birthday," Darla said, shooting me a grateful look. I didn't know if it was because I was picking Amanda up from school or because I didn't say anything about the FBI dropping by later. Amanda was already a little too obsessed with death and detectives for a eleven-year-old. If she found out Preston was missing she'd want to help investigate.

"Mom, can we put the tree up tonight?" Amanda bounced up and down on her toes. "My friend Clara said her mom put their tree up the day after Thanksgiving."

"Sure," Darla said. "We'll do it after we get home from dinner."

Not exactly my dream birthday, but if I couldn't be with Parvati then tree-trimming with my little sis wouldn't be too bad. I twisted the mug around in my hands to check out the painted surfboards one more time. Amanda was actually pretty cool for a kid. I hoped she would rub off on the twins as they got older.

After everyone headed out, I relaxed in front of the TV. There was still no word about Preston's disappearance, not even on the local news. I knew I should call Agent McGhee, but he probably didn't expect me to skip school. The twins would be at the babysitter's and my parents would be at the shop until sunset. I could give McGhee a call an hour before I had to pick up Amanda from school. That would be a convenient excuse to cut the "routine follow-up questions" short if things got tense. I couldn't leave my chronically ill little sister without a ride home, could I?

Slouching down on the sofa, I flipped through the channels. I heard Senator DeWitt's name mentioned on a local news show and paused, thinking maybe people were finally talking about Pres. Nope. It was just a couple of analysts speculating about who the new president would appoint to his cabinet.

I sent Preston another text—*Seriously dude. Please call or text someone*—and when that went unanswered I tried to call him. The phone rang four times before going to voicemail. I didn't leave a message. As I clicked the red disconnect button on my phone, I thought of something. Preston's phone couldn't be dead. If it was, it would have gone straight to voicemail with no ringing.

My stomach churned. Pres and his phone were never separated. To my knowledge, he had never lost it. For the first time, I thought that maybe the feds were right. Maybe something terrible *had* happened, and I was making it worse by covering things up.

TWELVE

I DOZED OFF FOR A couple of hours, and when I woke up I flipped through our measly fifteen channels again, but every show seemed to be about kidnappings or disappearances. I flicked off the TV with a sigh of disgust. Then I slapped together a salami sandwich and plunked down at the kitchen table. My stomach was growling, but my mouth was dry, my throat closing up as I tried to choke down bites of bread and meat.

It was hopeless. I needed to just get dressed, call McGhee, and get it over with. Otherwise I was going to sit around all day and worry about what he and Gonzalez wanted. I pushed my hair out of my face and headed for my bedroom. As I turned the corner into the living room, I skidded to a stop on the rug.

Parvati was sitting cross-legged on the sofa. I hadn't even heard the front door open or close.

"Jesus." I swiped at my mouth quickly, hoping there weren't any breadcrumbs stuck to my lips. "Ninja much?"

"Well, I didn't want any of your neighbors to see me loitering on the porch, just in case they know my parents."

Not likely. My street was full of blue-collar types. Waiters, retail workers, the occasional mechanic or plumber. Maybe her pool man lived in the neighborhood. "Much better for my neighbors to see a strange girl walking in like she owns the place," I said. "Aren't you supposed to be playing office assistant?"

"Aren't you supposed to be dressed?" she fired back, taking in my plaid pajama bottoms with an amused glance. "What is going on?"

"Preston still hasn't come home."

"I gathered that much. I get to school and there's no you and no Preston and then there's suits busting open both of your lockers and interviewing people—"

"Wait, what?" Shit. Maybe lying to the FBI had done no good at all. There were so many people who might blab about Liars, Inc. if McGhee or Gonzalez asked. "What did you tell them?" I asked, trying not to panic.

"Nothing. They didn't talk to me." She sounded a little bit hurt that she hadn't been interrogated. "They only talked to the teachers. And they tried to be slick about opening the lockers. They waited until everyone was in class. No dogs or anything. Just two guys in plain clothes. I saw them when I was sneaking out."

It sounded like McGhee and Gonzalez were still keeping things quiet for now. "They'll probably ask you stuff eventually. What if they're right and something bad happened, P?"

Parvati glanced around. Her eyes zeroed in on the front window. The sky had gone from clear to white. Thick, fluffy clouds obscured the sun. She dropped her voice slightly. "You think he's really missing? Like kidnapped?"

"I don't know," I said. "If Pres got arrested or something he would have called one of us, right? Maybe his phone got lost or stolen, and then his car broke down on the way back from Vegas. Maybe I should go look for him."

"But if he had car trouble he'd just flag down someone else or walk to town, wouldn't he?" Parvati tugged at the ends of her hair, something she only did when she was anxious. "Let's go by his house and see if Esmeralda will let us in his room. Maybe we can find this girl's address or phone number, figure out for sure where he went."

I had only been in Preston's bedroom a couple of times. We always hung out in the basement. I got the feeling he was really private about his stuff. Even when he had parties, people stayed downstairs or out by the pool.

I checked the time on my phone. I still had almost four hours before I had to pick up Amanda. Plenty of time to run by the DeWitts' and call McGhee afterward. "Okay. Good idea." I traded my pajama bottoms for a pair of black cargo pants and pulled a hoodie over my T-shirt.

Parvati and I hopped in my car and headed across town to the exclusive neighborhood where Preston lived. This whole area was done up in Christmas decorations. Swags of evergreen twisted their way down lampposts, and picture windows glistened with fake snow.

"Duck down," I told her as we drove through an ivy-covered stone archway wrapped in white lights. There was a much greater chance people who lived in *this* neighborhood might know her parents.

I slowed my car to a stop a block away from Preston's three-story house. There were two black Lincoln Town Cars parked in front that might have been FBI, as well as a couple of smaller sedans I didn't recognize.

Parvati stared at the line of cars. "It looks like they've got a whole command center set up already."

"I asked about that. Apparently, the fact that Preston is a

senator's kid means everything gets expedited. They have to assume this could be a political thing until they know otherwise."

"But Preston is eighteen. He can legally vanish anytime he wants. This doesn't make any sense." She turned to face me. "How long has it been since you've tried to call him?"

"A couple of hours."

"Let me try," Parvati said. "If he did just decide to bail for a while, he'd tell me."

Was she insinuating that he wouldn't tell *me*? I was the one he asked for the alibi, after all. I waited while Parvati found Preston's name in her contacts menu and pressed call. She put the phone on speaker, and I swear it took an eternity before it started to ring.

And then "Burst into Flames" started playing, ever so faintly. "Did you call me accidentally?" I asked. I pulled my phone out of the side pocket of my cargo pants, but the screen was black. What the hell? "Call him again," I said.

Parvati called Preston again. Once more, Alexis Destroyer, the lead singer for Kittens of Mass Destruction, started shrieking about how she was going to make me catch fire. It was almost like . . .

Both Parvati and I turned toward the backseat. It was empty except for a crumpled fast food bag and a couple of soda cans. "The trunk," we said simultaneously.

I reached for my key fob and popped the trunk. I slid out of the car, casting a wary glance at the vehicles down the street. As usual, no one was paying me any attention. Thunder rumbled in the distance. The sky had gone from white to gray. The breeze off the ocean was cool, but a heaviness hung in the air, a thick blanket of humidity that signaled an oncoming storm. *You know how fast things can change around here.* Had Preston been talking about more than just the weather?

I pawed through the camping gear that was still in my trunk. Parvati materialized at my side. She called Preston again. This time the music was louder. I shook the long nylon bag that his fancy tent was in. Nothing. Next I undid the top of my gear bag that was full of cooking equipment. Nothing. I pushed both bags to the side. Nestled at the very bottom of my trunk was a phone.

Preston's phone.

I didn't even know we had the same ringtone.

Parvati's pretty face looked up at us from the screen. It was a picture from when her hair was still long. Above her left shoulder, a red rectangle flashed a low battery warning. Without thinking, I reached for the phone, my fingers closing around it just as Parvati said, "Don't touch it." Her almond skin paled slightly. "You might mess up any fingerprints."

"It must have gotten mixed up with his camp stuff and he forgot it," I said. "No wonder we haven't heard from him. I'm surprised he even made it to Vegas without his cell."

Parvati was staring at my hand. She didn't seem to have heard a word I had said. "Max," she started. "Look at your fingers."

I looked down. My right hand was smeared with flecks of reddish brown. Something that looked like rust.

I transferred Pres's phone to my left hand as Parvati took my right hand in hers, bringing my fingertips close enough to her face so that she could smell them. Before I could stop her, she touched my index finger to her lips.

"It's blood," she said.

THIRTEEN

I PULLED MY HAND FREE from Parvati's and gave it a fierce wipe against the safe darkness of my pants. My fingers came away clean. "Blood? How could you possibly know that?"

"I tasted it," she replied. "Salty. Metallic."

"Gross," I said. "And not exactly scientific." My voice was sharp with doubt, but there was a part of me that believed her. She was usually right about weird things. Hell, she was usually right about everything.

Without warning, Alexis Destroyer started singing again, the tinny ringtone surprising me so much that I dropped Preston's phone. Parvati and I both watched as it landed facedown in the trunk next to a larger smear of brown on the upholstery.

More blood.

She wrapped her hand in her sleeve and reached out for the phone.

"Wait," I said. "It's mine this time." I fished around in my pocket, but the caller had hung up. The icon for a new voice-mail message appeared. It was from Special Agent McGhee. He and Gonzo were on their way over to my house. One of my teachers had probably told them I skipped school. "The feds are looking for me. I have to get home."

"No," Parvati said. "You can't go home." She headed back toward the passenger seat.

"What? Why not?" The world blurred in front of my eyes. My brain felt like it was barely functioning, like someone had put me on frame-by-frame advance while Parvati was operating on fast-forward.

"Because they *have* something on you, or they wouldn't be so hell-bent on questioning you again. Maybe they GPS'd this phone while your car was parked at home."

"Yeah, but I didn't put it in my trunk," I protested.

"I know," Parvati said. "But what makes you think the feds will believe you?"

"You're being paranoid. They've been waiting for me to call them all day. Maybe they just have new information," I said. "Or someone at school blabbed about Liars, Inc. and they figured out what happened. Anyway, I should fess up about

Pres going to Vegas to meet Violet, just in case she's some crazy stalker who has him chained up in her basement." It had been stupid not to tell them earlier, but they had treated me like a criminal from the second they saw me—especially Gonzalez—and I didn't want to give them the satisfaction of admitting any wrongdoing. Plus, back then I still thought Preston was going to show up any second and have a good laugh at my expense.

But what about now?

The phone. The blood. Parvati could be wrong—it didn't have to be blood. The trail leading down to the beach had clay mixed in the dirt. It could be that. Or it could be rust from my camp stove. Or maybe it *was* blood but Preston just had chapped lips or a cut on his hand. It wasn't a big pool of red, after all. Just a couple of brownish smudges. Somehow Pres's phone had gotten mixed up with the camp stuff he brought for me, and that's how it got in my trunk. He was probably fine, just sleeping off a sex-and-alcohol hangover.

Still, it would be shitty of me to let his parents worry. I could tell the FBI about the alibi without mentioning Parvati or Liars, Inc. That way they could make some calls, check out Violet, and see if Preston's car broke down or he got arrested for underage gambling.

"Don't worry, I won't bring up your name." I headed back to the driver's seat.

"I'm not worried about me," she said. "If you're going home, I'm coming with you. I want to hear what they say."

"We're supposed to be broken up, P. They could tell your dad—"

"They don't have to know I'm there. I'll hide in the kitchen or a closet or whatever."

"What about the Grape?"

"My car's still at school. I walked to your house."

I knew her well enough to know that when she got an idea like this into her head I wasn't going to be able to change her mind. "Fine," I said. "We'd better get going or they're going to beat us there."

Parvati slipped her tiny frame into our overstuffed living room coat closet, adeptly straddling a bouncy seat and other assorted baby stuff. The feds showed up a few minutes later. Gonzalez let the door slam shut behind him, and I twitched at the sharp noise.

"What's the matter, kid?" Gonzalez asked. "Awfully jumpy."

"I guess I've been a little on edge since my friend disappeared, jackass."

"Watch your mouth," Gonzalez barked.

I rolled my eyes at him. I was pretty sure calling an FBI

agent a jackass wasn't against the law. Especially since it was true.

McGhee eyed the seating options and selected the over-stuffed armchair. That left the sofa and the rocking chair. Gonzalez sat on the side of the sofa nearest to McGhee, and I plunked down in the rocker.

No one said anything for a moment. I swore I could hear Parvati's breathing, slow and steady, from the closet. Then McGhee flipped open his notebook and pulled a nubby pencil from the pocket of his shirt. My heart started pounding, getting bigger with each beat, crowding out my lungs so it was hard to breathe. What the hell was going on?

McGhee cleared his throat. "I just have a couple follow-up questions for you, Max."

"Yeah?" My voice actually squeaked. I wanted to kick myself. Or better yet, kick Gonzalez. I could see him fighting a smile. I raked a hand forward and then backward through my hair, leaving one of my eyes obscured by bangs.

"Did you and Preston argue the night of your camping trip?"

This again? I shook my head. "The answer is still no. Why?"

Gonzalez started to say something, but McGhee cut him off. "We received a call from someone who says they saw two boys arguing at the top of Ravens' Cliff Saturday night."

"Bullshit. We were walking along the cliff and Preston got too close to the edge for me. I told him to stop freaking me out. I wouldn't call that arguing."

"So there was no physical struggle? No pushing and shoving?"

"Preston outweighs me by at least sixty pounds. If there had been pushing or shoving, my broken ass would be floating out to sea right now."

McGhee abruptly changed the subject. "Did Preston take your ex-girlfriend to homecoming?"

I almost blurted out that Parvati and I were still together. "Yeah. So what? They went as friends. We're all friends."

"So Ms. Amos isn't dating Preston?" he asked.

"Nope," I said. "They've never dated."

McGhee nodded. "And Preston's car. You said he parked it next to you in the overlook parking lot?"

"Yeah."

"That's a problem, Max," McGhee said. "We have multiple witnesses that swear Preston's car wasn't at the beach parking lot on Sunday morning."

"Well, yeah, not after he went home."

McGhee flipped back in his notebook. "According to you, Preston left about nineish."

"Uh—" A wave was brewing inside my stomach. McGhee

had set me up when I was leaving the station with Darla and Ben. He waited until my guard was down to ask about the parking. "I might have been a little off."

"According to multiple eyewitnesses, Preston's car wasn't there at six, when the sun came up." Gonzalez leaned forward for emphasis.

Fucking Jacobsen brothers. It had to be. No one else was there. I bet one of them was the mysterious eyewitness who saw Pres and me "arguing" too.

"Can you explain how Preston's car was parked at the overlook parking lot Sunday morning and also *not* parked there?" McGhee asked.

"Isn't eyewitness testimony wrong a lot?" I asked. "My little sister is always watching detective shows, and it seems like I've heard that over and over."

"Sometimes." McGhee chewed on the end of his pencil. He sighed. "Look, I want to believe you, Max, but I know you're not being straight with me. I can help you if you tell me the truth."

"Or," Gonzalez said, "we can arrest you for obstruction of a criminal investigation if you keep lying to us."

I looked back and forth from McGhee to Gonzalez and didn't say anything for a few seconds. Then I blurted out, "Here's the deal. The camping trip was just a cover."

Gonzalez's eyebrows shot up, but he kept quiet for once.

"What do you mean?" McGhee had a knack for keeping his face perfectly expressionless. It was a little creepy.

I told him how Preston had asked me to cover for him so that he could go to Vegas to meet a girl. As I talked, McGhee made notes and Gonzalez made faces. Snarls and sneers, the kinds of looks you give to someone you think is totally full of shit.

I finished my story and McGhee sat in silence for a moment, looking at me, but not really. More like looking through me at the living room wall. He nodded to himself. "Got a last name for this Violet?" he asked.

"No," I said.

Gonzalez laughed. A brittle sound, like breaking glass.

"Something funny?" I asked him.

"What's funny is how often the stories start to change once we catch someone in a lie." He reached up to scratch the side of his neck. "Although you think quick on your feet, I'll give you that, kid."

"It's the truth," I said.

"Why wasn't it the truth yesterday?" McGhee asked, nibbling on his pencil again.

I shrugged. I still didn't want to tell them about Liars, Inc. It wasn't like any of our classmates had kidnapped Preston. "I thought everything was fine. I told him I would cover for him, so I didn't want to screw it up and get him in trouble."

McGhee nodded. "I see. He hasn't called you, has he?"

"No."

"But he should have his phone with him, wherever he is, right?" McGhee asked. "Preston's mom said he was always glued to his cell."

"Yeah," I admitted. My stomach lurched as I thought about Preston's phone still hanging out in my trunk.

"You don't mind if we take a look around, do you?" McGhee said. "It's not like you have anything to hide, right?"

I froze. "I, uh, I think my parents would want to be here for that."

"We promise not to disturb anything. We won't even go in their room," he said.

I could feel the blood draining from my face. My phone buzzed sharply. Gonzalez watched as I accessed the text message. It was from Parvati. One word: *warrant.*

I tucked the phone into the pocket of my hoodie. "Look. I have to go pick up my sister from school in a little bit. Now's not a good time for you guys to start looking around." Then, almost as if it were an afterthought, I added, "Anyway, don't you need a warrant to search somewhere?"

"We only need a warrant if you don't give us permission," McGhee said.

"I think my parents would want a warrant."

Gonzalez narrowed his eyes. "Just remember, Max. If you

make things hard on us we might feel inclined to make them hard on you."

"Well, it's all been easy and fun so far." I made a big show of pulling my car keys out of my pocket and glancing toward the door. "Talk to you guys soon, I'm sure."

"I guess we'll get out of your hair," McGhee said. The two agents exchanged a long look. I didn't know what it meant, but I didn't like it.

They got up and headed for the door. "Hey, Max," Gonzo called back over his shoulder. "You just turned eighteen, right?"

Just my luck that all of this was going down the exact day I legally became an adult. Happy birthday to me. "Why?" I asked. "Did you buy me something nice?"

He smirked. "Let us know if you're going to leave town, okay?"

FOURTEEN

PARVATI AND I FISHED THE phone out of my trunk the second McGhee and Gonzalez left. Of course the battery had died. I started scrubbing it down with a baby wipe. No more blood. No more fingerprints.

A giant clap of thunder came out of nowhere, shaking the windowpanes. Raindrops began to plink against the glass.

"Nice call on the warrant," I said.

"Yeah," Parvati replied, without looking at me. She was staring at the phone. "If they find that, they're going to arrest you."

"So let's just get rid of it." Even as I said the words, I knew we couldn't. We might need it to find Preston's mysterious girlfriend. There could be other clues on it too. I finished with the baby wipe and then set the phone on the coffee table.

Parvati reached for it. Using the sleeve of her shirt, she pressed the power button. The screen stayed dark. "At least if the battery is dead they won't be able to track it anymore." She sighed deeply. "But we can't just baby-wipe away the smears of blood in your trunk."

"You really think some random smudges that may or may not be blood are enough to prove I committed a crime?"

"No, but add the smudges to the fact that you had the phone and got rid of it, and that they have an eyewitness that says you and Pres were arguing. All that is more than enough to convince them to test your trunk for blood and go digging for other stuff."

"Other stuff they won't find."

She arched an eyebrow. "You sure about that?"

I shook my head. "I'm not sure about anything," I said. "Preston wouldn't make it an hour without his phone. If he thought he lost it he would have pulled over and gone through his whole car to find it. And then he would have realized he forgot it and turned around. How could it end up in my trunk?" *With blood on it.* "And who the hell told the cops Pres and I were arguing?"

Parvati rested her forehead against her hands. "It's almost like you're being—"

"Set up." Like I was a suspect in one of Amanda's detective shows instead of a high school kid. Like I had fallen into someone else's life. One that might look fun if I was watching it on TV, but sure as hell didn't *feel* fun.

I thought about the Jacobsens, the only other people at the beach. They had to be the ones who told the FBI about Preston's car not being parked at the overlook. But were they the ones who lied about seeing Pres and me fighting? If so, why? The surfing brothers had nothing against me.

At least, I didn't think so.

Too much had happened too quickly. I was still waiting for Preston to roll up in his car and tell me a big funny story about his adventures in Vegas. I hadn't completely wrapped my brain around the possibility that something bad had happened to him, let alone the possibility that someone else had hurt him and was setting me up to take the fall.

But then I remembered how weird Pres had been acting at the overlook. He was upset about something going on with his family. Bad thoughts started to creep in. "What if someone hired Violet to get close to Preston online? People are speculating about his dad getting tapped as Secretary of Labor. Maybe the FBI is right and some political nutjobs snatched him."

Parvati went quiet for a second as she mulled the possibility over in her head. "Did Pres have any enemies of his own that you know of?"

"He told me he owed Jonas Jacobsen money, but according to Jared that was a lie." I raked a hand through my hair. "Everyone else worships Preston, don't they?"

"Pretty much," she agreed. "If someone took him, his parents will get a ransom request." She paused. "But the FBI guys are still going to pounce on you once they find the blood in your trunk. I'll charge the phone and then drive somewhere and turn it on just long enough to look at the recent calls and texts. But you need to get rid of your car, or find someplace to hide out until we can figure out what really happened."

I couldn't just get rid of my car. Was I supposed to tell my parents that someone *stole* that twenty-year-old rust bucket? Even if I wrecked it or ran it off a cliff, the agents would still find it unless I set it on fire or something.

The idea of skipping town until all of this blew over was majorly appealing, but if the feds pulled Preston's body out of a back alley or some crazy bitch's apartment in Vegas, I was going to blame myself. "Screw that. I haven't done anything wrong. If I split I'll look totally guilty."

"And if you stay you'll look guilty, and you'll go to jail. I've heard my mom talk about stuff like this. Your parents won't be able to make bail on kidnapping, Max. Or worse. We're talking six figures, minimum."

Worse. Like murder. The agents had decided I was guilty of something from the moment someone had lied about Preston and me arguing, if not earlier. They'd see my trunk, test the blood, and arrest me. I'd never figure out what happened to Preston from inside a jail cell, and they might not waste time looking for other suspects once they had me.

"Plus they probably know about your assault charge," she added. "I'm sure that's not helping matters."

"The lawyer told me that couldn't be used against me," I protested.

"Probably not in court, but that doesn't mean those guys won't judge you because of it."

My assault charge. Technically assault and battery, but what a bunch of bullshit. It happened a couple years ago. Amanda was playing outside after school and I was supposed to be looking after her, but I was inside watching TV instead. I remember I had just found out I had to retake American History in summer school, so I was really pissed off. I peeked out at my sister during a commercial and saw these two boys out in the street hollering at her—calling her a freak. Just as I opened the door to get her safely inside, one of the boys picked up a crushed aluminum can and threw it at her. What kind of epic douchebag throws stuff at a little girl with a disability?

Props to my sister, though, because instead of running away to safety, she picked up the crushed can and threw it back. Then she screamed a word that Darla would definitely not approve of and grabbed a loose clod of dirt and threw that too. I was beside her in an instant, chucking the first thing my hands closed around, which unfortunately was a rock.

My aim was a little better than Amanda's.

Ben and Darla were furious when the cops came around to arrest me. Turned out my aim was so good that one of the little thugs had to get five stitches. I thought my parents were going to leave me locked up until my trial date. But once they shut up and let Amanda tell them what had *really* happened, they got me out the same day. I still got a lecture about violence, but Ben couldn't keep from smiling throughout the whole thing. He might as well have high-fived me and taken me out to dinner.

After that day I was Amanda's freaking idol. She was kind of my idol, too. The only thing that sucked was that the public defender said I might get tried as an adult, since I was sixteen and obviously knew what I was doing. (It probably didn't help that the kid I hit was eleven.) She said if I pled guilty I'd just get community service and probation since it was my first offense. If I pled not guilty I might end up going to jail.

So of course I pled guilty, and now a couple of asshole FBI agents probably thought I was the kind of loser that got my jollies beating up little kids. They'd use that info to paint me as some unstable whack job who jacked his rich, popular friend. Who cares if they didn't have a motive? Crazy kids committed random acts of violence all the time, didn't they? My brain was finally catching up to Parvati's. If I let them take me in, I was done for.

I started flipping through the possibilities of where I could go and what I could tell Ben and Darla so they wouldn't worry. Unfortunately, I wasn't coming up with much.

"Maybe I'll head to Vegas," I said. "See if I can locate this Violet chick. If you find her number on Pres's phone you can text it to me." I glanced down at my own phone. "I have to pick up my sister in twenty minutes."

"I'll get Amanda," Parvati said. "The teachers have seen us pick her up together plenty of times. I'll just tell her your parents needed extra help at The Triple S." She hopped off the couch. "Going to Vegas is a good idea if we can figure out for sure where Pres went. Otherwise it's just a waste of an entire day. Give me a few hours and I bet I can con my way into Preston's room. I'm sure the FBI took his laptop, but he keeps an external hard drive hidden away. There might be information on it."

"What am I supposed to do for a few hours?" My heart started banging out a drum solo in my chest. I didn't know how long it took to get a warrant, but I had a feeling I'd be seeing McGhee and Gonzalez again soon. Maybe I could clean my trunk. Can you even clean blood off fabric? You can't, can you? It's one of those things that shows up under those cool purple lights you see on TV. And trying to clean it would only make me look more guilty. Maybe I could just rip the upholstery out of the trunk. Maybe I could set the car on fire.

"Hide somewhere," Parvati said. "I'll grab the hard drive, meet up with you, and we can check out his files together. If Preston is in Vegas we can head there tomorrow after my parents go to work."

She made it sound so easy, like there wasn't anything to think about. Hide. Then find Preston. Get back to a normal life by the weekend. "I guess I could go camping again. Maybe a little ways up the coast, catch a few waves." I frowned. "Darla's going to get all freaked out, though. We were supposed to go out to dinner for my birthday."

On cue, a bolt of lightning cut the sky outside into two

pieces. The rain came down in sheets, blotting out my front yard and the houses across the street.

"Stupid weather." Parvati swore under her breath. "You can't camp in this. What about my dad's cabin?"

"Isn't it still full of his military pals?" I envisioned a few Navy SEALs launching themselves through the plate-glass front window in gas masks and full riot gear.

"I saw Dad detail-cleaning his rifles last week, so hunting must be done for this year. You should be okay."

Being inside was definitely preferable to riding out the storm in a tent. Plus, the cabin was isolated, and McGhee and Gonzalez had no reason to know about it. They didn't know Parvati and I were still together, so they'd have no reason to suspect she was helping me. Not yet, anyway. By the time they figured out we were still a couple and thought to question her, we'd be on the way to Vegas.

"I'll go back to Pres's house and talk Esmeralda into letting me in his bedroom," she continued. "Then I'll meet you at the cabin. We'll look at anything I manage to find and go from there."

"How are you going to get away with cutting class?"

She grinned. "The same way I'm getting away with it right now. 'I'm afraid Parvati's condition has not improved. It might be the influenza,' " she said in an exact imitation of her mother's lilting Indian accent. "Duh. Liars, Inc.

Self-alibis are free, right?"

I shook my head. "You're a piece of work, you know it?"

"A national treasure," she said, still speaking in her mom's accent.

"It's kind of hot when you talk like that." For a second, I almost forgot I was preparing to run away to avoid being arrested for a crime against my friend.

"It's hot no matter how I talk." Parvati leaned in and gave me a quick kiss on the lips.

Both of us smiled, and I realized how glad I was to have her on my side, how everything seemed a little less scary with her around.

FIFTEEN

WHILE I SCRIBBLED A NOTE to Darla and Ben about how I left to go look for Preston, Parvati helped me quickly pack a bag of things I'd need for a couple days in case I went straight from the Colonel's cabin to Vegas. Then she went to pick up Amanda while I headed toward the Angeles National Forest.

My tires quickly ate up the miles of dusty highway. I still didn't know if running away was a smart move. Parvati thought it was, but easy for her to say. She wasn't the one implicating herself in a possible felony. Still, thanks to her mom she knew more about this crap than I did, and what she said made sense. The FBI agents would present my lies to the judge, along with the bloody trunk and missing phone, and I'd be done for. They'd assign me another overworked public defender who would tell me to take a plea bargain, and I'd end up in jail. Not happening.

I puzzled over two main questions as I drove. The first: who would want to hurt Pres? He was our school's most beloved athlete, but his rah-rah go-team image was mostly smoke and mirrors. He didn't give a shit about school spirit or our classmates. He played football because he loved it, the feel of slipping between two hulk-like defenders, the thrill of beating the odds. It was the same reason he liked surfing and gambling. He liked taking risks, especially when he came out on top, which he almost always did.

In that sense, a lot of people might have wanted to hurt him. People who he had lied to or beaten. People who had gambled with him and lost. Or won. Jared Jacobsen said Preston might have moved on to bigger and better things. Was Pres betting with a professional bookie? Maybe that was why he was so secretive about his recent online activities. Maybe that was the real reason he went to Vegas. I thought about what happened in movies to gamblers who owed money. I hoped Pres wasn't lying bloody and beaten in an alley somewhere.

The other question was harder: who would want to hurt *me*? I was basically invisible at school and tried my best not to piss people off at the beach. I couldn't think of a single person who had anything against me. But someone had lied about Preston and me fighting at the top of Ravens' Cliff, and possibly planted Pres's bloody phone in my trunk. It had to be the Jacobsens, didn't it? No one else was there.

No.

Wait.

There was another car.

A gray SUV.

I had nearly crashed into a gray SUV just down the street from my house when I was daydreaming about Parvati. It could have been the same one that was parked at the beach overlook on Sunday morning.

My phone buzzed. Shit. If I left it on, the feds would be able to GPS me. I glanced down at the display before switching it off. Darla. My stomach tightened. I was screwing up every-thing—our birthday dinner, trimming the tree. I wondered if she and Ben had ever regretted adopting me, if they were secretly glad I was eighteen now so they could be rid of me whenever they wanted.

I'd been on the road for just under an hour when the turn-off for the cabin appeared. I realized I hadn't thought about what I should do with my car. Parking it in the Colonel's driveway didn't seem like a smart idea.

I turned off the winding two-lane road about a mile past the cabin when I saw a sign for a nature preserve. Gravel sprayed up on both sides of me as the car lurched and bounced down a shallow incline. I did my best to avoid the bathtub-sized potholes and low-hanging branches. At the bottom of a hill, a tiny parking area sat overgrown with weeds. I pulled the Escort as far into the high grass as I could. Anyone who came this way would find it, but it wouldn't be visible from the top of the hill.

A wooden trailhead, with a place for backpackers to register if they were going into the backcountry, stood at the edge of the parking area. If someone found the car, maybe they'd think I hiked into the wilderness to hide.

The camping gear from Preston's alibi was still in my trunk. If I remembered right, the cabin was pretty sparsely furnished. I'd need just about everything I had with me to survive comfortably there. I packed my sleeping bag, first aid kit, a thermos of water, and the bag of clothes and toiletries Parvati had gathered for me into my oversized frame pack.

I hiked back up the gravel road and stood at the edge of the trees, listening for cars approaching on the highway. The last thing I wanted was for some trucker to see me. When the road was empty, I jetted across the street and quickly disappeared into the underbrush on the other side.

As I hiked toward the cabin, I reviewed the events of the last few days in my head. On Saturday I went camping and Preston went to Vegas. On Sunday night, he didn't come home. The FBI was talking to me by Monday morning, and then again on Tuesday. Preston was eighteen and had a history of reckless and impulsive behavior. Senator's kid or not, the first idea should have been that Pres ran off on his own. Yet from the moment his disappearance was reported, the FBI was treating it as a crime. They knew stuff I didn't. That was the only explanation.

Thunder shook the sky. The dense foliage blocked out most of the daylight, making it seem later than it was. I ducked under a low-hanging branch, a carpet of pine needles crunching beneath my feet.

Preston might have come back to the overlook parking lot when I was already down on the beach. Let's say he was missing his phone. Maybe my car was unlocked (it usually was), so he popped the trunk without making his way down the steep trail to come find me. He found his phone at the bottom of the camping gear and then someone hit him on the head. That would explain the phone and the blood. Or maybe someone followed him from the beach overlook, jumped him when he stopped for gas or something, and then planted his bloody phone in my trunk afterward.

But why would anyone do that?

Unless . . .

Maybe I was just in the wrong place at the wrong time. Maybe I was just a convenient fall guy. If someone wanted to kidnap the school's MVP, why not pin it on the kid who gets paid to fake alibis? There was a certain poetic justice to it all.

I climbed up a small slope and escaped from the trees onto a winding dirt road, and there it was—the Colonel's cabin. Parvati had made me a spare key during the summer, back when we used to hang out there on a regular basis. I glanced around nervously, hoping no one was watching. I knew this whole area was full of similar cabins, most of which were probably deserted this late in the year.

I opened the metal storm door quickly and unlocked the inner door. It creaked as it swung inward, and the smell of rancid meat overwhelmed me. Covering my nose with my shirt, I flipped a switch on the wall, and the only bulb still working in the light fixture above my head crackled to life. The cabin looked pretty much the same as I remembered it: sparse but functional. The slick vinyl sofa sat against the back wall of the living room, and the wooden coffee table was bare except for a half-empty box of ammunition.

I ducked into the small kitchen, just to make sure I was alone. The fridge and stove were both smudged with dirty glove prints, and the steel countertop didn't look like it had been properly wiped down after the last person had cleaned his game. No wonder the whole place smelled funky. I dropped my gear in one of the two small bedrooms. They were just boxes with rollaway beds, a tiny bathroom between them. It was livable, but it wasn't anywhere I wanted to live for too long. Good thing I'd be out of there in the morning. I would have to keep moving if I didn't want McGhee and Gonzalez to catch me. That was another thing I had learned on the streets. Being homeless was like being a shark—survival was a matter of always moving forward.

Unfortunately, I couldn't do anything until Parvati showed up later. Desperate for a distraction, I plunked down on the sofa and flipped through the handful of TV channels. All I got were varying degrees of static. What were the feds doing? Gonzo had probably skipped right past the search warrant to the arrest warrant, and I couldn't even blame him. Maybe they were already looking for me. Or interviewing people at school about *me* instead of Preston. Someone would tell them about Liars, Inc. Someone would tell them Parvati and I still seemed like a couple. That would be enough for them to contact her, if they hadn't already. She was Preston's other best friend, after all. She'd definitely get questioned sooner or later.

I knew she'd lie to protect me, but I also knew her mother would insist on being present for any questioning. Would her mom see through Parvati's stories? Would she consider the possibility her own daughter might be aiding and abetting a fugitive?

Was I a *fugitive*?

I swore under my breath. Hiding out here had made perfect sense when I was talking to Parvati, but now I wasn't so sure. Maybe this was a really bad idea. Was it too late for me to go back? I could have her turn in the phone, explain why I ran. Innocent people ran from the cops on TV all the time. McGhee and Gonzalez might understand.

Or they might just let the pieces fall neatly into place . . . and crucify me.

I fiddled with a rip in the sofa, my fingers aimlessly pulling out bits of cream-colored stuffing. Three mounted bass looked down at me from the wall behind the television. Their mouths gaped low, like they were drowning. The more I looked at them, the more I felt like they were trying to tell me something.

Air. Fresh air would be good. I decided to go for a walk in the woods behind the cabin. I headed through the kitchen and out the back door, stopping for a second to pull a questionably squishy bag from the trash can. Maybe the rancid smell wasn't coming from the dirty countertop. I knotted the top of the bag without looking inside and dropped it outside the door. The forest stretched out around me.

The trail from the back of the cabin led through the trees to the edge of a cliff that overlooked a river. It was only slightly overgrown since the last time Parvati and I came here. We used to hide in the foliage and stalk deer. Parvati didn't want to hurt them. She just wanted to see if she could get close enough to touch one.

My eyes quickly adjusted to the waning light as I headed down the path. I could hear the water before I could see it. At the edge of the cliff I looked down. Fifty feet below, the river writhed and twisted, black water roaring through the turns.

I sat on the edge of the cliff, dangling my feet over the side. Parvati and I used to swim in the river. I still remembered the first time she dared me to jump from this spot. I wasn't going to do it, but then she did, so I had to. It was terrifying, the brief instant of free fall before crashing into the icy water. But it was exciting too. One day we must have jumped at least twenty times. We'd had so much fun during the summer. It sucked that I had to be here without her.

My stomach rumbled, reminding me I hadn't eaten since I choked down a few bites of sandwich much earlier. I wandered back to the cabin and into the kitchen. Unfortunately, the cupboards were empty.

I wondered if it was safe to hike back to my car and drive to the nearest town to get fast food. A crash of thunder and the sound of rain battering the corrugated roof put an end to that idea. I dug through the drawers and cabinets one more time, looking for anything edible. No such luck.

The digital clock on the microwave read five o'clock and I was ready to go to bed. Boredom will do that to you. I wondered if Parvati had managed to snag Pres's hard drive, if she was on her way to the cabin. I wished I could turn on my phone.

"She can wake me up when she gets here," I muttered under my breath. I unrolled my sleeping bag onto the cot in one of the tiny bedrooms. It was more comfortable than it looked, but it was low to the ground and only half the width of my bed at home. No matter which way I turned, one of my limbs hung over the side and onto the floor. After a few minutes of tossing and turning, I moved my sleeping bag out to the sofa in the living room. Slightly better, except my arm kept falling down in the cushions. One of the sofa coils was poking through the fabric and each time the sharp metal stabbed my hand I jolted back awake.

I pressed my hands to my chest, mummy-style, and was almost asleep when I heard the cabin door open. Even though Parvati was the only one who knew where I was, my heart slid up into my throat. I sat up quickly, praying she wasn't wrong about hunting season being over.

Her slim figure slipped through the door, and I exhaled deeply. "Hey, P," I said. "Find out anything interesting?"

"Maybe." She shook drops of rain from her curtain of hair.

"I brought you something."

"Please let it be dinner." My stomach was shrieking for decent food.

"Not quite." Parvati pulled a black handgun from her purse.

SIXTEEN

"WHAT THE HELL?" MY JAW dropped.

She tried to hand me the gun, but I pulled away at the last second and it landed on the floor between us. She ducked out of the way like she thought it might go off.

"Holy shit! That thing is loaded? Have you lost your mind?"

"What good is an unloaded gun?" she asked, like I was completely dense. She picked it up and handed it to me again.

I took it reluctantly, angling the barrel toward the ground. "Is the safety on at least?"

She shook her head. "There's no safety, Max. It's a Glock, like your FBI pals use. You just slide the lever and pull the trigger. It's made for dropping people."

"What, are you a gangsta now? Who exactly am I supposed to be *dropping*?"

Parvati hopped up on the sofa and sat cross-legged next to me. "If someone snatched Preston, who knows what else the guy is capable of? I just think we need to consider all of the angles. We need to protect ourselves." She tugged at the ends of her hair. "What if this wasn't about politics or some crazy internet girlfriend? What if it was closer to home? Maybe we screwed someone with one of our alibis."

The gun felt like a live grenade in my hand. I set it gingerly onto the coffee table. "What? Like some loser high school kid kidnapped Pres? I think this is bigger than that. Besides, he was mostly just our PR guy."

"Did he ever say anything about having trouble with that David guy he was helping in calc class?"

"David Nephew? He's about half Preston's height and one-third his weight. Even if David had a baseball bat and a tranquilizer gun, I'd still bet on Pres. And didn't you say he was all surprised when Preston didn't show up at school yesterday?"

"True. Can you think of anyone else?" she pressed.

"I don't think he set up many alibis by himself," I said. "I had to hook up Quinn with an excuse note that Pres forgot about, but other than that we haven't had any complaints."

"Do you know who he was always texting?" she asked. "Or what he was doing on his laptop all the time?"

"I figured it was online gambling," I said. "Or talking to this Violet girl. What was on his phone?"

Parvati pulled it out of her purse. The screen was dark. "I only turned it on for a few seconds, but everything before Saturday has been wiped. No videos. No pix. No texts."

That didn't make sense. Preston was always shooting videos and saving stuff on his phone. "So there's nothing on it?"

"Only a handful of calls and texts from me, you, and his parents." She slipped the phone back into her purse. "I just don't want whoever's gotten to him to get to you too, Max."

She said this all matter-of-factly, like Preston being "gotten to" was no big deal, but I knew better. I knew Parvati. I knew that the more things bothered her, the more she acted like everything was fine. That was why some swim team girl talking to me at school was enough to rile her up, but the news of a friend's disappearance didn't even seem to register on her pretty face.

"What about you?" I turned toward her. "Any of your call-ins go wrong? Anyone get busted?"

She shook her head. "Not that I know of."

"Well, if I'm in danger, you're probably in danger too."

"I'm a brown belt, remember? Plus no shortage of guns at the Amos compound." She raised her shirt just high enough to show me her shoulder holster.

I cringed at the thought of Parvati locked and loaded, but at least she wouldn't shoot off her own foot like I might. Her dad had taught her how to handle rifles and shotguns in middle school, and she'd been practicing with a handgun for at least a year. I'd only seen the inside of her bedroom a handful of times, but I would never forget her proud display of paper targets, all of which had ten hits in the inner circle.

"Besides," she continued, "no one is trying to kidnap me *or* frame me as far as I know."

"Have you heard anything new?" I asked, dreading the answer. "Is there a ransom note?"

"No," she said. "But I heard Astrid Covington say the Vista P cops were searching the water, that they think maybe Preston got pushed off Ravens' Cliff."

"So Astrid is telling everyone I killed him?"

"Well, she didn't say your name specifically, but—"

I cut her off. "Did you get the hard drive?"

Parvati's pupils widened, making her eyes look completely black. "Of course." She pulled a flat, metallic rectangle from her jacket pocket. "Esmeralda let me in, and for a while no one knew I was there. I also took some pictures of Pres's room." She slid her laptop out of her backpack, plugged it into the wall, and turned it on. While we waited for it to boot up we scrolled through the photos on her phone, looking for anything unusual.

I squinted at the screen. There was almost no hint of Preston in the blank white walls and black lacquer furniture. For the most part, it could have been anyone's room. Parvati and I studied the pictures one at a time. His bookshelf, prominently featuring a neat line of textbooks he probably hadn't opened all year. His dresser, a mess of toiletries—aftershave, deodorant, contact solution.

"I didn't know Preston wore contacts," I said.

"Me neither." Parvati flipped to another picture and pointed at Preston's open closet door. His rich-kid pants and designer sweaters hung on one side, a wash of deep blues and greens, muted tans and yellows. The other side was full of black rock-band T-shirts and ripped jeans. In private, Pres dressed like me, but his parents had bribed him to quit "looking like a thug" in public by buying him a second wardrobe and a brand-new BMW. I guess they thought if he dressed like a yuppie and drove the car of a forty-year-old that he'd join the country club and start building a stock portfolio instead of getting wasted and gambling away his allowance. It had never worked, as far as I could tell.

I looked back and forth between the wardrobes. If you didn't know Preston, you'd swear this closet belonged to two different people. There was a small ribbon of blank space in the middle.

"Normally it's overflowing with clothes," Parvati said. "I wonder if Pres planned on staying with Ms. Violet for more than just a couple of days."

The closet looked pretty full to me, but obviously Parvati had been in his room more than I had. "Or maybe Esmeralda was just behind with the laundry," I offered.

Parvati snorted. She scrolled to the next image. "Unlikely. I never saw that woman fall behind on anything. Did you happen to notice if Pres had a lot of stuff packed?"

"His whole car was full of camping stuff, but I thought it was just for the alibi. He gave me some, but I didn't go pawing through the rest."

"Did the FBI guys ever find his car?" she asked.

"Not that I know of, but they haven't exactly been keeping me in the loop."

Parvati's laptop beeped, and the start-up screen finally appeared. She plugged Preston's external drive into the USB port.

"Where'd you find that, anyway?" I asked.

She smiled enigmatically. She was good at that enigmatic thing. She pointed at her phone, at the picture of Pres's bookshelf. "False book," she said. "No one would ever decide to pull out *Essentials of Trigonometry* and start thumbing through."

"How did *you* know?" For the first time, I felt jealous of

Parvati instead of Preston. It was irrational—they'd been friends for three times as long as Pres and I had—but still, it kind of bothered me that she knew things about him I didn't.

"We made them together freshman year—razor-bladed out a square in the middle of the pages. It was my idea," she said proudly.

I could see them there, sitting cross-legged on Preston's bed, silver blades poised over the crisp pages of unused math books. Parvati looking conspiratorial. Preston with that usual relaxed grin of his. I wondered what else they'd done together, what other stories I'd never heard.

"Was there anything else hidden in there?"

She shrugged. "Just his passport and a few pictures from when he was a kid."

I stared at the laptop screen as a group of folders popped up, arranged in two orderly rows. The good thing about investigating someone who kept his external hard drive in a doctored trigonometry book was that he didn't think he had to encrypt his files. I scanned the folder names: docs, tunes, pix, vids.

"Let's try docs first," she said. "Maybe he saves emails."

No luck: it was full of school papers. Pix was more interesting. There were several sub-folders with two-letter names that seemed to be initials. I saw my own initials, as well as

Parvati's. Only one folder started with *V.* Parvati seemed to be sharing my train of thought. She clicked on the VC folder, and sure enough, three thumbnail images of a blonde girl came up.

Parvati clicked on the first one to enlarge it, and her jaw dropped slightly. "Is it just me or does she look kind of old?"

"It's not just you," I said. The girl stood in front of the pirate ship display at the Treasure Island Hotel. She wore the same short skirt–tall shoes combo that a lot of the chicks at Vista P were always rocking, but there was just something about the photo that made her look older. Maybe it was the hairstyle, or the way her shirt fit, or the hardness of her smile. I couldn't put my finger on it. The second picture was a headshot, a little blurry, like someone had snapped it with a cheap cell phone. The woman was pretty, but I could see ridges in her forehead and tiny wrinkles at the corners of her eyes that only came with age. She was wearing a bikini in the third picture, and although her body was banging, she was still clearly much older than Preston.

I squinted at the photo's background, but it just looked like a generic beach. It could have been taken anywhere. I guess a picture of her posing in front of her house, address prominently displayed, was asking a little much.

"Let's see if we can find her." Parvati connected the hard drive to her phone and transferred over the image files. She fiddled around until she got a decent signal and then opened a search engine page and pasted the first picture into the image search box.

I leaned over her shoulder. "I didn't know you could search by picture."

"Watch and learn." Parvati smiled as a social networking profile pulled up. I peeked over her shoulder, but the text was too tiny to read. "Get this," she said, in a voice that let me know a big reveal was coming. "I think I know why Preston didn't tell us about her." She paused for emphasis. "Violet Cain. Las Vegas. Thirty-five years old."

SEVENTEEN

THIRTY-FIVE YEARS OLD? WHAT WAS Preston doing hooking up with someone almost old enough to be his mom?

"Let me see that." I glanced back at the bikini picture, which was still open on Parvati's laptop. Violet's skin was tan, her body flawless. Okay, so she did have that going for her, but still. We had hot teachers younger than her, and Preston had never seemed interested in any of them.

"What else does her profile say?" I asked.

"Violet only shares some of her information." Parvati read from her phone. "For more about Violet Cain, send her a message or friend request."

"Should we send her a message?" I asked. "Maybe Pres is totally fine and just lost his phone."

"But if she's crazy, we'll be tipping her off that we know about her. Let's see if her address is listed." Abandoning the incomplete profile, Parvati found the page for Las Vegas directory assistance and typed in the name Violet Cain. There were three listings—two in Las Vegas and one in North Las Vegas. "If we went to Vegas ourselves, we could check out all three of these addresses in less than an hour," she said. "If we left here around seven tomorrow morning, do you think we could make it to Vegas and back by five?"

"Probably not," I said. "Not without speeding, anyway."

Parvati furrowed her brow. "Maybe I can just leave my phone off. When I don't come home from school, my parents will freak, but by that time we'll have found Pres, or Violet at least. I'll just tell them you forced me to go along with you."

"Great." I mentally added kidnapping to my list of alleged crimes. "With or without you, I'm definitely going to Vegas tomorrow." It wasn't like there was anything I could do hanging out around the cabin. The longer I stayed, the greater the chances were that McGhee and Gonzalez would find me.

Me, Max Cantrell, fugitive.

"You can go with me if you can figure out how to get away from your parents," I continued. Part of me wanted Parvati by my side the whole way. She knew all this stuff about spying and the legal system that I had no clue about. Plus, I wanted her because I *wanted* her. Not just for the sex, but because she had this gift for making terrible stuff seem okay. Almost fun. And with Parvati, it'd feel like we were two kids searching for our friend. Without her, I'd be one criminal running from the FBI.

But I didn't want her messed up in anything illegal. Not only because she could get shipped off to military school, but also because every day Preston didn't come home this whole thing felt more dangerous.

Parvati nodded. "That reminds me." She pulled a cheap plastic-looking phone out of her purse. "I got us both pre-paids so you can call me and no one will be able to trace it. My new number is the only one programmed in."

"A burner phone and a gun made for dropping people. Whose life is this again?" I tried to keep my voice light because I didn't want to lose it in front of her, but inside I was starting to crack. I just wanted Preston to come home and everything to go back to being normal. I wanted to spend my birthday like I'd planned, with Amanda and my parents, putting up the Christmas tree while Ji and Jo tried to eat the ornaments. I didn't want to be hiding from feds or thinking about whether my friend was dead.

"It's our life, until we figure things out."

"Good thing I have a master spy on my side." I forced myself to smile. "Your parents would be so proud."

"Hah. My mom would be horrified. She still wants me to

be a lawyer. My dad would probably ask me if I'd been reading his SERE manuals."

"What's seer?"

"S-E-R-E. Survival, evasion, resistance, escape," she said. "That's what he does now. Teaches new recruits to be badass. He used to be a combat controller before he got old."

I didn't know what a combat controller did, but anything with "control" in the title seemed like it would fit the Colonel.

Parvati looked sad for a moment, snuggling close to me on the vinyl sofa. "I have to leave in an hour. I called my mom to tell her my newspaper meeting was running late, but I need to be home by eight for some big dinner with my grandparents or I'll be the one needing to survive, evade, resist, and escape."

"Okay." I touched my cheek to her forehead. "Hey, can I hang on to your laptop until tomorrow? Maybe go through some more stuff on Preston's hard drive?"

"Sure. I'm going to leave his phone here, too, so I don't accidentally get caught with it." She laid her head back in my lap and looked up at me with her soft, dark eyes. "Poor Max," she said. "This isn't how I wanted you to spend your birthday."

I brushed her hair back from her face. "I'm just glad you're here."

"But you only turn eighteen once. I wanted it to be unforgettable for you."

"Unforgettable, huh?" I bent down and kissed her lightly on the lips. "I can think of a few things that might make today unforgettable."

"I was hoping you'd say that," she whispered. She pulled me down to her level. "Max time. My—"

I cut her off. "Yeah, yeah, your favorite time." Our mouths met. I forgot the feel of cracked vinyl and the rumbling in my stomach.

A folded gray blanket sat on the top of the sofa. Parvati yanked it down with one hand and shook it out so it unfolded over us. For the next half an hour, I quit worrying about Preston and FBI agents and thirty-five-year-old chicks from Vegas. I just let Parvati wish me a happy birthday.

Afterward, we both lay back, looking up at the light fixture with the burned-out bulbs.

"I don't know what I would do without you," I told Parvati. "I don't think I'd make it through everything that's happening."

"You'd be fine, Max." She slid out from beneath the blanket and started getting dressed. "Your past made you resilient so you don't fall apart in a crisis. I like that."

I thought about her words as I watched her get dressed. She wasn't very tall, but her legs seemed to go for miles. My eyes worked their way up her naked back. Just the slightest hint of tan line lingered at her shoulders. I had never considered myself resilient. I wondered if it was true, or if she was just seeing what she wanted to see.

"But I'm glad I can help," she continued. Skipping her bra, she slid her T-shirt over her head and then came to lie next to me again. She rested her cheek against my chest.

Warmth radiated through her skin into mine. I angled my neck to look down at her. "You know I didn't do anything, right?"

"Of course." She squeezed my hand. "We don't know that anyone did anything yet."

"Yeah, but you said they're searching the water." I wasn't sure how I would react if someone pulled Preston's body out of the ocean. I wasn't ready to accept that he might really be gone.

"They're grasping," she said. "Because they don't have anything else."

We lay there in silence, our inhalations and exhalations slowly coming to match up. I felt whole, like I could breathe, like I could figure this thing out. Together, we could find Preston.

When it was time for Parvati to leave, I walked her out to her car. The sky had gone gray; the thick billowy clouds were weighted down with rain. We stood there a few minutes, pressed up against the door of the Grape, kissing. I didn't want her to go. Ever.

"If I don't hear from you tomorrow morning—"

"Then it means I can't get away," she said. "And that you should go to Vegas without me." She tossed her hair back from her face. "Where's your car? We can trade license plates. If you have to go alone, it might keep you from getting busted on the way."

"God, sometimes I think you're a spy already, and just undercover as a high school girl," I muttered. But it was a good plan, and I had the tools in my trunk to make it happen.

"Uh-oh. I've been made." Parvati arched her eyebrows suggestively. "I'm actually twenty-four, but lucky for you I have a thing for younger men." She poked me until I cracked a smile. "Actually I saw it in some movie Dad was watching a few months ago." She opened the driver's-side door and climbed behind the wheel. I jogged around to the passenger side and got in.

Parvati drove me to my car at the trailhead, and after we were sure no one was around we quickly swapped our plates. She headed home and I headed back to her father's cabin, flipping up the hood of my sweatshirt as the first drops of rain began to fall.

Back inside, I blotted myself with a towel hanging over

the edge of the shower. I went back to browsing through Preston's hard drive, poring over each of Violet's pictures, looking for clues. I wished I could get into Pres's email, but even if I could crack his password there wasn't any Wi-Fi out in the sticks.

Off in the distance, thunder tore the sky apart. Rain pounded the metal above my head. I hated the thought of Parvati navigating the twisting mountain roads during a storm, but there wasn't much I could do about it. *Focus, Max. Find Preston.*

I skimmed through the list of other folders, looking for anything that caught my eye. None of the initials were familiar to me except mine and Parvati's. The PA folder had ten pictures, including a recent one of Parvati in her homecoming dress, a short spangly green thing that I got turned on just looking at. Again, I reminded myself to stay focused. The MC folder had three pictures of me. One of them was a pic of me, Darla, and Ben outside The Triple S. I didn't even remember Preston taking it.

There was a PM folder that turned out to be pictures of Parvati and me together. There were two of us posed at parties, and even one shot of us scrunched together at the lunch table that Pres had snapped with his phone. I couldn't believe his phone now had nothing on it except a call record that probably implicated me. Total bullshit. He lived on that thing. It should have been full of files.

Clues.

I flipped to the video folder, but it was empty except for a couple of clips he had taken at the latest Kittens of Mass Destruction concert. That seemed odd. Pres was always shooting videos of people he knew. Maybe he only saved them to his phone, or maybe . . .

I scrolled up to the top of the screen to the View menu. Holding my breath, I selected "view hidden files and directories." A list of subfolders appeared. There was no VC folder for Violet Cain, but there were folders for Parvati and me. I went to click on the PA folder, but my aim was a little off and I opened the PM folder instead.

Thumbnails appeared, laid out in a nice orderly grid, and my blood screeched to a halt in my veins. Preston had videos of Parvati and me having sex.

EIGHTEEN

WE'D ONLY HOOKED UP AT his house the one time, but he had obviously rigged the guest bedroom with cameras. The videos were shot from above and from the side. I didn't have to play more than a few seconds of any of the clips to know exactly what I was looking at. My face reddened. Parvati would die (or her parents would murder her) if these videos ever got out.

What the fuck? Did Preston have some sort of creepy voyeuristic fetish? Why had he recorded us?

And how, exactly, was I supposed to break this news to Parvati?

A giant clap of thunder shook the cabin, and the lights flickered out. The laptop went dark with the room, the thumbnails of us winking out of view. I remembered Parvati saying something about her laptop battery not working. Just my luck.

I used the faint glow of my cell phone to make my way back into the cabin's living room. Did this place have candles? Probably, but I didn't have anything to light them with. I debated going to Vegas right away, but the rain was really coming down and I'd be soaked to the bone if I walked all the way to my car. The best plan was to crash until morning. I'd head to Vegas as soon as I woke up, with or without Parvati.

I bedded down on the sofa, letting my mind wander back to her lying next to me. Closing my eyes, I listened to the rain pinging against the roof. Parvati's face slowly disappeared, replaced by Preston's. *You ever feel like you don't know anyone?* Could he have meant me, or Parvati? Is that why he was spying on us? Because he didn't trust us? No, it's one thing to spy on people. It's another thing completely to film them naked. Preston was apparently more screwed up in the head than I had ever known.

Turning over, I buried my face in my pillow. After an hour or two of tossing and turning, my brain faded to black.

But even in my dreams, I couldn't escape thoughts of Pres and Parvati. They were running through the halls of a school. Not Vista Palisades—some place I had never been before. It looked old, with pillars and high hallways and classroom doors inset with big panes of glass. There was a ringing sound, like maybe someone had pulled the fire alarm, but Pres and Parvati didn't seem worried. I watched as she used a bobby pin to pick a lock. The two of them ducked inside a classroom, laughing, and then came out with a handful of dusty books. Pres dumped them in his duffel bag and they proceeded down the hall, stopping at a door that had CHEM-ISTRY LAB stenciled in neat black letters across the glass.

The ringing was louder now. Pres turned toward me as Parvati worked her lock-picking magic again. I ducked into a recessed area of the hallway so he wouldn't see me. I heard footsteps, people speaking in hushed tones. I peered around the corner, and Pres and Parvati were gone. The corridor was empty, but the voices sounded so close.

And then I heard a creak, and a key in the lock. My body jolted completely awake.

Someone was coming.

I slid off the sofa, grabbed the gun, and headed for the back door, just as Agents McGhee and Gonzalez burst through the front door of the darkened cabin and everything got even more fucked up.

THE END

NINETEEN

December 6th

AND JUST LIKE THAT, MY birthday went from a sleeping dream to a waking nightmare. I barely remember brandishing the gun, running from the feds, leaping from the cliff into the frigid water below.

But I've passed the last fifteen minutes or so in the river, mostly beneath the surface. That's one good thing about surfing. You spend enough time getting sucked under by rogue waves, you get good at holding your breath.

My lungs finally give up the last little bits of air and I pop up into the night, just far enough to suck in a couple more deep breaths. Around me, the roar of the water sounds muffled. My ears are still throbbing from the sound of the gun going off.

With a start, I realize the gun is weighing down the side pocket of my cargo pants. I don't even remember putting it away. Hopefully, I won't need it. Pretty sure guns aren't made for swimming.

I let the current carry me to the opposite bank, where I hide in a tall patch of reeds and try to figure out what to do next. McGhee and Gonzalez will either call for backup from a police department around here or set up some kind of river blockade downstream. I'm not sure if I should get out of the water or use the current to float even farther away. I wish Parvati were with me. She'd know. She'd quote some military escape manual. But Parvati is gone. Unreachable. The phone she left me is back at the cabin. I still have my own phone, but even if by some miracle it works after it dries out, calling her on it isn't safe.

That gives me an idea. I reach my hand below the surface of the murky water and pull my phone out of my hoodie pocket. The screen stays dark when I try to turn it on, but I throw it as hard as I can up onto the riverbank. Maybe it'll buy me some extra time if it dries out and someone decides to track me by GPSing it.

I take in another big breath of air and let the water carry me farther downstream. *Think, Max.* Nine years ago, I was the survival expert, not Parvati. There were some seriously bad people trolling the streets and beaches where I lived, and avoiding their psychotic wrath took mad skills. Have I gotten soft since the Cantrells adopted me?

A patch of rapids appears out of nowhere and I adjust my body so that I'm heading into the whitewater feet first to protect my head. The river curves to the left and then back to the right. An owl, or maybe a bat, soars across my field of vision.

I glance up at the sky. It's black, just like the water. I have no idea what time it is. I think I finally fell asleep around ten thirty, and it seemed like at least an hour passed before McGhee and Gonzalez found me, so now it's probably somewhere around one in the morning. I'm hoping the feds got distracted by Preston's phone and hard drive—the thought of them finding those sex clips almost makes me want to drown myself—before they started looking for me. But either way, they won't stop until they find me. I need to either ride the river far enough away from the cabin that I won't get caught in a manhunt, or get out of the water and try to hide in plain sight.

I decide to take my chances in the river for a while. It's cold, but I feel safer in the water. And I'll be able to see anyone coming before they get close.

My wallet is still in the back pocket of my cargo pants. Thanks to Liars, Inc. I should have enough soggy cash to buy another prepaid phone and some food. All I have to do is eventually find a safe place to get out of the river and make myself into someone other than Max Cantrell. How hard can it be?

I stay in the water for what feels like hours, curling my body into the fetal position to maximize warmth. In a couple places, the river is so shallow that I have to slither along on my elbows and knees to stay hidden beneath the surface. Soft sticky mud clings to my hands and coats the fabric of my pants.

When the current carries me past a wide stretch of gravel and sand I recognize as a canoe pullout, I work my way over to the bank. There's a painted wooden sign here. I squint to read it in the dark: LAZY DAYS CAMPGROUND AND FLOAT TRIP-PING. Score. I peel off my waterlogged hoodie and let it float downstream. Maybe someone will see it, and McGhee and Gonzalez will think I went farther than I did. Maybe they'll think I drowned. Even better.

I follow a winding path through a dense grove of trees and emerge into a campground. Most of the tents are still zipped closed for the night, which is good. Even in the "anything goes" atmosphere of most campgrounds, I'd probably raise a few eyebrows strolling up from the riverbank soaking wet and covered in mud.

I find what I'm looking for along the far side of the clearing, where a few RVs sit in asphalt parking spaces—a clothes-line tied between two trees. Unfortunately, all I see is girls' clothing. Impossibly skinny jeans and ruffled tank tops. Not going to work. But then I see a plain oversized T-shirt advertising last year's Sacramento Fun Run. Good enough. It's a little damp, but not soaked. Either it didn't rain here last night or the trees' dense branches protected the clothes on the line.

I head toward the middle of the campground, past a smaller wooden sign pointing to the shower area. Is it stupid to take a shower when you're being chased by the FBI? Probably, but then being covered in mud is pretty conspicuous. Besides, when I lived on the streets, I sometimes found useful stuff lying around in bathrooms. Since I left all my belongings at the cabin, I should at least check it out.

Unfortunately, this bathroom doesn't have anything to offer except for a vending machine that spits out various toiletries. There's a two-pack of razors I can use to shave my head. It isn't much as far as disguises go, but it's a start.

I slip into one of the showers and decide to rinse myself off, even if I have to put my soggy pants back on. Wet hair will be easier to cut, or so I think.

After all that time in the river, the warm water feels amazing. I have to keep reminding myself that McGhee and Gonzalez could be closing in, because otherwise I'll stand under the steamy jets all day. I hack at my hair and give up on going bald almost immediately. The flimsy razors are not made for cutting through five inches of tangled mess. I fight through my knots as best as I can, stopping frequently to rinse out the blade. When I finally give up, my hair seems to be several different lengths, but all of it is shorter than it was before. My trademark long bangs are lying on the tile floor of the shower, surrounded by other irregular messy brown clumps.

I start to slide my wet pants back over my legs when I hear footsteps. I hold my breath as a pair of muddy tennis shoes moves past my stall. There are a few beats of silence, and then the shower next to me starts up with a creak of pipes and a whoosh of water.

I exhale hard. What kind of weirdo goes camping and gets up before sunrise to take a shower? I peek out the side of my stall door. Bonus. My shower neighbor has left a towel and a pair of khaki pants hanging on a hook. I've never stolen clothes before, not even when I was homeless, but I'm pretty sure I need these khakis more than he does. I give myself a quick pat-down with the towel before slipping into my new clothing.

The pants are too big in the waist and about two inches too short for me. One of the hems is coming unstitched so the left leg is actually longer than the right leg. Oh well. I almost leave my wet pants behind for him, but I decide not to risk it. I don't want to leave a trail for McGhee and Gonzalez. Something tells me my stuff wouldn't fit Shower Guy anyway. I ball my wet, heavy clothes up under my arm.

Cruising through the bathroom, I stop for just a second to check out my hair in the mirror. It's sticking up all over. I'm going to look like a douchebag boy band singer when it dries. Either that or a crazy person. Best to find a hat, but not here. I can just imagine skulking around the campsite looking to score a forgotten baseball cap and having Shower Guy catch me wearing his oversized pants.

I follow the main path through the campground to a tall building made out of logs. The sign says that it opens at six. I plop down on the porch for a few minutes, studying the sky's colors. I'm trying to decide what time it is, and whether I should risk hanging around, when an old sports car with a red eagle painted on the hood peels into the gravel parking lot. A kid my age gets out, wearing sunglasses and a T-shirt with the sleeves cut off.

"S'up?" he says as he fishes in his pocket for the key to the front door.

"I lost my hat," I say. "Just looking for a new one." I follow him into the store, which thankfully has a whole slew of hats. I skim past the ones with sayings like "fishermen do it with crappie bait" and find a plain black hat with a brown leather brim. It's still a little lame, but it beats getting arrested. I wear it forward, which is something I haven't done since I played on a baseball team in middle school. I put on the cheapest pair of sunglasses I can find, mirrored "cop sunglasses" I wouldn't normally be caught dead in, and check out my reflection in one of the tiny rectangular mirrors built into the glasses carousel. Along with the hat and shades, I'm sporting a couple days' growth of beard. Even I don't think I look much like myself.

I figure by now Shower Guy has realized that someone stole his styling khakis. He'll probably go back to his tent first and accuse whoever he's camping with, but I should still get lost, just in case he heads up to the store to replace them.

I grab a couple of energy bars and sticks of beef jerky and line my purchases up on the counter. The cashier is texting on his phone and listening to the radio. As I'm handing him my wet money, the song ends and the DJ comes on for a special announcement. I tense up and one of my soggy bills ends up on the floor. My hands start shaking. I almost make a run for it. But the special announcement turns out to be about a lunchtime interview with a San Francisco band, and I feel stupid for almost blowing it. I'm expecting everything to play out like the movies, where the airwaves and TV stations are full of grave voices announcing that I, Max Cantrell, am a fugitive, presumed armed and dangerous.

And then I realize with a start that I *am* armed. The Colonel's Glock is still in the side pocket of my wet cargo pants. Jeez! Good thing I didn't leave them behind for Shower Guy.

I finish paying for my purchases and gingerly slide my wet clothes, along with the gun, into the crinkly plastic bag I get from the cashier. It's time to get going. *Like a shark*, I remind myself. I lift my hand to touch my shark's tooth pendant and remember it's not there—I forgot to look for it in my camping gear. "Which way to town?" I ask.

"South," the cashier says. "Make a left when you get to the road."

I thank him and head out. I need to find a way to Vegas, but first I need to find civilization.

The Lazy Days gravel driveway ends at a paved two-lane road. All I see in either direction are rocks and trees. I don't dare walk along the street. Just because the radio stations aren't beeping in with special bulletins about me doesn't mean they won't be soon.

There's a ditch that runs along one side of the road, with a dense line of pine trees just beyond it. I duck behind the thick, feathery branches, just far enough to stay out of sight, yet close enough so that I don't lose track of the road.

The air is humid, but cool. I swipe at a cloud of gnats as I step across a fallen branch. Crickets chirp in the grass around me. An old truck with round headlights and a metal grill that looks like a face passes from the other direction. I hide farther back in the trees until the truck disappears from sight, and then I keep going.

After about a half an hour of walking, the sun starts to rise. I come across a green sign outlined in white that says EAGLE'S PASS: 8. Ugh. At least eight more miles to civilization, if a place called Eagle's Pass even counts. It doesn't sound like the kind of place that's going to have a wide variety of prepaid cell phones for newly minted criminals such as myself. I look down at the stiff khakis with their fraying hems. Grand theft pants. Not sure stealing these would even count as a misdemeanor. More like an act of goodwill.

It takes almost three hours to get there, but Eagle's Pass surprises me by having a gas station of unusual size—one of those trucker plazas with gas pumps, a Burger Barn, a doughnut shop, and a convenience store all rolled into one. There are little TVs mounted on the wall behind the cash register, and as I pay for a phone my eyes casually float upward. College football highlights are playing. No picture of me with a moving ticker tape of my alleged crimes flashing below it. So far, so good.

Only now I'm going to have to find a way to Vegas without a car, unless Parvati will come get me. I shouldn't involve her, but she'll get pissed if I don't. Part of me thinks she's been waiting her whole life for something like this—a chance to use the tactical skills she's been honing since she was old enough to know what her father did for a living. Plus, I have to at least let her know I'm okay.

I duck into the men's room and lock myself in one of the stalls. After quickly activating the phone, I realize I can't call her on her burner phone because I don't know the number. Swearing under my breath, I dial Parvati's regular cell. Just as I expected, she doesn't answer. I don't feel safe leaving a message, so I decide to just hang out here for a while to see if she calls back. It's possible her parents confiscated her phone or she doesn't have it on her since she's expecting me to call the prepaid. I'll give her until lunchtime and then continue on to Vegas by myself.

Somehow.

I have thirty bucks left after buying the phone. I want to spend all of it on cheeseburgers, but the Burger Barn doesn't open for an hour. Keeping the brim of my hat low, I grab a bag of chips and a turkey sandwich and take them to the front register, doing my best not to make eye contact with anyone in the store. I crack my knuckles and scan the items in the glass cases as the clerk rings me up: leather wallets, switchblades, a bunch of cool silver rings shaped like skulls. I've always wanted a ring like that.

The door to the shop trills mechanically, and I resist the urge to whirl around and see who it is. With slightly shaky fingers, I count out the money I owe the clerk and then take my bag and receipt. I carry the food back through the front door of the shop and out into the sun. I saunter around to the back of the parking lot and sit cross-legged against the brick wall of the gas station.

I let out a huge breath and try to relax my back and shoulders. I've been on high alert for so long that my entire body is rigid. As I unwrap the sandwich, my stomach rumbles in anticipation. I eagerly bite off a big hunk of meat and bread.

I watch the highway as I chew. I can see everything coming from both directions. I'm not sure exactly what I'll do if a parade of cop cars appears, but I feel a little better knowing nothing can sneak up on me.

About an hour later, I get a call from an unknown number. Warily, I press the button to connect it, but then don't say anything.

"Who is this?" Parvati's voice. She must be calling on her prepaid. Emotion floods through me and I have to choke back a lump in my throat before I can speak. "Hey," I say finally. "It's me."

"Oh my God. Are you all right?" she asks. "Where are you?"

I swallow hard again. "Eagle's Pass. Some place called the Flaming Engine."

She doesn't say anything for a minute, and I can almost see her furiously googling. "Damn, that's like fifteen miles from the cabin. How'd you get there?"

"The river, mostly. I had to leave my car." And the laptop. And the hard drive. And Preston's phone. Man, I really messed everything up.

"McGhee and Gonzalez interrupted our family dinner last night. They threatened to charge me with aiding and abetting if I knew where you were but didn't tell them." She sighs loudly. "My parents *freaked* this morning when they found out you had been at the cabin. I had to tell them you must have stolen my set of keys back when we were dating."

"Great. My alleged crimes just keep adding up."

"It was either that or end up under house arrest, and you need my help. When we find Preston and everything goes back to normal, I'll tell them I lied."

"Sure." I blink back tears. The lack of sleep combined with the craziness suddenly has me teetering on the edge of hysteria. Inhaling deeply, I lean against the building, watching an eighteen-wheeler swing out to the right in order to make a left turn into the lot.

"Can you find a safe place to hide?" she asks. "I can pick you up tonight, as soon as my parents are asleep."

"That would mean another ten hours before you can even leave, plus an hour to get here. I'll just start walking, or hitch a ride with a trucker. If you come, there's no way you'll get back in time for school tomorrow."

"Screw school. Screw truckers. They'll turn you in," she says. "And trying to walk all the way to Vegas will take days. Not to mention there's nowhere to hide out in the desert."

"But your parents will lose it completely if you disappear." Even worse than my parents are no doubt losing it at this very moment. Which is probably a lot. They seem laid-back, until something bad happens. Then Darla starts to self-destruct. I wonder what Amanda is thinking, whether she knows I ran away from the FBI.

"Let them lose it. It isn't like I'm sneaking out of the house to hook up with you. I'm trying to help you find Preston, and not go to prison for something you didn't do. Getting grounded, even getting shipped off to military school, is kind of worth it."

I was hoping she would say that, but I don't want her to feel obligated. "If you're sure."

"I'll call you when I leave, all right?" she says.

"Okay."

"See you later, Max."

I disconnect the call without answering. A black-and-white cop car is turning into the lot.

TWENTY

I QUICKLY TURN THE PHONE off and slip it into my pocket. Pulling the brim of my hat even lower, I walk casually toward the corner of the building. My first instinct is to lock myself in one of the bathroom stalls until the cop leaves. I take a couple of deep breaths and realize I need to give myself an escape route. Street Living 101: always give yourself an out.

I change direction, cutting across the parking lot like I'm going to eat at the Burger Barn. When I'm halfway there I glance casually over my shoulder. A policeman dressed all in navy is striding toward the door of the Flaming Engine with a white paper in his hand.

It could be nothing.

Or it could be a flyer with my face on it.

Once the cop is safely inside the truck stop, I head back to the road and plunge into the wooded area along the side of the drainage ditch. If I see more cop cars I can just run farther into the forest. The police might have dogs, but if I find my way back to the river they'll lose my scent.

I work my way deep inside a grove of evergreens and bend into a crouch. The backs of my legs press against rough bark, and the feathery green needles hide most of my form. Through the tightly woven branches, I can just barely see the front of the truck stop. My heart starts up a drum solo. Even though the day is windy and cool, beads of sweat form on my upper lip. Each time the glass door to the Flaming Engine swings open, I am ready to run.

It's a lady carrying a toddler and dragging a kid Amanda's age behind her.

It's a trucker with a carton of cigarettes and a bucket-sized drink.

It's the cop.

My heart stops. The breeze stops. I swear I can hear each of his footsteps on the asphalt parking lot. He's carrying a soda cup and what looks like a sandwich. What he's not carrying is the piece of white paper he brought into the store.

He's in his car now. Wheels moving. Backing up. I hold my breath as he turns onto the road. He's coming toward me. I inch backward, farther into the trees.

He's five hundred yards away.

Three hundred yards.

If I turn and run, will he see me?

Two hundred yards.

I hold my body completely still. My muscles betray me. My legs threaten to buckle.

One hundred yards.

A drop of sweat falls from my upper lip to the carpet of pine needles below my feet.

Fifty yards.

The black-and-white rolls past without slowing down.

I sink to the ground, exhaling sharply. My legs are shaking so bad that I almost wet my pants. Curling onto my side, I try to slow my rapid breathing. I'm fine. Everything is fine.

No, it's not fine. Preston is missing and the FBI is acting like I killed him. Everything is completely wrecked.

Still, there's nothing I can do for the moment except try to calm down and catch up on the sleep I missed last night. Shielded from view by the thick evergreen foliage, I lean back against a tree trunk and let my eyelids fall shut.

I wake up hours later, after the sun has set. Dusting the pine needles from my clothes, I creep out of the woods and cut across the road to the Burger Barn. I lean up against the back of the trash Dumpster and watch the Flaming Engine parking lot from a distance. The cars parked behind the gas pumps are unidentifiable black blobs. I turn my phone on just long enough to check the time and messages. It's right at 8:00 p.m. Parvati hasn't called.

I order more food and take it back to the woods to eat in safety. Every fifteen minutes I turn on my phone again to check my messages. Just before midnight, Parvati sends a text that simply says *here*.

Flipping the phone off again, I jog slowly toward the truck stop. Parvati is parked around the back in her mom's silver Honda. She's wearing a choppy blonde wig and pointy glasses that sit low on her nose.

"Your mom's car?" I say, sliding into the passenger seat. From grand theft pants to grand theft auto, just like that. I am so dead.

Parvati shrugs. "That's what she gets for confiscating my car keys." She gives me a pointed look. "Plus the Jetta is purple, and has your license plates, remember?" She leans under the leather brim of my hat to give me a kiss on the cheek. Then she peels out of the parking lot. "Nice look," she says. "Old-man chic?"

"You should talk. You look like a librarian." I glance down at her hoodie and baggy jeans. "Masquerading as a middle school boy. Are those your mom's glasses too?"

Parvati ignores me. She gestures to the fuel gauge. "We've

got enough gas to get to Vegas. I mapped all three addresses for Violet Cain."

"How long do you think it'll be before Colonel Dad notices your absence?"

She looks at her watch. "About five or six hours." She turns onto a bigger road.

"How long until we get to Vegas?"

"Four hours."

"We'll have to work fast."

"That's the plan," she says grimly. She bears down on the accelerator and then punches the buttons on the steering wheel to activate the cruise control. Trees quickly become desert, and before I know it we're on Interstate 15, the only highway into Las Vegas.

"So did McGhee and Gonzalez get you to give up my hiding place or what?"

Parvati shakes her head, and fake blonde hair swishes back and forth. "Of course not. But they grilled me about my relationship with you and Preston. Some of our wiseass classmates seem to think we have threesomes."

The videos on Pres's hard drive of Parvati and me having sex flood my mind. I swallow hard. Now is not the time to bring those up. "What'd you tell them?" I ask finally.

"My parents were listening, Max. I told them that you and I broke up and that the three of us are all just friends who hang out together, mostly in school."

"I guess they didn't buy it."

"Guess not." Parvati jabs at the radio's power button. "When they were done interrogating me they asked to speak to my mom and dad alone. I tried to call you to warn you, but you didn't pick up the phone."

The ringing sound from my dream—it was Parvati trying to call. I swear it felt like McGhee and Gonzalez busted in just seconds later.

"Still no ransom note?" I ask.

"Nothing." Parvati makes a face as she flips through her mother's presets. She mashes the tuning arrow with her finger until she finds a station playing something she knows we'll both like.

Miles of dark highway fly by. In the moonlight, I can just barely make out the mountains of sand and rock on either side of us.

"Are you tired?" Parvati asks me suddenly, tweaking the volume down on the radio just a hair.

I shake my head. It feels weird not having my bangs flop in front of my eyes when I do it. "I crashed out in the woods for a while today."

"You look exhausted. You should sleep more," she says. "I know the way to Vegas. I'll wake you when we get there."

"Really. I'm fine," I tell her, but I take off my hat and settle back against the seat anyway.

"Oh my God. Your hair," Parvati says. "It looks ridiculous. I love it."

You would, I think, letting my eyes fall shut. Parvati loves anything that most people consider weird. Something about the way the Honda purrs its way across the desert lulls me to sleep. The next time I open my eyes I see a line of bright lights in the distance.

TWENTY-ONE

THE CLOCK ON THE DASHBOARD reads 4:11. Less than two hours before the Colonel wakes up, notices Parvati and the Honda are missing, and calls the cops. By now McGhee and Gonzalez have me on obstruction charges and whatever crime it is to point a loaded gun at two FBI agents, not to mention what they might have tacked on to the list if they found my car and the blood in my trunk. I'm seriously screwed if we don't find Preston in a hurry.

"We made it?" I ask, rubbing sleep from my eyes.

"Almost." Parvati tosses me a Megaburger from the Burger Barn.

My mouth waters on cue. "You are the best girlfriend ever."

That makes her smile. "It's a couple hours old. I went

through the drive-through right before they closed. You didn't even wake up."

I sit up in the seat and start to unwrap my burger as Parvati takes the exit for North Las Vegas. The burger is gone in about five bites. Time to check out our three Violet Cains.

The first listing is for a simple brick home in a lower-middle-class neighborhood. These people are going to think we're crazy waking them up so early, but there's no time for skulking around. I head straight up the driveway to the porch and bang on the front door. A wreath made of tiny green bells jingles each time my knuckles meet wood. No one answers. I knock again. I see the curtains flutter out of the corner of my eye.

"What do you want?" a female voice yells through the front door. "Do you have any idea what time it is?"

"Sorry," I say loudly. "It's an emergency."

Parvati stands beside me, one hand resting on my lower back. She transfers her weight from one foot to the other as we wait to see if the woman will open the door.

The door opens a crack. A woman peeks out. She's got brown hair instead of blonde, but she looks about the right age. "Yeah?" she asks sleepily.

"Are you Violet Cain?" I ask.

"I was. It's Violet Armstead now."

"Are you friends with Preston?" I ask.

"I don't know no Preston." She rubs her eyes. "Is this some kind of joke?"

I take a closer look at her. Her face is the wrong shape, and even in baggy pajama bottoms and a T-shirt I can tell she doesn't have the same body as the girl in the pictures.

Parvati comes to the same conclusion. "It's not her," she says.

"Not who?" the woman asks.

"Sorry to have bothered you," I say. "I think we have the wrong house."

The next address is in an apartment complex. We head up three flights of stairs and knock on the door, but no one answers. Parvati rests her ear against the wooden door. "I think I hear the TV," she says.

I press my face next to hers. Sure enough, I can make out occasional snatches of what sounds like the early morning news. I cup my hands around my eyes and try to peer through a crack in the curtains. Nothing but darkness and the slightly distorted reflection of my own face.

Parvati pulls her sleeve over her hand and tries the knob. The door is locked.

"Think we should try to break in?" she asks.

"Let's try the other place. We can always come back."

The last address on the list is in a neighborhood just a few blocks off the Strip. It's a little green-and-white cottage with a mailbox shaped like a birdhouse. It isn't the mailbox that catches my eye, though.

It's the wall of fire, extending upward from the roof.

TWENTY-TWO

BLACK SMOKE BILLOWS FROM THE windows. Flames lick their way up the sides of the house. Fuck. I am out of the car in an instant, racing toward the front door. Parvati is right behind me. The heat scorches my skin, radiating straight through the front wall of the cottage.

Parvati grabs my arm, hauling me back just before I reach the porch. "Max, wait. You can't go in there."

I know she's right, but I try to shake her off anyway. "What if Preston is inside?"

"Then we have to wait for the fire department." She yanks me back a couple more steps until we're standing in the middle of the tiny scrap of grass that makes up Violet Cain's front lawn.

Sirens sing in the distance. High and shrill, low and honking. An EMS cavalry is on its way. Around us, neighbors are popping out onto their porches. Silhouettes of children peek between their parents' legs.

"We should get out of here," Parvati says. Her blonde wig sits crooked on her head.

I don't want to go. I want to rush into the house. Preston is here. I know it. I can feel it.

A section of roof caves in, sending up a shower of dazzling embers. The neighbors murmur and point. Flames explode out of the gaping hole. Fingers of fire claw at the dark sky.

Parvati pulls me backward again. "Max, come on. It's not safe."

We both know she's not just talking about the fire. The rescue vehicles are close now, and the cops won't be far behind. Sirens crescendo as fire trucks and an ambulance turn the corner onto the block. Around us, the clouds of smoke blink flashing red.

We stumble through the haze, getting back to the car just as a hook-and-ladder truck roars to a stop at the curb. Firefighters leap off, dressed in heavy coats and gas masks. They huddle together in the middle of the lawn. What are they doing? Why aren't they rescuing Preston? I hurry across the grass, intending to ask them what the holdup is.

"Max." Parvati hollers from behind me. "Run!"

I spin around and move toward her but skid to a stop in the middle of the street. Agent McGhee has her up against the side of the Honda. Shit. How did they get here so fast? The fading moonlight glints off a pair of silver handcuffs.

"Run!" she repeats.

Leaving her feels so unnatural that it takes my body a few seconds to process my brain's request. Gonzalez sees me just as I take off down the street.

"Stop!" he screams.

I turn toward the neon lights of the Strip. I came here once with Ben and Darla and nearly got lost in the herds of people milling up and down the sidewalk in front of the big casinos. If I get up to Las Vegas Boulevard, I know I can disappear. I race up the driveway of a little brick house and vault my lanky body over a silver chain-link fence. I cut across the darkened backyard, hurdling what looks to be a giant cactus. The fence rattles behind me as Gonzalez clambers over it. I'm already at the other side of the yard, lifting myself over the next fence. He'll never catch me.

The next couple of yards are unfenced. I can still hear Gonzalez huffing and puffing behind me. I'm only a block from the Strip now. Adrenaline propels me. I lengthen my stride, pumping my arms and legs as I cut across the parking lot of a sleazy motel and explode out onto Las Vegas

Boulevard. Left or right? I go right, toward the Bellagio and Caesar's Palace. There seem to be more people that way. I push past a loose knot of what looks like bachelor party guys heading home after a long night. Shirts are untucked. Gelled hair is starting to droop. I dodge a couple of old men handing out advertisements for strip clubs. Somewhere, a girl screams. It's a playful, laughing noise, but it's enough to make me wonder what's happening to Parvati. Did McGhee really arrest her? Is she scared? I glance quickly over my shoulder. Several sets of headlights are prowling the Strip, but I can't make out any individual cars.

The toe of my sneaker catches a seam in the sidewalk. I fall forward, landing on my hands and knees. As I scramble back to my feet, someone tackles me from behind. The side of my face slams into the asphalt and something round and hard presses against my spine. At first I think Gonzalez actually has his gun out, but then he leans down to cuff me and I realize it's his knee that's planted in the small of my back. Around us, I see the clunky white sneakers and high heels of a small group of tourists. Camera flashes light up the night, like I'm just one more attraction in Vegas, something to occupy time while people wait for the Bellagio's water show to begin.

Gonzalez's phone rings in his pocket and he jams his knee

even farther into my spine as he goes to answer it. "Yeah," he says. "Good. I just got him." He hangs up and bends down so I can see his face.

"Max Cantrell," he barks, like my ear isn't literally two inches from his lips, like maybe he's auditioning for a role on *Law & Order: Las Vegas*. "You're under arrest for obstruction of justice, flight to avoid prosecution, and assaulting a federal agent."

TWENTY-THREE

December 8th

LATER THAT MORNING, I GET arraigned. My court-appointed lawyer, a mousy-haired woman in a dark suit and sensible shoes, comes to get me from my holding cell. She introduces herself but I'm not paying attention, so I don't catch her name. I'm too busy thinking about how "holding cell" is now part of my vocabulary—how I'm back in one of those detective TV shows I never, ever wanted to be a part of.

My lawyer takes one look at my insane haircut and rumpled, stolen clothing and forbids me to speak in court. "I'll handle entering your pleas," she says. "I'll handle everything. Just don't . . . speak."

The courtroom is smaller than what you see on television and is set up like a church—vaulted ceiling, rows of long wooden pews, and a raised platform at the front. The judge is a white-haired black guy who looks like he might have had a long career as a drill instructor. With my luck, he's friends with Parvati's dad. There are only a few other people here, and I don't recognize any of them. My lawyer and I take a seat at a wooden table in front of the pews. Across from us, at another wooden table, sit a man and a woman I've never seen before. They're both wearing the same eyeglass frames and sharp expressions.

"The prosecution," my lawyer whispers. The next fifteen minutes are a blur of incomprehensible legal jargon. I do my best not to piss off the judge, standing when my lawyer stands and sitting when she sits. The only words that stick out to me are my lawyer's name when she introduces herself for the court reporter—it's Kathleen—and the word "murder" tossed around repeatedly by the prosecution and always quickly slapped with an objection by my lawyer. Later, as things seem to be coming to an end, I hear five more words that I understand: "flight risk" and "bail is denied."

Kathleen leaps from her seat, but puts a hand on my shoulder when I go to do the same. "Your Honor, may I approach?"

The judge nods.

"Stay," she tells me.

She and the prosecutors approach the bench. A heated conversation takes place, complete with head tossing and hand waving by the prosecution. I'm not close enough to hear any of it.

She returns to our table a few minutes later wearing a cocky grin.

"What happened?" I ask in a low voice.

"Bail happened," she says.

"Bail set at two hundred thousand dollars." The judge sounds bored, like he's ready to move on to a more interesting case.

"Two hundred grand?" I hiss. "That's your big coup? My parents could sell everything they owned and not come up with that money."

She starts to answer, but then the judge clears his throat and then bangs his gavel twice.

And just like that, I'm officially a criminal.

I don't get much time to think about it, though, because instead of going back to my cell, I get to go back to the interrogation room.

It's another fun session with my two favorite FBI agents. McGhee is wearing the same unreadable expression as always. Gonzalez's smirk can only be described as triumphant. I don't know if it's because McGhee is actually letting him do something besides fetch water or because he's day-dreaming about my trial.

"Nice hair," Gonzalez says.

"Where's Parvati?" I've asked this question to anyone who would listen since Gonzalez hauled me up off the Vegas pavement and packed me into the backseat of McGhee's unmarked sedan. The FBI opted to take me straight back to Vista Palisades, since my alleged crimes were committed in California and I was a "person of interest" in Preston's disappearance. I have no idea what happened to Parvati. All I know is that they didn't let her ride back to Vista Palisades with me.

"We're the ones asking the questions, Max," Gonzalez informs me. He's actually being nicer now that I've been arrested. I swear his smile couldn't get any bigger, not even if my lawyer hopped up on the table and started doing a striptease.

"I'll answer whatever you want if you tell me what happened to Parvati."

"He doesn't mean that," Kathleen interjects. "He's speaking under psychological duress."

I turn to her. "No, really. I don't have anything to hide. I just want to know if my girlfriend is okay."

"Thought she was your *ex*-girlfriend," Gonzalez says. "Just one more lie?"

"Her parents forbade us from seeing each other, so we pretended to be broken up. You didn't arrest her, did you?"

"You answer our questions and we'll tell you what happened to Ms. Amos," Gonzalez says.

I glance at McGhee. "Do you promise?"

McGhee nods. "We'll tell you what you want to know."

Kathleen clears her throat. "Max, I can't help you if you make these kinds of deals with them. You do know that anything you say to them can be used—"

"Yeah, yeah. Court of law. I got it."

Kathleen sighs deeply and makes notes on her yellow legal pad.

"Tell me about the time you assaulted an eleven-year-old," Gonzalez says. "How old were you again? Sixteen?"

"Fuck you," I say. My lawyer puts a hand on my shoulder, but I shake her off. "That kid was picking on—"

Gonzalez doesn't let me finish. "Pretty violent tendencies. Was Ms. Amos part of it? Or did she just come pick you up after you set the fire?"

"Why don't you ask her?" I say. "She was with me the whole time I was in Vegas. She'll tell you I didn't burn anyone's house down."

"You'll have to forgive me if I don't find either of you to be the most credible of witnesses," Gonzalez says. "Why don't you tell us about Liars, Inc.?"

Kathleen raises an eyebrow but then quickly says, "You don't have to answer that."

My first instinct is to tell Gonzalez to go fuck himself again, but suddenly it feels like every decision I've made in my whole life is coming back to haunt me all at once. Maybe I should go against my gut and tell him the truth. "It was just a stupid thing we were doing at school to make money," I say. "Forging permission slips. Covering for kids so they could get away from their parents. That kind of thing."

McGhee nods. "Kids like Preston."

Kathleen sighs deeply and makes some notes on her pad. "Let's not talk about that anymore until after you and I have met in private," she says. I can almost hear her writing my case off as hopeless.

Gonzalez clears his throat. "I figure it like this. You find out your best pal has been hooking up with your girlfriend. You attack him on top of Ravens' Cliff, but he gets away. He knows you're crazy, so he decides to skip town for a few days until you cool off. Only instead of cooling off you make a plan to find him and finish the job."

"Genius," I say sarcastically. "Too bad my best pal *wasn't* hooking up with my girlfriend." I hold my face rigid, unblinking. "Just because they went to homecoming together doesn't mean anything. Your lame revenge theory doesn't work because Parvati and Preston were never more than friends."

"No?" Something in the way Gonzalez utters that single syllable makes me hate him more than I've ever hated anyone in my life. He opens a manila envelope. Glossy pictures slide out onto the table. Pictures of Preston and Parvati. The top one is of the two of them kissing. They're sitting at the edge of Preston's pool. Parvati has a towel wrapped around her shoulders. The image stings a little, but it isn't a betrayal. I know exactly what day it's from. Preston's New Year's Eve party, junior year, the night Parvati and I met.

I spent most of the evening swilling free beer and wandering around the DeWitts' cavernous mansion, checking out the Bristol Academy chicks from a distance. They were richer than most of the girls from Vista P, but other than that they were the same: tight dresses, lots of makeup, too much drama. I almost left early, bored by the usual bullshit. I was halfway out the door when I saw a shadow in the DeWitts' in-ground swimming pool. It was a cold night for Southern California—definitely not swimming weather—so I ducked out onto the deck to make sure no one was drowning.

A girl's lithe form moved beneath the wind-rippled water. Her dress flared up and exposed her slender thighs with each stroke. She finished her lap and then popped above the surface. "Hi." She dipped her head backward into the pool so that her long dark hair stayed slicked back out of her face.

"Are you okay?" I was pretty sure she wasn't okay. She was swimming in what was probably an expensive dress, and even though her teeth were chattering, she showed no signs of getting out of the water.

Instead of answering, she flipped onto her back and did a lap of backstroke. Her hair streamed out around her in a thick ebony halo as she glided across the pool. She looked otherworldly, like a ghost or a hot alien chick. She hit the far wall, did a graceful flip beneath the surface, and headed back toward me. Her arms barely made a splash as she cut the water with them repeatedly. When she got to the side, she saw me hovering above her and stopped again. "You're still here," she said.

"I'm enjoying the show," I admitted.

She stared at me for a long moment. "You don't belong here."

"Why? Because I'm not rich?" A note of defensiveness crept into my voice.

She twirled her body in another back flip and then came up treading water. "No, silly. Because Preston's friends are all sheep."

"Aren't *you* one of Preston's friends?"

"Sometimes I think I'm the worst sheep of all," she said, her eyes dropping to the water for a second. Her olive skin was starting to look a little blue.

She didn't look like a sheep to me. The sheep were inside getting drunk and acting stupid. "Are you going to come out of there anytime soon?" I asked. "I could get you a towel."

Her teeth chattered again and she ducked low so that everything but her face was submerged. "Do you know that SEALs have to stay in the cold water in their clothes for more than twenty-four hours? It's part of their training."

"I didn't know seals wore clothes," I said. Maybe hypothermia was already setting in.

"Navy SEALs, silly." She laughed, and for the briefest moment I debated jumping in next to her. "My dad's friend was a Navy SEAL. He's teaching me to be hard core."

That was twice she had called me silly, but for some reason I didn't mind. "I think it would be hard core if you got out of the pool." Not to mention how hot she'd look shivering in her clingy little dress.

Her dark eyes widened. "So cute. You just met me and already you're worried." She took in my unkempt hair and casual clothes. "Are you one of those hippies? Philosophically opposed to the military?"

"I'm philosophically opposed to hot chicks freezing to

death." It wasn't the kind of thing I usually said to girls. I didn't usually say anything at all. I just stayed in my own world and hung out with the occasional cute girl who hit on me.

She smiled. "I need to finish my laps, but I promise I'll get out before I die, okay?"

I knew a blow-off when I heard one, so I left her even though a huge part of me wanted to stay. Instead, I found Preston inside and told him a crazy chick was doing SEAL training in his pool. "That's just Parv," he said. "She's a freak."

I didn't tell Preston that I kind of liked her. I didn't even admit it to myself until the next time I saw her, three months later, when she showed up in my English class.

Gonzalez rattles the photograph under my nose. "Where'd you go, kid?"

"Nice try," I say, reluctantly letting go of the memory. "That's from New Year's Eve. Everyone kisses on New Year's Eve—it doesn't mean anything. And I didn't even know her back then."

"So you're saying Preston and Ms. Amos were never an item?" Gonzalez asks.

"No. They were not."

"Check out the rest of them," he says.

"I don't need to," I say. "I don't care what kind of bullshit you think you have on my girlfriend. She wouldn't lie to me."

"It's not bullshit. We like to call it motive." He flips to the next photograph.

My eyes betray me. It's Parvati and Preston in his bedroom. In his bed.

They look like they're sleeping. He's lying on his back; she's curled on her side, her head resting against his chest. The covers conceal their bodies, except for one of Parvati's bare arms.

A fist tightens in my stomach. "That doesn't prove anything," I say, but my voice wavers and I hate myself for having doubts. *We made them together freshman year—razor-bladed out a square in the middle of the pages. It was my idea . . .* What else had they done together alone in Preston's bedroom?

The next photo answers my question. I train my eyes on my lap, but not before I catch a glimpse of Parvati on top of Preston. Long silky hair obscures her naked breasts. The photo tech has blurred out part of the image, but it's still obvious what's going on. "Where did you get these?" I ask. As soon as the words leave my mouth, I know the answer. From Preston's hard drive. These are stills made from the videos. Of course if he has videos of Parvati and me, he has some of the two of them also. Preston and his obsessive fucking recording of everyone. "So they were together at some point," I whisper. "That doesn't mean she cheated on me."

It just means that both Preston and Parvati had lied to me about fifty times.

"And then there's this one," Gonzalez says. "Looks like they've been pretty close for a while."

I can't help it; I look. Then I bite back a gasp. It's Parv and Pres going at it again, but the room looks like a dorm room and Parvati looks like she's about fifteen. It has to be from Bristol Academy, which means not only have Preston and Parvati hooked up and lied about it, they've hooked up for years. Gonzalez fans a few more photos out on the table and then reclines back in his chair.

My fingers are shaking. I want to kill everyone. I imagine leaping over the table and wrapping my hands around Gonzalez's throat. "Her hair is l-long in all these pictures," I stutter. "She cut it at the end of summer, soon after we started dating. Unless you have some photos where she has shorter hair, then you don't have any proof they hooked up after Parvati and I were together."

But Gonzalez can see that he's getting to me. He abruptly switches tactics. "Where's your car?"

Jeez, they didn't even find my car? I figured they would have combed the woods all around the Colonel's cabin. What a bunch of morons. I shrug.

"What is Preston's connection to Violet Cain?" Gonzalez asks. "We found the hard drive with her pictures. We know you two searched for her online."

"I told you that already," I say. "The last time you questioned me. Preston said she was some chick he met on the internet."

"Did you know she was twice his age?"

"Not until we found her profile." We. Me and Parvati. I can't keep myself from looking at the pictures spread across the table, at the seductive smile on Parvati's face. At her hair. Her legs. At the way she's positioned on Preston in a manner that makes it seem like they've spent a lot of time naked together. If they lied about having a relationship, God only knows what else they lied about.

"Is it Violet Cain's body?" Gonzalez asks.

Did he say *body*? I look away from the photos. "What?"

"Don't play dumb. The firefighters pulled two bodies out of the house, burned almost beyond recognition. One of them was a woman. Was it Violet Cain?"

Wait. Did he say *two* bodies?

"Don't answer that." Kathleen puts a hand on my arm. I almost forgot she was in the room.

I remember the certainty in my gut as I raced toward the flaming house. Preston was in there. I could feel it.

"You found bodies?" My voice raises in pitch. "Dead bodies?" The room goes fuzzy. This isn't happening. It can't be.

"Give it up," Gonzalez says. "There's no point in lying."

"What bodies?" I ask.

"Two bodies," McGhee repeats slowly. "The body of Preston DeWitt, and an as-of-yet-unidentified female."

My mind is spinning like a hamster wheel. If someone kidnapped Preston because of something political or because he owed them money, there would be no point in killing him.

"Preston can't be dead," I say.

"I'm sorry, Max," McGhee says. "His father made a positive identification."

It takes a few seconds to sink in. Then I double over, my hands clutching at my gut as I feel stomach acid burning its way up my throat. My lawyer thrusts a trash can beneath my chin just in time. I throw up for so long my stomach practically turns itself inside out. I hang my head low for a few minutes afterward. A strand of saliva drips from the left corner of my mouth. Preston. Dead. Burned to death. All I can think about is how he might be alive right now if I hadn't lied for him.

"Is this yours?" Gonzalez asks.

I have to force myself to look up. Gonzo tosses a ziplock bag in my direction. Son of a bitch. My shark's tooth pendant is inside, blackened from the smoke but not destroyed. I don't know why I'm surprised. One more nail in my coffin.

I wipe my mouth on my sleeve and then bend over the trash can again.

"We have no comment," Kathleen snaps. "I think we're done here for now."

"It doesn't matter, Max," Gonzalez says. "The forensics report on this and everything else from the fire will be back in a few days, and it's going to link you—irrefutably—to Violet Cain's house. And when it does, we're charging you with arson . . . and murder."

TWENTY-FOUR

I LEAN BACK AGAINST THE wall of my cell and let my eyes fall shut. Tears push at my eyelids. It was bad enough when Preston was missing and someone was trying to set me up. But now Pres is dead and Parvati is a liar and maybe a cheater too. I have never felt so alone in my whole life, not even back when I was homeless. At least then I knew I was the only person I could count on. Whoever said it was better to have loved and lost was completely full of shit.

I haven't seen Parvati, and I don't expect to. After they were done grilling me, McGhee and Gonzalez informed me she was charged with aiding and abetting and then promptly bailed out by her parents, who filed a restraining order against me on her behalf. I don't even care anymore.

I'm glad she's not here. I wouldn't be able to look her in the face without thinking about those pictures of her and Preston.

She probably thinks she did me a favor by lying, that if I knew she and Pres had been together for years I'd be jealous all the time. But she had to know I would find out eventually. Unless she thinks I'm a complete idiot. She does tend to think most people are stupid. Preston is like that too.

I mean he *was* like that.

I should be pissed at him, too, for lying and for making those video recordings, but I just feel hollow. I kind of understand why *he* lied to me. To admit he liked her—that they used to be a couple—would be like admitting she preferred me to him. Preston was never any good at losing.

Also, it's hard to be mad at a dead guy.

My lawyer stops by to read me the riot act about talking to the feds in exchange for information about Parvati. She stands on the other side of the bars, ignoring the guy in the cell across from me who is hooting and making rude gestures with his fingers and tongue.

"Do you want to go to maximum security prison for life?" she asks, flipping Hooting Guy the bird without even turning around. "If not, you'd better start listening to me."

"How can they charge me with Preston's murder? I'm innocent."

"Prosecutors charge innocent people with murder all the time." Kathleen plucks a piece of lint off the collar of her suit. "But remember, right now you've only been arraigned on obstruction, flight, and assault charges."

"Oh, is that all?" I can't keep the sarcasm out of my voice. "Can you get rid of the assault charge? It's not like I was really going to shoot anybody."

"Any time you threaten someone with bodily harm, it's assault," she says. "You would have gotten charged with felony theft, too, but your girlfriend admitted that she took the car and gave you her dad's gun."

"Great." I sigh. I had actually managed not to think about Parvati for two whole minutes, but the images of her and Pres come rushing back.

"At least I got you bail," Kathleen says hopefully, like she's trying to cheer me up. "I had to reference a ton of precedents to get that."

"It's not like I'm going to get out of here, anyway. My parents don't have that kind of money."

"They only have to come up with ten percent of it and a bail bondsman will get you out."

"Oh, only twenty grand?" I cross my arms. "Still not happening."

Her demeanor softens. "Look, Max. We'll talk privately later about everything that happened during the questioning, okay? We're going to need to come up with a plan of action regarding the pictures and the shark's tooth."

I nod, even though I have no idea what the two of us could possibly come up with to explain away a motive for murder and physical evidence linking me to the fire.

TWENTY-FIVE

"CANTRELL." THE UNIFORMED GUARD SAYS my name uncertainly.

"What?" I ask. I'm sitting on my cot, my back leaning against the cinder-block wall. I've spent the last few hours trying to puzzle through everything that's happened. "Another visitor?" Darla has been here twice, a brave face and red eyes both times. I don't think I can handle seeing her again today.

"You're out." The guard slips a key into the lock on my cell. The door slides open with a soft scratching sound.

"Out of what?" *Luck? Time?* "What are you talking about?"

"You made bail. Hurry it up. We got a line for this cell."

"My parents are here?" I can't help but think it's some twisted joke thought up by Gonzalez to break me down even further. Like they're going to let me get all the way to the front door and then tackle me and say they made a mistake.

"No. Some guy who says he's your uncle."

I pause for a second. Both Darla and Ben have brothers, but they live in different states, and I don't think either one of them would have twenty grand to spend on some kid they barely know. Still, I guess anything is possible.

The guard rattles his keys. "You sure don't seem anxious to leave. You and Clemens here bonding?"

Clemens is the guy in the cell across from me who made the lewd gestures at my lawyer.

"I'm coming," I mutter.

The guard directs me toward a desk where a woman in uniform pulls out a handful of forms.

"Sign these," she says crisply. She hands me a pen and turns back to her computer screen, where she's in the process of buying what looks like a throw pillow shaped like a Doberman.

I scribble my name on a pink form and a yellow form, not even really paying attention to what they say. Something about being treated humanely and having all of my belongings returned to me. The woman picks up her phone and barks something into the receiver about my stuff. Another uniformed officer brings up a clear plastic bag with my wallet, my keys, and the prepaid cell phone I bought in Eagle's Pass. I'm surprised they're not keeping the phone as evidence, but I guess they can always subpoena the call records from the service provider.

I shove the stuff in my pocket and turn toward the door. There's only one guy standing in the lobby, and he sure as hell isn't my uncle. Not unless my uncle is black.

"Hello, Max," the man says.

Go figure. There's something vaguely familiar about him, but if we've met before, I don't remember it. "What's up, *Uncle*?" I say. "Thanks for springing me." The late-afternoon sun slams me in the face as I glide past him through the exit. I raise a hand up to block out the abrasive light so that I can make my way down the concrete steps in front of the police station.

A handful of people are waiting for a bus. One by one, they turn around to look at me with blank, cold faces. I wonder if they know about Preston's death already. Maybe the whole town thinks I'm guilty.

"Need a ride?" my fake uncle asks. He smoothes the lapels of what looks like a very expensive pinstriped suit.

I'm tempted to tell him I'd rather walk, but then my

curiosity gets the best of me. "Who are you?" I ask. "And why the hell did you post my bail?"

"Let me give you a ride home, and I'll explain everything."

"Sure. Okay." The bag of stuff buzzes in my hand. I stop at the bottom of the steps and yank out the phone. I have three voicemail messages. My chest feels heavy. I know they're going to be from Parvati, because she's the only one that has this number. I shouldn't listen to them. I should throw this phone in the trash can next to the curb. I line up like I'm going to take a free throw. Phone. Trash. Two points.

But I'm a masochist, so I don't do it. Instead, I play the messages while Uncle Expensive Suit looks on.

"Max. It's me. I'm at home. Look, there's something I have to tell you about Pres. Call me the second you get this."

Now Parvati has something to tell me? Maybe something about how she screwed Preston every which way from Sunday? In my hurry to delete the message, I stub my toe on the uneven sidewalk and nearly fall flat on my face. A sharp beep signals the beginning of the next message.

"Max. It's me—"

Delete. Next message.

"Max. I—"

Delete. Somehow, I feel a tiny bit better. I probably can't avoid her forever, but I don't have to talk to her when I'm pissed. Forget pissed. I'm wrecked. I'm not even sure if I'll be able to tell her I know about her and Pres. I keep imagining the inevitable confrontation, but every time I open my mouth to speak, no words come out. How, exactly, do you tell the girl you were crazy about that she's a lying bitch?

"Messages from Ms. Amos?" Uncle Suit asks.

I nod without thinking. How does he know that?

"Gum?" He holds out a pack of spearmint sugarless.

"Sure." I haven't had any water for hours. My mouth feels like crap.

As I unwrap the gum and pop it in my mouth, I motion for him to hang on a second and dial my home number. As the phone rings in my ear, I watch the cars pass both ways in front of the Vista Palisades Police Station and Municipal Jail. The babysitter answers and I hang up. I'll just go by the shop and let my parents know I'm out.

Uncle Suit gently removes the cell phone from my hand. "We're in a bit of a hurry," he says.

"Well then, why did you offer to—" I stop short, just in front of the parking lot. There's a gray SUV with tinted windows parked in one of the first spots. It looks just like the car from the Ravens' Cliff parking lot. "Actually, I just remembered somewhere I need to be." I spin around, but Uncle Suit grabs me.

"There is only one place you need to be," he says, his voice as smooth as water, like he should be narrating a nature documentary. "And that's with me." I feel the blunt tip of a gun poking into my side.

TWENTY-SIX

"WHOA," I SAY. "THERE'S NO need for that."

He presses a button and the doors to the SUV unlock with a snap. There's another guy in the driver's seat, wearing all black. He's got pale blue eyes and close-cropped blond hair that's going gray at the edges. Uncle Suit nudges me with the gun.

"You guys sent the black guy to pretend to be my uncle?" I shouldn't be smarting off considering there's a gun pressed into my ribs, but I think it's my brain's way of not focusing on what's really happening—that I'm being abducted, maybe by the same guys who took Preston. The driver reaches back to grab my shoulders, and Uncle lifts me up and tosses me inside the vehicle like I'm a sack of potatoes.

He shrugs as he slides in beside me. "I only do the things that need to be done well. Besides, you've got Chinese sisters, right? Is it really that much of a stretch?"

"They're Korean," I say, as the SUV's doors lock with an ominous click. "And if you know that much about my family then you know no one can afford to pay any ransom, so what exactly do you guys want with me? Are you going to kill me like you killed Preston?"

The driver glances back at me in the rearview mirror, his expression disturbingly neutral. He pulls the SUV out of the lot.

"We didn't kill Preston." Uncle chuckles as he slides the gun back into his pocket. It looks a lot like the gun Parvati gave me. I wonder what happened to that, anyway. It was wrapped in my clothes in the backseat of her mom's car when we got arrested. I bet the feds have it. Gonzalez is probably testing it against the ballistics report of every unsolved crime on the books.

"I apologize for my impatience," Uncle continues. "I just didn't want a large number of people to see us together." He gives me a brief smile. It looks all wrong on his face. "We're not going to hurt you, Max. We just want to debrief you."

"Debrief me?"

He nods. "We needed you out of jail so we could speak privately. My name is Langston, and that's Marcus." He gestures toward the driver. "We work for Senator DeWitt."

I cough and nearly swallow my gum. "DeWitt paid my bail? Why would he do that?"

Langston doesn't answer, so I keep thinking out loud. "I've only spoken to Preston's dad twice in my life. He must really think I'm innocent." Unless, of course, he really thinks I'm guilty and decided to hold his own trial, presided over by a couple of thugs with guns.

"The senator doesn't believe you're a killer." Langston strokes his well-trimmed goatee. "And he's unconcerned about the money, since he'll get it back eventually. He *trusts* that you won't do anything foolish like try to run away again."

I finish the thought in my head: *But we'll come find you if you do.* The SUV turns onto the main road that leads out of Vista Palisades. "Where are we going?" I ask. Langston doesn't answer. Houses and strip malls whiz by. People walk their dogs along the cracked sidewalks. Kids with giant backpacks head home from school.

Too bad no one can see me through the tinted glass.

"We're just going for a drive." Marcus turns on the radio. Classical music has never sounded so creepy.

"I need my phone." I tap one foot, rapidfire, against the SUV's floorboards. "My parents are going to worry."

"We only need a little of your time. It's better if your parents think you're still in jail for the time being."

"Yeah, that would work, except my mom's probably planning on visiting me two more times in the next hour," I say. "At least. She's having a little trouble dealing with things." It feels weird to call Darla my mom, but now doesn't seem like the time to explain my entire history to Langston.

He tosses the phone back to me. "Fine. Tell her you don't know who bailed you out, that you're with friends, and you'll be home later."

Except I don't have any friends anymore. "Great," I say, knowing that explanation won't be enough for Darla. Hopefully she's still at work. I dial my number again, expecting the babysitter. It goes straight to voicemail. Ji and Jo are probably doing their lethal tag-team screaming act. I leave a quick message assuring everyone I'm fine and that I'll explain everything when I see them. Luckily, Ben and Darla are about as low-tech as it gets and don't have caller ID. They won't be able to call me back and demand more information.

"So who are you guys?" I ask. "Like private investigators or something?"

"Sort of." Langston crosses his legs at the ankles. He's wearing shiny black shoes with white wingtips, like something you might see on a golf course.

Marcus weaves his way through a neighboring suburb and turns onto the interstate. I lean against the window and watch the highway fly by. We're heading toward L.A. In front of us, a dump truck spits occasional bursts of sand and gravel onto the road. My mind starts doing that hamster-wheel thing again. How bad would it look if word got out that Senator Remington DeWitt had bailed the leading suspect in his son's murder out of jail? He has to have an agenda. But what is it?

"What do you guys want to know?" I ask. "Where's Senator DeWitt?"

"The senator and his wife just returned from dealing with things in Las Vegas," Langston says. "Due to the politically delicate nature of Preston's murder, the DeWitts have tasked Marcus and myself to follow up on some leads."

"They think Preston's death was politically motivated?" I fiddle with my seat belt.

"Let's just say they know you aren't responsible."

"I wish they'd tell the feds that."

Langston smiles slightly. "The FBI means well." He pauses. "But Senator DeWitt hasn't made them privy to all of the pertinent facts. Some of the relevant information is too classified."

Something pings hard against the front windshield. I flinch, even though it was probably just a pebble from the truck in front of us. "So why am I here if I'm so innocent?"

"We need to make sure we know everything that *you* know. We're gathering information to track down the real killer."

I nod. "What if I can't help, though? Are you going to toss me back in jail?"

Langston's smile widens. "You knew to go to Las Vegas. Tell me about that."

There's something about him that makes me want to talk. Maybe it's because I don't feel like I can talk to Parvati anymore. Or because I'm so hurt by her lies that I finally care more about finding the real killer than about protecting her. I tell Langston about the cover story, how Pres and I pretended to go camping. And then about snatching Pres's hard drive. I don't tell him it was Parvati who took it. I'm not sure I could even bring myself to say her name right now.

"Did he ever mention Violet Cain to you before?"

"He mentioned a girl named Violet when he asked for the cover story. He said he played online poker with her. I thought it was weird, Preston meeting chicks on the internet. He could've dated almost any girl at school."

"But didn't Preston despise most of his classmates?"

It was true. That was probably the main reason Pres and I stayed friends after he enrolled at Vista Palisades and basically took over the school. He might have excelled at playing Mr. Popularity, but beneath the surface he was a loner, just like me. Just like Parvati. A lot of kids think high school represents the best years of their lives, but others recognize that it's mostly irrelevant bullshit, and that life doesn't even begin until afterward. All of us belonged to the second group, but Preston had always done an excellent job of pretending.

"How did you know that?" I ask. Then it hits me. This guy has already gotten to Parvati. That's probably why she tried to call me so many times.

Langston reads the expression on my face. "She's an interesting girl, Ms. Amos."

"Yeah, she is. But I don't want to talk about her."

"Fair enough." Langston nods.

Marcus exits onto a different highway, and the SUV heads north, away from the city. The lanes opposite us are backed up, bumper to bumper with traffic.

"Did Preston ever tell you about his childhood?" Langston asks.

I blink hard. "I don't really know anything about him from before the day we met. Just that he grew up rich since his dad is in business and politics."

Langston strokes his goatee. "I see."

I don't see how any of this can possibly be relevant to Preston's murder. I also don't understand how DeWitt can be convinced of my innocence, unless he somehow knows who killed his son. But in that case, why would he need me? "Look," I say. "I appreciate you getting me out of that shithole. But what does any of this have to do with who killed Pres?"

"For several months the DeWitts have been blackmailed about their son." Langston pops his gum. "I have been on retainer with them for years, so naturally they asked me to investigate. The blackmailer was exceptionally clever, and I never figured out who was behind it. Eventually the senator grew weary of being abused and decided to stop paying. That was a few weeks before Preston disappeared."

"You said blackmailed *about* Preston?"

"I did, didn't I?" Langston's mouth tightens into a hard line. "Let's just say there are things about Preston that the senator needs to remain a secret."

"What? Was he like a superhero or something?" I ask, only half kidding. Charismatic. Natural aptitude for everything. Invincible on the football field. The ability to fly or start fires with his eyes doesn't seem completely outside the realm of possibility.

"I'm not at liberty to discuss what Preston was or wasn't," Langston says abruptly. "But you and Ms. Amos probably knew him the best. If anyone can help find his killer, it's one of you two."

I nod. I need to find Preston's killer just as much as these guys do. If someone does want me to go down for this crime, they're probably not finished framing me.

I take a deep breath and then tell him about the anonymous tip that claimed Pres and I were fighting, about the bloody phone showing up in my trunk. "Do you know why anyone would try to set me up?"

"Nothing comes to mind. Do you still have the phone?" Langston asks. "That could be helpful to me."

"It got left at Colonel Amos's cabin, so I'm sure the FBI has it. But it didn't have anything on it—no files, no apps. Just a few calls from me and his parents."

"Did you find anything else in your car?"

"No. Preston left some of his camping equipment, but that's all," I say. "I hid my car about a mile away from the cabin in a nature preserve. Apparently, it hasn't been recovered."

"Marcus and I will find the car and make sure it stays hidden from the feds. We'll tell you if we find anything of interest," Langston says. "In the meantime you should go back to your normal life. Let us know if anyone approaches you about Preston, but otherwise stay out of it. These people are dangerous, Max. They won't hesitate to kill you if you get in their way."

I nod, but my mind is still spinning. Langston seems all right (now that he's put his gun away), but I can't just sit back and rely on him and Marcus to find Preston's killer.

Parvati and I came *so* close to finding Pres. The fire in Vegas couldn't have been burning for very long if we beat the fire department to the scene. If only I was a few minutes quicker somewhere along the way. If only I had acted instead of reacted, my friend might still be alive.

I try to think about what I would have done next if I hadn't gotten arrested in Vegas. Probably go back to the hard drive. Which I can't do. So then . . .

"Can you get me inside Preston's room?" I ask. "Like you said—I know him best. I might see something helpful."

Langston strokes his goatee again. "I went over the bedroom and basement myself after the FBI finished up, but I suppose it can't hurt for you to take another look."

I nod. I'm not sure if there's anything in Pres's room that'll help me find his killer, but I don't know what else to do. My only other option is to call Parvati back, and every time I so much as think her name, I see her and Preston naked in his bed. I hear both of them telling me how they're just friends, have never been anything but friends. It's a shitty feeling when you realize the two people you trusted most in the world are liars.

TWENTY-SEVEN

IT'S DEAD QUIET IN PRESTON'S house. Apparently, the federal agents all split once Pres's body was identified. No point in hanging around hoping for a ransom call anymore.

The inside of the house is dark except for the white glow of a TV screen. Preston's mom sits on the sofa in the living room, her cat curled protectively on her lap. One hand mindlessly strokes the animal's fur as she stares glassy-eyed at the wall-mounted flat-screen. It's the nicest TV in the house, with a better picture and sound quality than the one downstairs, but I've never seen anyone but Esmeralda ever watch it before. Preston always wanted to hang out in the basement. He said the living room felt cold and dead, like a funeral home. Funny considering it's filled with his baby pictures.

Claudia DeWitt doesn't even seem to notice me. There's a little brown pill bottle on the glass coffee table, along with a mostly empty bottle of wine.

"We need to look in Preston's room," Langston explains. "We'll just be a few minutes."

Claudia works the keys on the remote control, slowly scanning through the channels. She doesn't even look at us.

We pass the study on the way to the stairs. The door is open just wide enough that I can see Senator DeWitt seated at his desk, his pale face illuminated by the glow of his computer. Behind him, a trio of deer heads hang on the wall.

Marcus mutters something about updating the senator on our progress. He knocks on the doorframe outside the study and the Senator DeWitt gestures for him to enter. Langston and I continue upstairs. I stand in the center of Preston's bedroom, trying to see if anything sticks out as unusual.

Langston leans against the wall just inside the door, watching me scan the room systematically. "You see anything?"

"Give me a few minutes." I turn a slow circle. Plain white walls, black lacquer dresser and desk. Bookshelf. Bed. No, not the bed. I can't even peek at the wrinkle-free navy comforter without seeing the tangle of cream-colored sheets, Parvati, the curve of her naked back.

"Max?"

"I said hang on." Irritation creeps into my voice. Probably not a good move toward a guy with a gun strapped to his armpit. I force my eyes away from the bed and turn toward the closet instead. The sliding door is still partially open. Surprising. Maybe the feds haven't been letting Esmeralda clean in here.

I pull the closet open the rest of the way. Half empty, according to Parvati, but still twice as many clothes as I own.

"We did a thorough check of the closet," Langston says.

Ignoring him, I flip through all of Preston's clothes, patting down the pockets, checking for keys or notes or anything else small that could be a clue. No luck. Several pairs of tennis shoes and shiny loafers are lined up on the floor of the closet. I shake each of the shoes, but nothing falls out except some sock lint and a couple of tiny pebbles. The shelves above my head are mostly empty except for some old yearbooks and a couple of empty shoeboxes.

Next, I move to the dresser. The top is a mix of sports trophies and toiletries. A picture of me, Preston, and Parvati clowning around at a party is tucked into the side of the mirror. I check each drawer. Boxers. T-shirts. Socks. A junk drawer full of computer cables. Surf wax. Small bottles that look like energy drinks but are labeled as "Herbal Detoxifying Elixirs." I uncap one of them and peek inside. Ugh, it smells terrible, like a rotten starfish.

The desk is empty except for a tangle of cords.

That leaves the bed and the bookshelf. Reluctantly, I pull the mattress away from the box spring, trying not to think about Parvati. There are a couple of porno magazines stashed near one edge. Langston raises an eyebrow as I reach for the first magazine. Preston hid stuff inside of a book. Why not inside of a magazine?

But there's nothing there except for Señorita Septiembre's *chichis grandes*.

I move to the bookshelf. The top shelf bows beneath a row of snooty-sounding novels he probably had to read for his English classes at Bristol Academy. Below it are this semester's books from Vista Palisades. The trigonometry book that doubles as a hiding place is on the bottom shelf. Maybe Preston carved out more than one secret stash book. Leaving the trig book for last, I pull out each of the books and shake them. None of them are hollow, but random things rain out from the pages onto the carpet—a ticket stub from a concert we went to together, a couple of receipts, a picture of Parvati at a school dance. I glance through the receipts, but nothing seems relevant.

I pull the trig book from the shelf and open it.

Langston leans in, popping his gum as I flip through the secret compartment. There's a passport, a picture of Parvati (clothed, thankfully), and a couple of pictures of a brown-haired kid that must be Preston when he was about nine or ten. Beneath them is a tiny ziplock bag of white powder. I'm pretty sure it's not baking soda. I wonder why Parvati didn't tell me Pres had cocaine. Maybe she didn't dig all the way to the bottom.

I hand the ziplock to Langston and start to put the pictures back when something about one of them catches my eye. Preston is sitting on crumbling stone porch steps, the kind that ought to lead up to an old Victorian mansion. The house isn't in the picture, but there's a pair of carved lions flanking the steps. The lions are made of reddish-gray stone, and the left one has a chip off one side of its mouth so it appears to be snarling. My jaw drops a little. I know that lion.

I know that place.

"Were you aware Preston was using cocaine?" Langston asks.

I barely hear him. I'm still staring at the picture of Preston, at something that seems impossible. "Was Pres adopted?" I blurt out.

Langston pockets the coke and tries to take the photograph from me, but I don't let go. I give everything a second look. The kid's hair is curly and a lot darker than Preston's, but the shape of his face, his smile, it's the same. It has to be him, or a really close relative.

And Preston doesn't have any brothers.

"Of course not," Langston says. "His birth is a matter of public record." But now there's something different in his voice. Something taut. Nervous.

Something that makes *me* nervous.

I back off immediately. "Sorry. This picture just reminds me of a place where I used to live. A group home."

"Group home?" Langston pauses. "Like an orphanage?"

"They don't call them that anymore," I say. "But yeah. Homeless kids, runaways, the occasional juvenile delinquent."

Langston recovers almost immediately. His voice flips back into nature-documentary mode. "Why would you think it's the same place?"

"It had lions like this. I thought they were cool when I was a kid." I don't tell him about the chipped stone on the lion's mouth, about how I'm 99 percent sure this is a picture of the Rosewood Center for Boys. I don't tell him how much I hated the place, or how one of the "lifers," a kid named Henry, supposedly set a drunk homeless guy on fire once "just to see what would happen."

As soon as I arrived there I started planning my escape. I had been surviving okay on the streets. I wanted to go back, find some other kids to hang with. We could protect each other if we banded together. And then I found out I was getting adopted and decided to give the Cantrells a chance. I wasn't thrilled about the idea of new parents, but they lived by the beach and worked on the boardwalk. Surfing was the one thing that still connected me to my dad, so I was willing to try living with them if it meant being close to the ocean again. Plus they wanted to adopt me, not just take me for a foster-kid test drive, so I wouldn't have to worry about getting dumped back at the group home just as I got comfortable.

Langston shakes his head. "Lots of houses have stone lions. This could be in a completely different state, or country for that matter. Preston spent some of his childhood at boarding school. *If* this is even Preston. Maybe it's a friend from his childhood."

Right. A childhood friend that could basically be his twin. Langston knows something, but he's not going to give up any info that might be damaging to the senator. I would swear to it that Preston is standing in front of the very same building that my parents adopted me from eight years ago.

"Yeah. You're right," I tell him, bobbing my head and trying to sound convincing. I figure it should be easy enough to check if Langston is lying. Pres's dad has been a politician for a long time. A birth or an adoption in the DeWitt family should have been newsworthy enough for someone to report on. Too bad my disposable phone won't get me online. I'm going to have to go home to do some research on the matter.

Langston is still hovering behind me. Something about this picture freaks him out, and he's not going to let me keep it. But I need it. I know I do. "So how do you know that's coke?" I ask. As he goes to pull the ziplock bag out of his pocket, I pretend to put the picture back into the hollowed-out trig book but palm it and slide it in the center pocket of my hoodie at the last minute. That's a trick I learned from an older kid when I was homeless. Misdirection usually works, but not always, so only steal what you absolutely need.

Langston holds up the tiny baggie. "Powdered cocaine looks a lot like baking soda, but I tested it on my gums. Cocaine causes a numbing sensation."

I nod. "Sorry, I guess that probably won't help you find Pres's killer, will it?" I slouch my shoulders forward and pray that Langston can't see the rectangular outline of the photograph tucked in my hoodie pocket.

"We're not inclined to think Preston's murder was drug related, but it's another lead we can follow up."

We head back downstairs where Pres's mom is still curled up on the sofa, stroking the Himalayan cat and staring at the television. She notices me for the first time. Her fake tan blanches white and her lips twist like she's been sucking on a lemon.

I steel myself, wondering if she agrees with her husband or if she's going to call me a murderer.

Instead, she starts to cry. "Oh, Max," she wails. "I'm so sorry. I don't know why he's doing this to you."

TWENTY-EIGHT

"WHO?" I ASK. "DOING WHAT?"

She doesn't respond. Her sobbing escalates. Langston ushers me past the living room and out of the house. He's still got a hand on my shoulder as we start heading across the grass toward the SUV.

"What the hell was that about?"

"She's drunk. Distraught. She doesn't know what she's saying."

"Really, because she sounded pretty fucking lucid to me. Almost like she knew who was setting me up." He doesn't respond, so I keep talking. "Come on, if you guys know something, don't I deserve to know too? Who is *he*?"

Langston's dark eyes blend in with the night. "She was

probably just talking about me, bringing you into your dead friend's room. Or perhaps about the senator involving you in this mess."

It's plausible, but I don't believe him, not for a second. I slide into the passenger seat of the SUV and have him drop me off a couple of blocks from my house, just in case my parents are awake and happen to be looking out the window.

Our front lawn is full of garbage. Bottles, old newspapers, just random crap like someone emptied their trash can onto our grass. As I scoop up some of the bigger pieces of paper and dump them in our metal can, I see the brick that's left a fresh dent in the hood of Ben's pickup truck. There's a note tied to it: "Bring back DeWitt before next week's game, or else."

I guess Pres's disappearance must have made the news, but not his death. Nice. People are dead and the local idiots are worried about the outcome of a high school football game. They'll probably come burn down the house when they find out Preston is never coming back. I wonder how long Senator DeWitt can keep the details out of the media, if he's got a bunch of political analysts crunching numbers and gathering data on how to best capitalize on his own son's demise. Shaking my head, I let myself into the house.

The first thing I see are the boxes of Christmas decorations pushed to the corner of the living room. Amanda was dying to put the tree up, and I was supposed to help. It takes so little to make her happy, and I couldn't even manage that. Once this is over, I'm going to have to make it up to her somehow.

I turn away from the boxes and listen for the sound of creaking doors or footsteps that would indicate someone is awake. Thankfully, all I hear is my own breathing. How could I even begin to explain all of this to my parents? Why I hid from the FBI, why I went to Vegas, how I managed to make bail? It's madness. It doesn't even make sense to me.

With a pang, I realize how much I miss Parvati. She was the one person I could tell everything to. She had a way of making the pieces come together. I think about calling her for a minute, but I don't.

Ben has a home office set up in a cramped little room next to the nursery. I make my way through the darkness and flip on his old desktop computer. It takes forever to boot up. While I wait, I trace a question mark in the dust with my finger and mull over what it might mean if Preston was adopted. I have no idea if it would be relevant, but somehow finding that picture doesn't feel like a coincidence. If Pres was adopted, it's a major life thing we share and he never told me. If he kept me in the dark about something so huge, who knows what other secrets he's kept? I think back to his closet, to the clothes belonging to two people. Maybe there was a whole other side to Preston that I never saw. I didn't even know he wore contacts. Maybe I didn't know him at all.

The computer beeps twice and Ben's desktop fills the screen. He's used the same picture for wallpaper since he bought the computer a few years ago—a picture of him, Darla, me, and Amanda at Disney World. I was fourteen and pretended everything was lame all day, even though I kind of had fun. Amanda was seven and dragged me around the park by my arm. By the end of the day, my parents and I were exhausted, but Amanda was still going strong. So much for cystic fibrosis being a disability. She kicked all of our asses. I wonder if she's taking any crap about me at school, or if kids her age are too young to know what's going on.

I open a search box and type in "Remington DeWitt." Hundreds of hits come back: news sites, opinion sites, websites for the state of California and the U.S. Senate. Too much boring crap to wade through. I add "baby" to the search box. Still too much to sort. I change it to "birth announcement." Four sites come back.

The first one shows DeWitt visiting a children's hospital during his campaign for the U.S. Senate. The second site is what I'm looking for. It's a link to the *Los Angeles Times*, a small news blurb about the birth of one Preston Abbott DeWitt to then-Governor Remington DeWitt and his wife, Claudia. There's a tiny picture with the article. Sure enough, a younger-looking DeWitt is smiling down at a swaddled infant.

I flip through the third and fourth links, but they don't have anything new to tell me. I feel like I'm back to square one. If Preston *wasn't* adopted, then why was he at Rosewood?

TWENTY-NINE

MY PHONE BUZZES AND I jump. It's Parvati. Indecision stabs me in the chest. Two seconds and then I answer. I need info. She might have it.

"What were you trying to tell me about Preston?" I ask.

"Oh my God, Max. So it's true? They let you out?"

"Yeah," I say, not bothering to explain. Every syllable out of her mouth hurts me. All I can hear is her saying Preston's name as she rocks back and forth on top of him. I squeeze my eyes shut, as if the visual is playing out on the patterned wallpaper of Ben's office instead of the inside of my skull. "What were you trying to tell me?" I ask again.

"What's wrong? Are you mad because I got us caught?" She's still talking, but I hold the earpiece away from my head because I almost can't stand it anymore. "My parents will drop that stupid restraining order once they find out you're innocent and—"

"I know about you and Pres." The words come out sharply and suddenly, like I'm vomiting up bowling balls.

Dead silence. And then a tiny breath. "What?"

"Your *friend* Preston? I know you guys . . . slept together."

"Max." Her voice softens. "I can explain."

"No, P," I say. "I don't want to hear about how it was all practice for being a spy or maybe a school project you two did together on the Kama Sutra." My voice starts to crack. I am dangerously close to losing it. "All I want to know is what was so important that you left me three messages."

"All right." She sounds hurt. I don't think I've ever raised my voice to her before. Never had a reason to. "I think maybe Preston was adopted, and Violet Cain was his real mother."

"Why would you think that?"

"I was going through all of my texts and emails from Preston, looking for anything that might be a clue. One of them reminded me of something that happened a couple years ago."

"What?"

"I found a lot of money in the trig book, like thousands of dollars. I asked Pres about it and he said his parents gave it to him. Said they were always giving him money because they felt bad about the adoption."

"What did he mean?" I ask.

"I don't know," Parvati says. "He was drunk at the time, and after that he never brought it up again."

Probably because they were too busy getting naked. Bile surges up into my throat. I swallow it down, try to keep from pushing the entire computer onto the floor. "Well it's an interesting theory, given her age. But she can't be," I say, "because I have a birth announcement in front of me, DeWitt and his wife holding baby Preston, back when DeWitt was the governor."

"Damn it. I thought for sure I was onto something," Parvati says. "I just keep thinking about Violet being thirty-five. There's no way Pres would be hooking up with someone that age. He's never shown any interest in older women. There has to be some other reason he went to see her."

"Uh-huh." I'm trying to focus, but my brain keeps flashing back to those pictures of Parvati and Preston.

"Are you at home?" she asks, oblivious to my thoughts. "I'll sneak out. We can go through all the information together."

"No," I say tersely. "I've got to go. I'll double-check the adoption angle, just in case."

"Come on, Max. You know we work better as a team."

"I thought we did," I say. "But that was back when I thought we told each other the truth." I hang up before she can answer. She calls back, but I let it go to voicemail. She sends me a text and I turn the phone off without reading it.

Using just the light of the computer screen so as not to wake anyone up, I scan the entire study, looking for Ben's giant key ring. I don't see it, so I head into the hallway, planning to check the kitchen next. My foot collides with something hard and plastic and I trip over a bouncy seat parked outside the nursery. "Son of a bitch," I say, just a little too loudly. One of my sisters stirs in her crib.

Uh-oh. The whole house shakes with the wailing of a healthy-lunged baby, which is shortly joined by the wailing of a second healthy-lunged baby.

Darla stumbles out of her bedroom in a flannel night-gown, her hair sticking up on top. "Max?" She stops like she isn't sure I'm real. "We got your message, but—"

"I know," I say. "I owe you an explanation, and I wish I had one."

I follow her into the nursery, where she picks up Jo Lee and gestures for me to get Ji Hyun. It might be the first time I've really held one of my little sisters.

"Sorry," I say. "I think I scared them when I bumped into their bouncy thing."

"It's okay." Jo fusses in Darla's arms. Darla rocks her back and forth and motions for me to do the same with Ji.

Gradually, Ji's screaming fades to wailing and then

sniffles before subsiding. I smile despite everything that's happening. The babies are cute when they're not screaming, but why Darla wanted to adopt more kids when she's over forty is beyond me.

"What happened?" Darla asks. "Did the charges get dropped?" Her voice is so hopeful that it kind of breaks my heart to tell her no.

"But who could have possibly posted your bond?"

"I don't really know," I hedge.

Darla looks worried. She lays Jo down in the crib, and I do the same with Ji. "Max, you're not involved with drug lords or the Mafia or anything, right?"

I snort. "Darla. I don't think the Mafia employs a lot of high school kids."

Her cheeks go pink and droopy, like one of those half-dead roses that gas stations sell around the holidays. I know she's given up hoping I'll start referring to her as "Mom" some-day, but she still wilts occasionally when I say her name. I don't call her Darla to be mean. It's just that my real mother died giving birth to me. It seems like the least I can do after that kind of sacrifice is not replace her with someone else. Besides, as hard as she tries, Darla just doesn't feel like a mom. More like a cool aunt, but I know that isn't what she wants to be.

"No drugs?" she asks.

I shake my head. "No drugs." I sigh. "I need to ask you a favor, though." The kind of favor a mom wouldn't do but a cool aunt just might.

She raises a finger to her lip and heads for the hallway. I follow behind her. She goes into the kitchen and fills the coffee carafe.

I check the clock. It's cruising toward midnight. "Seriously? Coffee now?"

"Something tells me you're not going to sleep anytime soon, and I could drink an entire pot of coffee and still be out before my head hit the pillow." She yawns. "What do you need?"

I don't answer right away. I feel guilty for lying about Langston, but I can't exactly tell her the senator's shifty henchmen bailed me out. That would invite too many other questions. And every minute I waste, Preston's killer might be getting farther away. It's like Amanda's newest cop show, *The Clock Is Ticking.* In the opening credits, a movie preview voice-over man informs viewers that only forty percent of criminals not apprehended in the first forty-eight hours are eventually brought to justice.

I hear the telltale drip as the coffee starts to brew. I turn away from Darla to grab a pair of chipped coffee mugs from the cabinet. "Your car," I say finally. I give Darla the Humane Society mug and keep the surfer mug Amanda painted for me. "Or Ben's truck. Is there any way I can borrow a vehicle, just for tomorrow?"

"When do you think you'll be getting *your* car back?"

She must think that the police impounded it as evidence. Instead of correcting her, I trace one of my mug's surfboards with my finger. Behind me, coffee rains down into the glass pot, filling the kitchen with an earthy smell. "I'm not really sure," I say.

"I see." Darla's face does its drooping thing again. We both know I'm not telling her the whole story.

"But I have to find Pres's killer, because everyone thinks I'm guilty, and I'm not." The coffeemaker hisses. "You believe me, right?" I jump up to grab the coffee, almost sticking my hand in the cloud of steam it belches out at the end of the cycle. I'm afraid to look at her right then. I know what she'll *say*, but what if I see something different reflected in her eyes?

Her voice is soft. "Oh, Max, of course I believe you. I just wish you had come to us for advice before you ran off."

I turn around slowly, but there's no doubt or judgment in her face. Just a divot of sadness between her thinning eyebrows.

I set the mug of coffee down in front of her. She always drinks it black. I add a slosh of milk to mine, and a spoonful of sugar big enough to kill most of the coffee taste. "I got scared and I messed up," I say. "But I'm coming to you now." I give her my most hopeful look.

I don't tell her where I'm planning to go with the car—back to the Rosewood Center for Boys. I never told her how much that place sucked, but she knows I hated it. We had to return for visits with the social worker, Anna, for the first couple of months after I got adopted, just until a caseload spot opened up for a Vista Palisades social worker. Anna was the nicest person there, but I still used to get all tense in the car on the way, as if part of me was afraid the building would swallow me up when I went back inside. As if I'd spend the rest of my life getting my ass kicked by Henry the Happy Sociopath. "I need to find out the truth."

Darla runs one finger around the rim of her coffee mug. "What you *need* is to let the police handle that. Go to school. Make up the work you've missed. Graduate."

School? Seriously? "Darla. The FBI is just waiting for the forensics report to link me to the fire in Vegas. They think I killed Pres. Probably everyone at school does too. I can't go back there."

She shakes her head like I'm being overly dramatic. "I don't want you to drop out. That could wreck your whole future. Just tell the truth and everything will be fine."

I never believed that, not even before someone put a bloody phone in my trunk and called the cops to tell them

Preston and I were arguing at the top of Ravens' Cliff. The truth doesn't get you very far on the streets, or in a group home, or even in high school. That's probably why the idea of Liars, Inc. appealed to me. Everybody lies. You might as well get paid for it. I shake my head in disbelief as I think about sitting at the cafeteria table with Pres and Parvati, joking about our new business venture. It seems like a million years ago. "I tried," I say finally. "They didn't believe me."

"What does Parvati think about all of this?"

"Who cares?" I mutter, stirring my coffee violently.

Darla's eyes widen slightly. She's never heard me say anything even remotely unflattering about Parvati. "Are you two fighting?"

"I wish that was all." I glance up for a second and then train my eyes on my coffee again, trying not to think about how the creamy, tan color reminds me of Parvati's skin. "Let's just say she lied to me about some important stuff."

"Do you want to talk about it?"

"Fu—hell no," I say. "I don't even want to think about it."

"Does it have to do with the investigation?"

"Sort of." I pause. It might feel good to tell someone, to release a little bit of the rage inside me. Maybe I would be able to think more clearly afterward. "You really want to know? The FBI found videos on Pres's computer of Parvati and him together," I blurt out.

Darla almost chokes on her coffee. "She cheated on you? Could they have been from before you started dating?"

"Maybe. Does it matter? Either way she lied to me. According to her, she and Preston were never more than friends." My sharp voice cuts through the quiet kitchen. I take a deep breath and try to tone it down so I don't wake the babies again.

Darla reaches across the table and pats my hand. "I'm sorry. I'm sure you feel betrayed, but maybe it's not as bad as you think. Maybe she has an explanation."

I shrug. "You think it's okay to lie about stuff like that as long as you have a *reason*?"

Darla shakes her head. "No, but everybody lies sometimes, Max. And I've never seen you happier than when you're with Parvati. It seems like she's the only person you actually confide in." She sips her coffee. "I wouldn't be too quick to kick that person out of your life."

Darla is right that Parvati was the only person I really talked to. She knows so many things about me that other people don't. But I always assumed that was a two-way street. Finding out she kept something so major from me . . . cuts deep.

I don't think I ever lied to *her*.

Darla adjusts the collar of her nightgown. "Do you love her?"

I slouch forward. "I don't know. What does that even mean?"

A smile plays at her lips. "Remember when you hit that kid with a rock because he was bullying Amanda?"

"Yeah." Not my finest hour, but he kind of deserved it.

"It's like that. When you care about someone so much that you'll do anything—even stupid or destructive things—for them."

"That sounds more like mental illness than love."

Darla doesn't respond. She's staring down into the bottom of her cup as if she could tell my future by the inch of remaining coffee. "You know, before we adopted you, your dad almost left me because of a lie."

"You? Seriously? I always thought you were perfect."

"No one's perfect." She laughs under her breath. "I really wanted to adopt a child, but the shop had been struggling and Ben thought we should wait until we were financially stable. I thought that would never happen. I ended up getting back in contact with a guy I dated in college."

I hold up a hand because I'm not sure if I want to hear this story. If Darla tells me she cheated on Ben I'm going to wonder if *any* relationship anywhere ever is safe from crushing betrayal. "You don't—"

"Nothing happened," Darla says quickly. "I just needed someone to talk to and didn't feel like I could talk to your dad. But I lied to him in order to go meet the other guy, and he found out about it."

"But then he forgave you?"

She smiles fondly. "Yeah. You and I are both pretty lucky that happened."

She's right. As much as I complain about babysitting and stuff, growing up with Ben and Darla has been pretty solid. "So . . . Parvati . . . you're telling me to forgive her?"

"I'm just saying to give her a chance to explain," Darla says. "And don't do anything rash."

I don't know. It sounds good, and Darla's pretty smart. Maybe I can think about it after my brain stops playing imaginary sex tapes of Preston and Parvati on infinite repeat. Until then, I'm more concerned with finding out who's trying to frame me. But I nod like I'm in total agreement. "And if I take this advice of yours, does that mean I can borrow your car?"

She sighs. "If I tell you no, you're just going to do something stupid like steal one, aren't you?"

I wouldn't really steal a car, but I don't answer. I can tell she's mulling over in her mind whether to help me or not. Things always work out better for me when I don't rush them. It's like surfing. You can't just chase wildly after every wave. You have to wait for the right one to come to you.

"Do you promise," she continues, "not to break the law in

any way while you're gone?"

I raise my hand like I'm swearing an oath. "I won't even roll through a stop sign."

"Where are you going to go?"

"Nowhere far, I promise. I just need to check out a couple of leads."

She sighs again, like maybe she's already second-guessing herself. "Take the truck, as long as it's only for tomorrow. Just please be careful with it. That pickup is your dad's baby and he'll kill us both if anything happens to it." She leans forward to pat me on the hand. "And you be careful too, okay? I know you're eighteen now, and that you don't think you need a mom, but that doesn't mean I don't need my son."

My throat tightens and I look away. I wish I'd been a better kid, that I'd given her a real chance, but it's too late to start playing house now. "You can tell Ben I took the truck without asking if you want," I offer.

She shakes her head. "We both agreed we wouldn't lie to each other ever again. I try hard to keep my end of that." She stands up to take her coffee mug to the sink.

I take it from her hand. "I got this. You get some sleep."

On cue, one of the twins starts crying. "I may never sleep again," she grumbles, but her lips curl into a smile as she says it.

"I'll see you soon," I say.

"Be safe." She stops just before rounding the corner. "By the way, I like your hair."

I snort. "It's not polite to lie."

"No, really. I can finally see your face," she says. "You're actually kind of cute. Who knew?" Her eyes sparkle in the dim light of the hallway, and for the first time in years I go to her and give her a hug. Her body stiffens in surprise, and then relaxes. She squeezes me tight. "You're a good kid, Max. I love you."

I swallow hard and start to tell her I love her back, but before I can get the words out, the other twin begins to wail. Darla breaks away and heads to the nursery, and the moment passes me by.

THIRTY

December 9th

IT'S BEEN A WHILE SINCE I've slept and I don't want to wreck Ben's truck, so I decide to crash for a bit before driving to Rosewood. I won't be able to find Anna until at least 7:00 or 8:00 a.m. anyway. I set the alarm on my phone to wake me at five. My mind is still racing as my head hits the pillow. Everything that's happened is all tangled together, twisted up and matted like a half-eaten ball of yarn barfed up by Preston's cat. My brain yanks at the knots, reviewing the suspects and the chain of events, until it finally gives up and I fall asleep.

When my phone wakes me, I sneak through the still-darkened house, stepping extra cautiously as I pass the nursery. It takes two tries to fire up Ben's pickup. The motor grinds and gurgles before sputtering to life. I baby the clutch as I drive toward Los Angeles, keeping one eye on my rearview mirror, watching for cops. I'm not supposed to leave town. Is driving to the far side of the city a violation of the terms of my bail? I don't think so, but I keep to the speed limit just in case.

I pull off the highway at the Rosewood exit and make my way through the suburban streets. I pass the elementary school some of the other boys attended and the corner park where Anna took us to play four square. It's like traveling back in time. I even *feel* younger—unsure, afraid. When I pull Ben's truck over to the curb, my eyes are immediately drawn to the crumbling porch steps and the stone lions on either side. I slide Preston's picture out of my pocket for comparison. There are a few more cracks in the stone, but it's the same porch, just like I thought.

I turn the truck's engine off, but I don't get out right away. It's amazing how the house hasn't changed. It has the same pink-and-white-painted wooden front with ash-colored shingles. The paint is still peeling, the roof still looks in danger of collapsing in a couple of places. My heart knocks hard against my breastbone and my sweaty fingers are clinging to the steering wheel. I'm being stupid. It isn't like I got tortured by the staff or violated by my fellow residents. I got beat up a couple of times. Big deal. Henry was older than me. He's probably dead or in prison by now. I'm not going to walk through the door and get punched in the stomach.

I force myself out of the truck and across the gravel front lawn. The screen door opens with an impressive creak and I step into the front room of the house, which doubles as a waiting area. The walls, formerly dusky gray, are now a sunny yellow that almost matches the hair of the receptionist. She looks up from behind a plain oaken table that is serving as her desk.

"May I help you?" she asks. Her eyes flick downward for a second and I wonder if she's got an emergency button that'll summon a couple of goons to come tackle me if I get out of line.

"Does Anna still work here?"

The receptionist takes a long time to answer. She looks down at the desk again, furrowing her brow.

"Social worker," I add, trying to be helpful.

"She's here," the girl says. "Just trying to see if she has any free time. Do you have an appointment?"

I shake my head. "I used to live here," I say, hoping she'll feel sorry for me.

"She's in meetings all day." The receptionist flips through a leather-bound book. "I can make an appointment for you the day after tomorrow."

"Sure." I give her my name and number and watch as she jots down my information. I don't plan on waiting two days to talk to Anna, but I figure a normal person would make an appointment, so that's what I do. "Do you mind if I look around?" When she looks perplexed, I add, "I just have a lot of memories about being here." Half of me is hoping she says no. The other half figures I might as well give the center a quick look-over, just in case I see something that clicks all the puzzle pieces into place.

"Guess it'd be okay," she says. "But I'll have to go with you."

I fidget nervously as the receptionist takes her time shutting the appointment book and straightening the pens and pencils on her desk into a neat line. She pushes back her chair and motions for me to follow her.

The main floor hasn't changed much except for the sunny new paint job. There's the small hallway with offices for the director and social worker, the kitchen at the back of the house, and the living area with a TV and bookshelf. I used to hide behind the books people donated to us. I would pull them out at random and pretend to be reading, just so no one would talk to me. It worked pretty well too. People are reluctant to disturb someone lost in a story.

We pass a desk with an old computer on it that might even get the internet. That's new.

"All the boys are at school right now," the receptionist says.

I nod. I turn toward a creaky staircase and she follows me. Upstairs, I duck into one of the dorm rooms where the boys sleep. Four beds are arranged the same as I remember, so close to one another that if you happened to thrash around in your sleep you might accidentally slap the kid next to you. A Christmas stocking with a glittery name is pinned above each boy's bed. I can't stop myself from reading them, even though I know it's ridiculous. Obviously, there's no one named Preston. Or Henry. There are several more rooms, but wanting to look in each one will only make the receptionist suspicious. I rack my brain trying to remember all of the kids who were at Rosewood with me, but I was there for such a short time and never talked to any them, so they blur into a stream of faceless strangers.

I give up and let her lead me back downstairs. "Thanks for your time," I say.

I head back out into the cool sunshine. My plan is to hang out in the truck and stalk the place until I see Anna leave at the end of the day. No need to sit around for hours, though. I kill time driving around town and grabbing some food at the diner on the corner. It's decorated just as I remember it—stark white walls with vinyl records glued above each booth. Ben and Darla took me here while they were waiting for the adoption paperwork to be drawn up. I remember how they told me I could order anything I wanted. Of course I ordered way more food than I could eat, but Ben helped me eat some of it and the rest Darla had boxed up and sent back to the center with me. I hid it under my bed, even though I'm pretty sure it was eggs and biscuits and gravy, and should have been refrigerated. Henry snuck over to my bed after lights-out and ordered me to hand over the food. I did, and he punched me in the stomach anyway.

I hang out in a small city park for part of the afternoon, but I'm back in front of the center by three thirty, just in case Anna goes home early. I check my phone messages while I wait. There's another voicemail and a text from Parvati, both of them begging me to call her. It takes all my willpower to focus on the task at hand instead.

"Whipped," I mutter under my breath. But the sharp pain of her betrayal is starting to dull a little bit. It shouldn't matter that much that she and Pres used to be together, should it? Parvati never cared about the girls I dated before her.

But I never lied about them.

I wish there were some way I could go back in time and never see those pictures. But I can't, so I do my best to forget about them and focus on the Rosewood Center.

Just after four o'clock, a woman exits the front door and cuts across the grass. She's got wide shoulders and frizzy hair that's pulled back in a low ponytail. She doesn't look much like the pretty social worker I remember, until she glances

257

in my direction. Same blue eyes and round face. My heart starts slam dancing around in my chest. Questions flood my brain. Will she remember me? Will she run away like I'm a crazy person? Has she heard about my arrest? What, exactly, am I supposed to say to her?

She makes it to her car before I even get out of the truck, so I end up following her to a fish taco restaurant a couple of blocks away. Great. Now she'll think I'm a stalker for sure. Oh well. Everyone else thinks I'm a murderer, so "stalker" feels like a promotion. I wait for her to order and then tap her on the shoulder while she's gathering her napkins and salsa packets.

"Anna?" I say.

She turns around. "Yes?" Her brow furrows and I can almost see her mentally flipping through her group-home-kid Rolodex, trying to identify me.

"My name is—"

"Max Keller!" she blurts out. "Oh my God, look at you. Different body. Different face. Same messy hair."

I freeze up for a second. No one has called me Max Keller in years. But then I smile. It feels good to be remembered.

She shakes her head in wonder. "I didn't know if you'd ever talk," she says. "You never spoke to anyone."

"Yeah," I say, once again at a loss for words. I want to tell her how she's the one good memory I have of Rosewood. How if it weren't for her I would have run away from the center, and who knows where I'd be. I don't say anything, though. It's like there's a statute of limitations on thank-yous. Like I should have said all that stuff the day I left, but I didn't, and to say it now would be weird.

"But I don't remember the name of the people who adopted you," she says.

"The Cantrells," I say. "They've been great."

"I'm glad." The corners of her eyes crinkle up as she smiles. "I remember how Mrs. Cantrell instantly fell in love with you."

"Can I ask you something?" I cut her off before she can tell the much-repeated story.

I pull the picture of Preston sitting on the Rosewood steps out of my pocket. "Do you know him?"

Anna's jaw goes tight, like she's grinding her molars together. "Yeah." She squints. "Adam. Lyons. He was at Rosewood . . . after you, maybe? I can't remember exactly." She shakes her head. "Nice kid."

"Are you sure about the name?" I don't tell her I think it's a picture of a young Preston DeWitt, and that he's dead now.

"Yeah. He disappeared from Rosewood and the center got audited because of it." She glances around. "We almost lost our state funding. Child Protective Services had to come and recertify us."

"Do you know what happened to him? Or where he is now?"

Anna takes a step back. "Why are you asking me all this?"

"I can't explain it," I say. "But it's really important."

"He just went to school one morning and never came back." She fiddles with her handful of napkins, rolling them into a cylinder between her palms. "The teachers said he never made it to class."

I stare hard at the picture. The hair is much darker than Preston's. Could I be wrong? Could it really be a picture of some other kid? But then why the hell did Preston have it? "Do you remember when it was that Adam disappeared?"

"Maybe eight or nine years ago?" she says. "The *LA Times* did a piece on how we might lose our funding. I'm sure you can find the information there."

"Number four-forty-one," the counter guy calls.

Anna looks down at her receipt and accidentally drops one of her napkins. For a second she freezes, like she's debating whether she should rescue the napkin from the sticky floor or just leave it.

"I got it." I bend down to get the napkin, which has tumbled its way across the floor and is sticking to the bottom of the trash can. I ball it up and toss it in the trash.

"Thanks, Max." She bites her lip again. "It was nice to see you, but I have to go. My daughter has a soccer game tonight and I'm running a little behind."

I nod. "It was nice to see you too, Anna." Once more, a bunch of sappy gratitude swells up on the tip of my tongue. "You were . . ." I crack my knuckles as I try to come up with the right words. "The one thing about Rosewood that didn't suck." By the time I spit it out the cashier has abandoned Anna's order to ring up the next person in line.

Anna smiles faintly. "Thanks. I hope everything is okay, Max."

"It will be," I say. She leaves and I order a trio of tacos and a drink for myself. I stare at the photograph of who I thought was Preston while the food is being prepared. Now what?

The cashier calls my order number in a monotone voice. I grab my tray, load up on napkins and soda, and take my food to a booth in the corner. I set the picture on the bench next to me and unwrap the first taco.

Could Preston have a twin or brother I don't know about? It seems far-fetched, the wealthy and powerful DeWitts giving a kid up for adoption, but who knew what politicians were capable of? I finish the first taco in about four bites and crumple the waxy wrapper into a ball. I suck in a long drink of soda. Parvati thought Violet was Preston's mom. Maybe she was closer than I thought. Maybe DeWitt had an affair and this Adam kid is Preston's half brother.

I bite into my second taco. A couple of diced tomatoes and chunks of flaky cod fall from the shell and land on my paper-lined tray. Tomato juice runs down my chin and I swipe at my mouth with a napkin. Maybe Preston somehow figured all of this out and went looking for his half brother, not knowing that Violet had actually given her child up for adoption. Violet might have gotten upset about being found, about Preston tricking her into meeting him, but why did they both end up dead? I crumple another wrapper and take a gulp of soda.

And then it hits me like a twenty-foot wave. Maybe Preston and Violet were the people blackmailing Senator DeWitt! I try to remember if one of the folders on Pres's hard drive was called RD, or anything else that might stand for the senator, but the two-letter folder names are just a jumble in my head. It makes sense, though. If Pres had video cameras rigged in the spare bedroom, surely he had them in other places around the house too. Who knows what he had caught his father saying, or doing?

And what if Adam was in on it, and he's still alive somewhere? Maybe Langston is looking for him and he thinks Adam will try to contact some of Pres's friends.

Maybe DeWitt bailed me out as bait.

My fingers shake a little as I finish the third taco and ball up the wrapper. Wiping my hands hard on a napkin, I stare down at the scuffed tabletop, at my three crumpled paper balls. Preston. Adam. Violet. What if the three of them had threatened to expose DeWitt's affair and subsequent abandonment of his other son just as DeWitt was about to get appointed to the president's cabinet? I know how much Preston liked money. I wonder how much he could have gotten for keeping a secret this big. But would he really sabotage his father's entire political career just to make a quick buck? Maybe he was so angry about being lied to and denied his only family that he wanted everyone to pay for it. Either way, I still couldn't believe that Senator DeWitt would really kill Preston to shut him up. Politics couldn't possibly mean more than his own children.

Did Preston ever tell you about his childhood? I glance around, suddenly nervous. If DeWitt did kill Preston, that means Langston and Marcus know about it. And that means they're just keeping tabs on me to make sure I don't figure it out.

THIRTY-ONE

IT'S TIME TO DO MORE research. If I head home now I'll get caught in traffic, so instead I drive through the streets of Rosewood until I find a small brick building with a sign that says LIBRARY out front. It's mostly empty inside, but a handful of college students and older people look up curiously as I stroll through the metal detector. A librarian with thin lips and a cone-shaped pile of graying blonde hair on top of her head stands as I approach the desk. It's like she's already judged me as a troublemaker and is preparing to throw me out by my ear.

"Yes?" One word. Curt. Sharp.

"I need to, uh, is it possible to use the internet?"

Her mouth twists like I just admitted to a hard-core porn

addiction. "Do you have a library card?"

"No." I'm about to tell her I don't live in Los Angeles when I get a better idea. I lower my voice. "I'm from Rosewood Center, you know? The group home."

Her voice loses a bit of edge. "Why do you need the internet?"

"Research," I say. "School project."

"So why not use the internet at Rosewood?"

I look down at the floor. "I got in trouble there. For online gaming. I'm not allowed any internet or video games for a week, but I've still got to get this paper finished."

"Ah. Well, I suppose I can set you up with a one-day pass," she says. "But they'll have to get you a library card if you're planning to come back."

She hands me a little plastic card printed with login information and then directs me to a glassed-in room with two tables of computers. I find Number 9 and log on.

I type "Adam Lyons" into the search box. Hundreds of pages pop up. I add "disappearance" and "Rosewood" to my search criteria, which narrows the results to just two pages. The first one is an article from a few years ago about the problem of runaways in warm-climate states. It only mentions Adam's name in passing, as one of several kids who disappeared from group homes in the Southwest. The second link is to the article from the *LA Times* that Anna mentioned. It doesn't say much, only that Adam Lyons was the second ward of the state to disappear from the Rosewood Center for Boys in the past five years. The article goes on to question some of the Rosewood policies and call into question whether the staff members are qualified to care for "at-risk" youth. There's a tiny black-and-white picture of Adam embedded in the article. It's grainy, but it still looks a lot like Preston. There's no mention of the exact date that Adam disappeared, but the article is dated February 11, almost eight years ago.

I try Preston's name with "Rosewood" and then Preston's name with "Adam Lyons." No hits. Other than the picture, there's no evidence linking Preston to Rosewood *or* Adam Lyons. I try the name "Violet Cain" with all of the other search terms. Nothing. I drum my fingers on the tabletop, not sure what to look up next.

I'm missing something important, but I don't know what it is. I turn back to the computer, intending to log off, but instead I type something completely unrelated into the search box: "Alexander Keller Los Angeles."

A whole string of hits come back. I click on the first one and my father's picture pops up next to a news story. I study his piercing eyes and square jaw. I wish I looked more like him.

"UCLA Professor of Oceanography Alexander Keller died this morning of an apparent heart attack . . ."

My phone buzzes. Stern Librarian glances up from her desk. She points at a sign that says NO CELL PHONES. Damn, how can she even hear it from way over there?

It's Parvati, of course. I let her go to voicemail. There's nothing else for me to find here. I take one last look at my real dad's picture and then log off the computer. I turn in my internet card as I pass the librarian's desk on the way out.

The railing for the library steps is a low cement wall, and I hop up onto it and let my feet hang down. I don't know where to go next. The FBI could probably access more information about Violet Cain or Adam Lyons, but there's no way McGhee and Gonzalez would believe a crazy story about Senator DeWitt putting out a hit on his own son to cover up some affair he had almost twenty years ago. I can't even believe it myself.

Drumming my fingers on the cement, I stare off into the distance. The sun is starting to set. A neon sign on the parking garage next to the library crackles to life. Reluctantly, I listen to the message Parvati left.

"Max. I need to see you. There's something else that you should know. Please call me when you get this."

Maybe she's got new information. I breathe in and out a few times and then dial her number.

"Max!" She sounds so happy to hear from me that it kind of makes me feel sick.

"You said you had something else to tell me?"

"Yeah, but not over the phone. I need to see you."

"I'm not home right now." I'm also not ready to see her yet. I glance down at the manicured lawn at the bottom of the railing and try to quell the jittery feeling in my stomach. It's not like what she has to tell me could possibly be any worse than eight-by-ten glossies of her and Pres having sex. "Just spit it out, P."

"Sooner or later you're going to have to let me explain the Preston thing."

"Yeah? Well, I choose later," I say. "There are more important things than us right now, like finding Preston's killer. So unless what you want to tell me has to do with that . . ."

There's a long pause. "No," she says finally. "At least I don't see how it could."

I hear a voice in the background. It sounds like the Colonel. "Isn't this the day you stay late for newspaper class?" I ask.

Parvati sighs again. "My parents pulled me out of school. I'm going to finish up at Blue Pointe Prep in the spring."

"What about this semester?"

"I'll have enough credits that I don't need it," she says. "Another thing I wanted to tell you in person."

"Sorry," I say tersely. "Didn't mean to get you in trouble."

"It's not just because of you," she starts. "My mom was

snooping around in my room and found—"

Condoms? Sex tapes? A lump starts to form in my throat. "I have to go," I say quickly.

"What? Go where?"

I don't answer her. I just click the disconnect button and slip the phone back into my pocket. I'm still sitting on the wall, my dangling feet growing heavy in my sneakers. People pass back and forth in front of me, colored blurs against the gray sky.

I spent most of my life being no one, and not really minding. And then I met Pres and Parvati and started to feel different. Not because they were popular or had money— I never cared about any of that. With them, I was part of something. Only maybe I wasn't. Maybe it was never the three of us. Maybe it was always the two of them, and me. Either way, Preston is gone and I kind of wish Parvati was too, even though that would clearly make me no one again. It kind of sucks having nothing to lose, but it sucks even worse having everything good taken away from you.

Or to realize it was never yours in the first place.

THIRTY-TWO

LANGSTON CALLS ME ON THE way home. I flip on the cruise control and turn down the music.

"Marcus and I took care of your car," he says.

"Do I want to know what that means?"

"It means that it's gone for good."

"Shit. I guess I'll be walking everywhere from now on." I drum my fingertips on the steering wheel.

"Sorry." He pauses. "Better than life in prison, though, right?"

Corporate campuses rush by me on both sides of the highway. I pull the truck into the exit lane to switch highways, swearing under my breath as I nearly sideswipe a black BMW that was hovering in my blind spot.

"There was nothing useful in the trunk. Anything new on your end?" he asks.

"No. I've been staying out of it, like you said I should," I say quickly.

Langston chuckles. "You sound anxious. What's wrong, Max? Still worried we're going to revoke your bail?"

"I just don't know how all this stuff is going to play out." I swerve around a dead possum, trying not to notice the guts spread all over the highway.

"Everything will be fine. I'll be in touch." He hangs up.

I crank the radio volume, zoning out a little as the truck eats mile after mile of open road. The sky has gone from gray to navy blue. The hard-rock station starts to broadcast an interview with a band I hate. I flip through the rest of the stations, but everything else sucks, so I turn the radio off.

The silence quickly makes me crazy. What am I coming home to? Had news of Preston's death been made public yet? Could Pres really have blackmailed, and then died at the hands of, his own father? The questions swirl together inside my head, and I can't answer any of them.

But I know who possibly can. Just the thought of Parvati's throaty voice makes my insides ache. She's always been able to make me feel better, and now I'm avoiding her because every time I talk to her it hurts me. And every time it hurts me I get one step closer to realizing the two of us are over. But maybe I should stop hiding and just deal with things. Darla's right—I need to hear her out, even if talking to her means officially breaking up. Plus, she's smart, and she's the only one who understands this whole Preston mess. If she can help me find his killer, I should let her.

She picks up right away. "Are you all right?"

"Yeah," I say. "I'm sorry I hung up on you." She doesn't respond right away, so I keep going. "I've been doing a really shitty job of dealing with things. Finding out about you and Pres from the FBI was not ideal, you know? But I can't avoid hearing the whole truth forever . . . even though I kind of want to."

"I know it was wrong to lie to you, Max. I guess I just didn't want to screw up our friendship. Would you have wanted to hang out as a group if you knew Preston and I . . ." She trails off.

"The feds have pics of you guys from Bristol Academy, Parvati. How did you not know Pres was recording you two having sex for *years*?"

Parvati shudders audibly. "I'm sorry you had to see that. I knew Pres liked taping stuff, but I had no idea how far it went. I swear to you, all the feelings I had for him are in the past."

"I just don't get why you both felt the need to lie. I talked to him before I asked you out, and he said you guys had never been together."

Parvati's voice goes hoarse. "Probably because to him we never were. I'm fairly certain he only saw me as a casual hookup."

"Oh." I'm not sure what to say to that. Parvati is smoking hot, but the thought that someone could appreciate her sexiness but not get totally sucked in by how fun, and smart, and strong she is baffles me.

"Are you going to forgive me?" Parvati asks. "Or are we . . . breaking up?"

Did I mention her straightforwardness? "I don't know, I mean, jeez, what do you want me to say?"

"Say you forgive me for lying to you. Give me another chance."

"It's not that easy, P. I never lied to *you*. Ever. Let's say I do forgive you. That doesn't mean I'm not still pissed."

"I understand. Just don't make any decisions yet, okay? Maybe we can talk more tomorrow?" she asks. "Are you going to the funeral?"

This is the first I've heard about a funeral. "Preston's death is finally public news, huh?"

"Yeah," she says. "It was on TV this morning. The funeral is tomorrow at four p.m."

It all feels so . . . final. But if DeWitt actually killed his son, I guess it makes sense he'd want to bury the body before anyone started asking the wrong questions.

"Do you think Preston could have been blackmailing his own father?" I ask.

She hmms. "I wouldn't put it past him. Why?"

"The guy who bailed me out said that DeWitt was being blackmailed."

"Who bailed you out?"

"Just this guy," I say. "He works for Preston's dad."

"I think I know the guy you're talking about," she says wryly. "Talk, dark, and creepy?"

"That's the one. Do you think it's possible Pres got carried away blackmailing his dad and DeWitt or some of his thugs killed him?"

"His own son? They never seemed close, but that would have to be some serious blackmail."

"Well," I say, "you know politicians. Most of them have a lot of skeletons in their closets." I fill her in on what I learned about Adam. "Somehow, Preston is connected to this kid. I'm thinking DeWitt had an affair with Violet, and Adam and Pres are half brothers. Maybe the three of them decided to blackmail the senator about his kid out of wedlock."

"So when Preston told me his parents gave him money because of the adoption, he was talking about this other kid, a brother he never got to know." I can almost see her nodding her head, her black hair swishing forward. "It all kind of works."

"Well, if it's true, I have to find the information Preston was using for blackmail, because that's the only way I can clear my name. Either that or find Adam Lyons, if he's even still alive."

"But if DeWitt did it, why would he report Preston's disappearance to the police?" she asks.

"Probably so he didn't look guilty when they found his body."

"And why bail you out?"

"Good question. Maybe as bait. Maybe they think Adam's still out there and might go to one of Pres's friends for help." I shiver as I think about how Langston and Marcus could have killed me, or how easily they could finish setting me up to get convicted for Pres's murder.

"It makes sense, in the most screwed-up way possible." Parvati pauses. "You should come to the funeral. Pres would want you there And we can talk more afterward. My father won't make a scene in front of the whole town."

"You don't think?" She's got more faith in her dad than I do. "I don't know if I'm going to go. I feel like time is running out, you know? I'm the only suspect and McGhee and

Gonzalez seem sure I did it. I probably only have a day or two before the forensics report comes back from Violet Cain's house."

"So?"

"So they found my shark's tooth there."

She sucks in a sharp breath. "Oh my God."

"I know, right? I thought I lost it in the ocean, but I guess I left it in my car. Whoever put the phone in my trunk must have taken it at the same time."

"I hate that you're going through this alone. Will you at least meet up with me tomorrow night?" Parvati pauses. "We don't have to talk about us. I want to help you figure this out, Max. I'm not going to let you go to jail for something you didn't do."

"Okay. I could use your help." I sigh. "And we can talk about whatever." Maybe it's her voice, or the news of the funeral, or the stuff Darla said to me slowly sinking in, but suddenly part of me wants to give her another chance.

I can't help it. I miss her.

THIRTY-THREE

December 10th

I DECIDE TO GO TO Preston's funeral after all. The cemetery is on the other side of Vista Palisades, a ten-minute bus ride or a thirty-five-minute walk. I loiter at the closest bus stop, but when the bus pulls up, it is full of people I know: classmates, teachers, the guy who rents kayaks in front of The Triple S. Their faces are ghostly white circles pressed close to the windows, monsters with blurry features distorted by the smudgy glass.

I decide to walk.

Cars line one side of the road leading into the cemetery, and both parking lots are full. Mrs. Amos's Honda is parked in the north lot, right inside the gates. I suddenly remember the restraining order. I hope the Colonel won't freak out and attack me in the middle of the service—I don't want to do that to Preston's friends and family. But at the same time, Pres was one of my closest friends, regardless of the secrets he kept. I deserve a chance to grieve for him.

The gravesite is on the far side of the grounds, near the south parking lot. I hang back along the fence, away from the crowd, so I can say good-bye without causing Parvati's dad to have a meltdown. I inch closer until I can see clearly. A mix of high school students and important political types stand gathered around a gaping hole in the earth. A priest gestures with one hand as he speaks. There are faces in the crowd I don't recognize—private security guards for DeWitt and his political friends, students from Bristol Academy. I look around for Langston and Marcus, but if they're here then they're keeping a low profile.

Astrid and the other All-Stars are huddled together at one end of the crowd. Quinn and Amy stand off to the side with some of the student council and a handful of Vista P teachers. Even David Nephew, the kid Preston cheated with in calculus class, is here, although he's standing at the very back of the mourners, as if he thinks the popular kids might push him into the grave if he gets too close.

The coffin is made of dark wood with shining trim that occasionally catches the sun and sends light bouncing around the pale tree branches. *Preston would like it.* What a weird thought. There are flowers piled on top. Lilies, maybe, or orchids. Some kind of blossom with big floppy petals.

Looking at that rectangular box of death makes it all feel real for the very first time. Preston is gone. We will never go surfing together again. He will never throw another New Year's Eve party. I will never get to confront him about his past with Parvati or about him spying on us.

My eyes move from the coffin back to the mourners. Parvati is standing between her parents. It's easy to pick her out because she's wearing white. It's tradition in India to do this at a funeral. I don't know how I know that, but I do. The wind billows the loose fabric of her sari around her like wings. She looks like an angel floating in a dead gray sky.

The coffin begins to descend into the ground. All of the women in the front row are holding roses. They drop them into the open grave one at a time, starting with Preston's mom. Parvati is last. I watch the red rose fall from her fingertips, like a single drop of blood.

The pallbearers begin to scoop dirt onto the coffin. The crowd starts to disperse. Half of the people head for the south parking lot, where their drivers are waiting. The students break apart into smaller clusters, some following the politicians, some heading in my direction. I retreat farther, toward the strip of woods that forms the western boundary of the graveyard, away from the winding stone path that connects both parking lots.

My breath catches in my throat as I peek through a layer of branches. I know what happens next. After everyone leaves, the graveyard caretaker will dump the rest of the soil on top of Preston's coffin with a backhoe. It just seems so undignified. Like he's nothing more than a hole to be filled in by a construction team.

I lean up against a tree trunk and wait for Parvati and her parents to pass by. I just want one tiny glance. I'm nervous about seeing her later. She needs to say something huge, something that will make me think I can learn to trust her again. Otherwise our relationship is over.

I don't want it to be over.

Everyone who passes by is wearing black. A lot of the girls look more like they're dressed for a fancy night out than for a funeral, their tiny velvet dresses looking strangely formal next to their mothers' frumpy suits and skirts. I crane my neck to see through the milling herd. No one in white. No Parvati. Maybe that wasn't her mom's Honda just inside the gates. Maybe her parents parked over at the south parking lot, with the politicians. I creep back through the trees and duck behind a tall obelisk monument. I peek around it, at the gravesite. Parvati is still standing in front of the hole in the ground. Her parents are nowhere to be seen. She must have asked for a moment alone.

I wonder if I can make it to her side before her mom or the Colonel notice. I maneuver closer, ducking between the tall gravestones to hide myself from anyone in either parking lot.

Parvati spins around as if she can sense me. The tail of her sari flaps in the breeze. She smiles tentatively.

But then something severs the connection between us. She flicks her head over at the woods. Her back arches as her neck cranes forward. I follow her gaze. A shadow moves among the trees.

Danger. The feeling comes out of nowhere, a fly slamming into a spider's web.

"Parvati," I say. It's just a whisper. I start running. She moves toward the tree line, clearly in pursuit of someone or something.

I can't see what she sees. She takes another step. And then another. My feet are flying across grass and graves. I want to call out to her, but I'm afraid her father will hear me if I do.

She moves with purpose. No looking back. The fir trees begin to swallow her.

She's half a girl.

One-quarter.

She's just a ribbon of white flying through the woods.

THIRTY-FOUR

"PARVATI," I YELL. "WAIT."

She doesn't wait. The white of her sari disappears completely into the foliage. I veer off the path and head toward the tree line. Boots thud on the hard ground behind me.

It's the Colonel. "Cantrell, you little shit! You're not supposed to be anywhere near my daughter."

I duck through the first layer of branches just as he catches up to me. He grabs my shoulder and spins me around. My feet get tangled up and I stumble. I fall backward, my head slamming against a knot on the nearest tree trunk. I end up on the damp ground.

"What did you say to her?" the Colonel thunders. "Where

did she go?" Typical overprotective dad—attack first, ask questions later.

I clamber back to my feet. "Nothing. I don't know." I suddenly have the urge to vomit. I double over and then stagger to the side. Reaching out for the tree that assaulted me, I collapse against the trunk. My skull feels like it got hit by a rocket-propelled grenade.

The Colonel advances on me. "If something happens to her, I'll kill you myself." His face contorts into a snarl.

Now there are two of him, dancing before me like a pair of prizefighters. Blinking spots float lazily through my field of vision. Yellow-black-yellow-black. "Not me," I say. It takes everything just to point in the direction that Parvati went. "Someone else. She went after someone. Go find her."

The Colonel turns away from me and crashes through the brush like a wild animal. He's probably carrying at least two loaded guns. I don't know what Parvati saw in the trees, but if whoever killed Preston lured her into the woods, right now her father is my best chance to get her back.

I want to go after him. I want to help too, but it's not just the spots that are blinking before my eyes now. The trees are blinking in and out, and so is the sky. From somewhere far away, I hear Parvati's mom say, "Oh, Max. Why does trouble seem to follow you everywhere you go?"

I try to answer her, but my tongue is thick and the words come out slow and garbled. I feel the rough tree bark pressing through my T-shirt. It scrapes its way up my back as I slide down the front of the trunk. My legs fold under me as I slump to the hard grass.

Rough hands shake me awake. My mouth is still dry and my whole skull is throbbing. When I reach up and touch the back of my head, my fingers come away red. Parvati's dad is looking down at me. His expression is bleak. Broken. Something pale flutters in the breeze. A torn triangle of white fabric embroidered with a repeating pattern hangs from the Colonel's right hand. It's a piece of Parvati's sari. She's gone.

I want to go look for her, but when the Colonel hauls me to my feet, my wobbly legs can barely support my weight. The ground spins slowly and yellow circles float in front of me like amoebas on a microscope slide. I think that bastard gave me a concussion. Well, him and the tree. Talk about a lethal tag team. I scan the shrubbery for any sign of movement, once again fighting the urge to throw up.

Nothing.

"Did you see which way she went at least?" There is a raw, animal-like quality to my voice that I have never heard before.

The Colonel shakes his head. "I didn't see her at all." He

holds up the scrap of white fabric. "I found this hanging from a bush. It looks like she was moving fast and it just got caught."

The fluttering cloth reminds me of all things bad—surrender flags, ghosts, burial shrouds. "Call up your goons," I say. "Combat guys. Navy SEALs. Whoever. They need to tear these woods apart today, now, before it's too late."

"It doesn't work like that, Max," he says. "First we need to call the police."

What the hell happened to the guy who grabbed me? Where is the animal-like desperation in the Colonel's voice? He is all coolness and collectedness now, like he activated some sort of mission switch in his brain. I am shaking, sweating, on the edge of losing it completely. "The police are idiots," I protest. "So are the feds."

Parvati's mom has appeared from somewhere behind me. "He needs to go to the hospital," she tells her husband. "He might have a concussion." Mrs. Amos's lilting accent reminds me of the day Parvati called herself in sick.

"Idiots or not, they're going to want a statement," the Colonel says. "Do you want to wait here or should I tell them to find you at the hospital?"

I imagine hanging out here with Parvati's dad, the two of us standing next to each other, awkwardly making small talk about sports and the weather. The cops would arrive and start doing their insanely slow cop things. Marking off the area with yellow tape, dusting tree trunks for fingerprints, collecting invisible fibers in plastic bags. No thanks. I'll go insane.

"I'll go to the hospital," I say, even though I have no intention of doing so. Five hours in the ER? Worse than waiting for the police to finish their slow-ass procedures. Even if I do have a concussion, it won't magically fix itself because I see a doctor. Preston got plenty of concussions on the football field. *You just have to wait it out*, he always said. *Don't go to sleep.*

I can wait out a head injury, just not Parvati's disappearance. I've got to do something about that right this second. I don't know what, but something. I'll figure it out on the way home. "Tell the cops not to screw around." I turn toward the parking area. My legs buckle slightly.

"If you're going to the hospital I'll drive you, of course." Parvati's mom steers me in the direction of her car.

"Okay." The hospital is on the way back to my house, at least. I let her tuck me into the passenger seat and sit hunched over and mute as she pulls out of the cemetery parking lot. How can she be so calm? Why is she not flipping out?

Mrs. Amos glances over at me. "Her father and I, we taught her to take care of herself, Max," she says. "The universe will bring her back. You just have to have faith."

I nod, but don't answer. Faith seems to be something people develop when their lives are going good. It's always been in short supply for me.

When Mrs. Amos pulls into the ER parking lot, an ambulance is there unloading a gurney. Even though we both know it can't be Parvati, we don't say anything until the wheels hit the pavement and we see the pasty, wrinkled body of an old man, his face partially obscured by an oxygen mask.

"Would you like for me to wait with you?" Mrs. Amos asks. "Or call your parents while you check in?"

"I'll call them," I say. Man, the lies are really rolling off my tongue today. "You should go back to the cemetery."

She looks dubiously at the back of the open ambulance, at the big glass doors that slide open to admit the paramedics and the man on the gurney. "You're sure you'll be all right?"

"Absolutely," I say. One more lie.

THIRTY-FIVE

I PASS THROUGH THE SLIDING glass doors and pretend like I'm heading up to the front desk of the ER. Instead, I turn toward the waiting area, hoping my head wound isn't totally obvious. I grab a magazine from a low metal table and flip through it.

"Can I help you?" the girl behind the counter asks in a chirpy voice. She's wearing black scrubs with gold embroidery on the pocket. It's probably supposed to look staid and official, but it just makes her look like an undertaker.

"Nope." I flick a glance at the parking lot. Mrs. Amos's car is gone. I duck out of the ER and start walking toward home. I check the time on my phone: it's almost six o'clock. Parvati seemed hell-bent on talking to me after the funeral. That half smile she gave me—she was going to head in my direction before she got distracted by something in the woods. She wouldn't disappear like that and stay gone for no reason. I consider a pair of possibilities, one grimmer than the other: 1. Whoever killed Preston lured Parvati into the woods and snatched her. 2. Parvati saw something suspicious in the woods and ran off on her own to investigate. The probability of each feels about equal.

The sun is dropping in the sky, and the breeze is picking up. The cool air clears some of the haze from my brain. As I turn the corner onto my street, I debate calling Langston. I bet he and Marcus were at the funeral somewhere. Maybe *they* lured Parvati into the woods for a little extra debriefing. It's not any weirder than Langston pretending to be my uncle and bailing me out of jail, is it? I try to make that possibility seem real. Then I see the dark sedan parked in front of my house. McGhee and Gonzalez are walking up my driveway as I approach.

McGhee kneels down and puts his cigarette out against the cement porch. "Got a minute?" he asks, slipping the butt into his pocket.

"Can I say no?"

"We can do this somewhere else if you'd prefer."

"Might as well get it over with." I hold the door open for McGhee but let it bang shut on Gonzalez as he tries to enter. He swears under his breath.

My sisters are all parked on the sofa watching television. The sagging upholstery is threatening to swallow Ji and Jo whole.

Darla enters from the kitchen, her face red from standing over the stove. Her lips flatten into a hard line when she sees me with the agents. She bends down and gathers one twin under each arm protectively, as if she thinks FBI agents eat babies for snacks. "It's almost dinnertime," she says.

"We'll only be a few minutes, ma'am." McGhee nods to her.

"Don't you think your lawyer should be present for this, Max?" Darla asks nervously.

My lawyer. Right. Probably, but who knows how long it'd be before she could get here?

"It'll be okay," I say. "I'll just tell the truth like you said." Once again, I pray that my hair is doing a good job of hiding my head wound. Darla will freak if I start dripping blood onto the carpet.

"If you're sure . . ." She trails off. Ji and Jo squirm in her arms. "Come on, Amanda."

"I want to stay and watch," my sister says. She mutes the TV volume and stares at the agents in fascination.

"Trust me, they're boring." I reach out and ruffle her

scraggly hair. "I'll tell you the story later and it'll be way cooler."

"Promise?" she says, looking reluctantly at McGhee and Gonzalez.

"Promise."

"Okay." Amanda clambers down off the sofa and follows Darla into the kitchen.

McGhee clears his throat. "Mind if we take a seat, Max?"

"Go for it." I sit in the old recliner and let the agents share the sofa. McGhee ends up on the sagging side, and I almost feel bad for him. His knees are approaching his chin, and it looks like he's going to need help getting up.

He grimaces and adjusts his weight, pulling a plastic dinosaur out from underneath his thigh. He sets the toy gently on the ground. "We've spoken to a few people who were present at the funeral today. Did Colonel Amos assault you?"

"He grabbed me," I say. "But a tree did most of the damage."

"Are you going to press charges?" McGhee pulls his mini notebook out of the pocket of his shirt.

"Nah." Tempting, but what good would it do? It won't bring back Parvati, and I get why he did it. I probably would have attacked him too if our roles had been reversed.

"Due to her relationship with Preston DeWitt and the ripped fabric recovered at the scene, we're treating Ms.

Amos's disappearance as possibly related to Preston's murder until proven otherwise."

"Are you guys here to blame me for her too?" I ask.

"Should we?" Gonzalez smirks. "Want to make a full confession?"

I resist the urge to give him the finger. "Here's what I have to *confess*. I showed up at the funeral around four. I stayed away from everyone and watched. It was about four thirty when I saw her go into the woods. I tried to stop her, but once she decides to do something it's pointless to intervene."

"Do you think what happened is connected to Preston's death?" McGhee asks.

"Duh."

"Why are you so sure?"

"Preston disappears. Someone tries to frame me. Preston turns up dead. And now Parvati is missing too? The three of us hung out together. Is anyone *else* dead or missing? How could all of this not be connected?"

"Violet Cain is dead," Gonzalez says. "How does she fit in?"

I shrug. I'm not ready to tell them I think Violet and Senator DeWitt had an affair, that somewhere out there she has a son who is Pres's half brother. They won't believe me without proof. "What do you guys think?"

"Do you know anyone who has it in for you?" McGhee asks.

I shake my head, which disorients me a little. Gingerly, I reach up and touch the back of my scalp. There's still a damp spot, but it feels like my blood has clotted at least. "That part blew my mind at first. Who could possibly hate me enough to screw me over in such an epic way? Then I realized maybe it had nothing to do with me, maybe whoever decided to set me up just picked the most convenient target. Preston's poorer, less popular friend. How could you go wrong?"

McGhee scribbles something in his notebook. "What about Ms. Amos? Enemies?"

"Only the dudes she beats up in karate class."

"And Preston?"

"Rich guys always have enemies. I'm sure plenty of people were jealous of him."

"Jealous enough to kill?"

Jealous enough to burn down a house? That'd be pretty jealous, all right. "Who knows?" I say.

"Why exactly do you think Ms. Amos went into the woods?"

"I think she went to pick fucking blueberries." This is what I mean about cops. Why does everything have to be as drawn out as possible? I sigh. "Come on, guys. Obviously she saw something suspicious."

McGhee scribbles in his notebook again. "What or who do you think she was looking at?"

"I don't know. Maybe Preston's killer."

"But then why would she go after him and put herself in danger?" Gonzalez asks.

I snort. "Did you even *talk* to her parents? Parvati *lives* for danger. Nothing scares her."

"Preston was a bit like that too, wasn't he?" McGhee asks. "I saw him on the gridiron at homecoming."

"Missed it," I say tersely. "I'm not into football."

"Not even to support your best pal?" Gonzalez stretches one arm out along the back of the sofa and rests his other on the armrest. I'm pretty sure it's a ploy to look bigger and more menacing. It's not working. He just looks like he's trying to put the moves on McGhee.

"Preston owned the school," I say. "He had plenty of support without me." I look down at the carpet, focusing on a dot of color that looks like the remnants of a stepped-on crayon.

"Was it intimidating, having two best friends who were both popular and fearless?" McGhee asks.

"What? No. It was cool." I don't even bother to hide my frustration. "Look, I didn't hurt either one of them. Why can't you guys see that?"

McGhee flips his notebook closed. "Thanks for your information. We'll be in touch." He leans against the armrest of the sofa as he gets to his feet. Gonzalez bounds up after him, still moving with a weird feral energy.

"Just find her," I say. "She thinks she's invincible."

What I don't say is that I can't handle the thought of losing her too.

After the feds show themselves out, I poke my head in the kitchen to let Darla know I'm okay. The twins are sitting in their high chairs playing with a batch of her famous edible clay. Amanda is leaning over the counter slicing carrots. Her face is a mask of concentration, her fingers gripping the knife so tightly that her knuckles are blanching white.

"Dinner in fifteen minutes, okay?" Darla says.

"Sure." I duck into the bathroom and use a hand mirror to look at the back of my head. It's hard to see through my hair, but the bloody spot on my scalp looks like it's only a couple of inches long. I probe the area gently with my fingertips to make sure it's not still bleeding and then shake out my hair. Time to make a quick phone call.

I slip out onto the front porch and call Langston. A car drives by while I wait for him to pick up. A girl wearing sunglasses and a baseball cap yells, "You're going to burn, murderer!" I don't think I've ever seen her before. Whoever is in the passenger seat bursts into applause. They honk the horn twice, and then the car screeches off in a cloud of smoke.

"Langston here."

I decide to skip all the bullshit formalities. "Do you know where she is?"

"Max? You sound agitated. Where who is?"

"Parvati disappeared right from Preston's funeral. I'm sure you guys were skulking around somewhere. Did you see anything?"

"Marcus was watching the ceremony, but I was handling something . . . off-site. So Ms. Amos has gone missing? That is most unfortunate."

"Hell yeah, it's unfortunate. So if you or one of your thugs took her somewhere for more *debriefing*, just tell me. Don't let me freak out over nothing."

"It wasn't us, Max," he says. "I'll look into it. But the people we're investigating don't have any connections to Parvati Amos. She's kind of a wild girl, isn't she? And I'm sure she was upset by Preston's death. Maybe she's just acting out, looking for a little extra attention."

Acting out? That was definitely Parvati's style, but not to get attention, at least not from her parents. She preferred it when they ignored her. Plus she's been trying to get me to talk to her for days. She wouldn't skip out on that meeting unless she had no choice.

I humor Darla and spend five minutes sitting at the dinner table picking at what is probably really delicious fried chicken. I can't eat, though. All I can do is worry about Parvati. "I'm going for a walk," I say suddenly, pushing my chair back and bolting to my feet.

Darla looks up from feeding tiny spoonfuls of mashed potatoes to the twins. More is ending up on the floor than in their mouths. "Be careful, Max," she says.

I head back to the cemetery. It's the only thing I can think of to do. By the time I get there, it's a little after eight o'clock and the cops are gone. The wind is cool, but not cold. The sky is overcast, only the brightest stars managing to penetrate the thick layer of clouds. The high wrought-iron fence glints in the shrouded moonlight, and the elaborately carved headstones cast deformed shadows across the lawn. I've never been in a cemetery at night, and now I know why. This place is seriously scary.

Something rustles in the high grass in front of me, and I flick on the small emergency flashlight I snagged from Ben's truck. I scan the grounds and see the golden eyes of a possum looking back at me. Creepy, but not a killer.

I don't know where to start, so I opt for the stretch of woods that makes up the graveyard's western border. It's slow going in the dark. I walk straight lines, up and down from one end of the trees to the other, scanning for footprints, fabric, for any sign of Parvati. Leaves slap me in the face and branches claw at my skin. "This is crazy," I mutter, pushing my way through another layer of foliage. But I keep going.

It takes over an hour to search the woods, and I come up

empty. Next, I trace the perimeter of the cemetery, looking for anything unusual or out of place. Bats swoop low overhead. A few dry leaves flip end over end across the grass. Behind me, the graveyard gates clank in the breeze. I find a hole beneath the southeast corner of the fence where some kind of animal has been tunneling in and out of the grounds.

But there are no clues; there's nothing that doesn't belong here. Except for me. My flashlight starts to go dead and I almost give up. But there's one more place I feel compelled to check out: Preston's grave.

I stand in front of the mound of dirt, watching as the wind scatters the top layer of soil across neighboring graves. The number of flowers here is astounding—there must be at least a hundred arrangements. I think about Preston, in a box, below the ground. About Parvati missing. About how just a few weeks ago we were hanging out and everything was normal. "How did we get here?" I ask.

It's tempting to blame it on Liars, Inc., but I would've provided that alibi for Pres no matter what. I wanted him to go to Vegas and hang out with Violet so things would stop being weird between Parvati and him. I remember when I finally admitted that I liked her. He had seemed so nonchalant.

It was back in May, a few weeks after Parvati transferred to Vista P. Pres and I were hanging out in his basement, eating

Megaburgers and watching some crappy reality-TV show full of college kids who were clearly addicted to drama.

"So that girl Parvati from your party is in my English class," I started.

"Oh yeah?" Pres took a bite of his burger. "She get in trouble yet?"

I laughed. "No. She doesn't say much. Is she really that bad?"

"She's pretty bad." Preston smiled to himself. "In a good way."

I finished my burger and crumpled the foil sleeve into a ball. "You guys aren't, like, hooking up, right? You're just friends?"

Preston grabbed the remote and flicked off the TV. His lips twitched. "You want to hit that shit, don't you?"

"I mean, she's really hot. But she seems cool too. I just . . ." I trailed off.

Preston laughed. "Oh, it's like that, huh? Maximus has a crush."

"Screw you," I said, tossing my foil ball at him. "I should have just asked her out without saying anything."

Preston snorted. "She would have told me. She tells me everything. Blah blah blah, girls." He grinned. "But you don't have to ask my permission. Parv and I aren't like that. Friend zone, you know?"

I believed him at the time. Maybe because he was convincing, or maybe just because it was what I wanted to hear.

I reach down, my fingers closing around a handful of loose dirt. I let it trickle out of my fist like sand from an hourglass. "Where is she, Pres?" I ask. "I know you felt the same way about her as I do."

My phone buzzes sharply and I almost drop my flashlight. For a second I'm afraid to answer it, positive that if I do it'll be a dead guy on the other end of the line.

THIRTY-SIX

THE PHONE RINGS AGAIN. I force myself to look at the screen. The caller's number shows up as UNKNOWN. My eyes flick nervously around the darkened graveyard. Suddenly, I am not alone anymore. The gravestones are eyes; the night bulges inward, like ears struggling to hear.

Exhaling deeply, I answer the call. "Hello?"

"Max?" It's only a tiny whisper.

Parvati.

"Where are you?" I try not to yell.

"I'm at the cabin."

"Why?" I ask, my voice still louder than it should be.

"He says you have to come here. Alone."

"Who?"

I hear the crunch of static that means someone is covering the phone speaker. Then, a muffled voice in the background. Male, I think. I can't make it out.

"Parvati. Are you okay?"

"You have until midnight to get here," someone whispers, low and growly. It's a man, but he's purposely distorting his voice. "If you call the cops, she dies."

"What do you want from us?" I ask. "Why are you doing this?"

The phone disconnects, leaving a silence as still as death.

If you call the cops, she dies. "And if I don't call the cops, we probably both die," I mutter. "This is too much for me." I slip McGhee's business card out of my wallet and dial the number on it with shaking fingers. When the call connects, I dial his extension.

And get his voicemail.

In his gravelly voice, McGhee invites me to leave a message or to call 911 if I'm "experiencing an emergency situation." 911 won't help. They'll think I'm some crackpot lunatic if I try to explain what's happening. Even if the dispatcher believed me, the local cops would probably show up in uniform and knock calmly on the front door of the cabin. I can't risk Parvati getting hurt. I don't want anyone else's death on my conscience.

I leave McGhee a semi-coherent message informing him

Parvati is being held at her dad's cabin and that I'm on the way up there. Hopefully he's the kind of guy who stays up late and checks his voicemail after hours. If not, it looks like I'm on my own.

I check the time. Midnight is less than two hours away, and it'll take me close to thirty minutes to walk home. Man, I miss my car. Abandoning the cemetery, I break into a jog and make it home in record time. I creep inside and snag Ben's keys, which are thankfully in plain view on the coffee table. I grab my black hoodie from the back of the sofa and slip it over my head, pulling the hood up around my face. Quietly, I slink back out into the night.

It takes multiple tries to get Ben's pickup to start. "Come on come on come on!" The clock on the dash reads 10:47. I turn the key again, and pray. The truck lurches forward as I shift into drive, and my knees ram into the console. I turn out of the driveway and onto the street. I figure there's about a 50 percent chance I'll make it up to the Colonel's cabin without the engine falling out.

My breath whistles in my throat and I realize I'm gripping the steering wheel so tightly that my fingers are going numb. I need music. Music keeps me calm. I flip on the radio. There's a commercial on my favorite station. I make my way through Ben's presets. Classic rock. Talk radio. Static. My finger is hovering over preset number four when

I hear the word "DeWitt." The signal is weak, so the speaker's voice is broken up by bursts of static, but he's definitely talking about Senator DeWitt.

". . . apparently not only decided against . . . Secretary of Labor . . . also resigning from the Senate . . . entire D.C. community shocked . . . wake of family tragedy . . ."

Holy shit! Preston's dad is leaving politics because of Preston's death. Why would he do that if he just killed off the only witnesses to his crimes?

". . . rumblings of a possible divorce . . ."

I turn the volume up, hoping to hear more, but the radio station fades out.

The sprawling suburbs dwindle, gas stations and strip malls giving way to patches of vegetation and then the hills of the Angeles National Forest. I alternate between watching my rearview mirror for cops and watching the minutes on the dash clock tick forward. 11:18. Forty-two minutes to find Parvati.

As I lose the lights of the suburbs, the winding roads seem to fill with shadowy ghosts, swirls of darkness that condense and dissolve in the ravine at the side of the highway. I blink hard. It's just the residual effects of my head injury, combined with fatigue. But the twisting shapes at the corners of my vision don't go away. Suddenly, one of them darts out into the road, and I slam on my brakes. The shadow grows in size as it approaches the truck, but when it gets close I realize it's not just a shadow.

It's a boy, about my age.

Preston.

THIRTY-SEVEN

HE TAPS ON THE GLASS as I slow to a stop. I roll down the window, almost like I'm in a trance. Crickets sing in the high grass. Darkness wraps around the truck.

"Boy, Maximum Overdrive, am I glad to see you." His hat obscures part of his face, but the voice is unmistakable.

I reach forward and flick on my emergency flashers. Obviously, that tree trunk did some permanent damage. Only Preston doesn't seem like a hallucination. He looks real, sounds real, he even smells real—a little sweaty, like he's been running.

"What the fuck, dude?" For a moment I'm at a loss for words. I touch one hand to the back of my head. The spot where I hit the tree is tender, but it's not leaking brain matter or anything. I blink hard again, rub my eyes. But Preston doesn't disappear. My throat constricts a little as I choke out, "We just . . . buried you. Everyone thinks you're dead."

"Not everyone," he says. "They grabbed us in the woods by the cemetery and took us to the cabin. I managed to escape because Parvati created a diversion, but we've got to go back for her."

Parvati! Preston's materializing out of the swirling dark like some horror movie phantom almost made me forget that I was on the clock. 11:33. Twenty-seven minutes. "Who? Who grabbed you?"

"DeWitt's goons."

"Your dad seriously hired guys to kidnap you?" Even though I've been thinking the same thing, it still seems so unreal. "Are you sure? I found cocaine in your room. Can't that shit make you paranoid?"

"That's not my coke and DeWitt's not my dad," Preston says. "My name isn't even Preston."

A pair of headlights appears over the crest of the hill. Both of us turn in unison to watch as the car cruises past. Neither of us speaks. The scarlet taillights dissolve into the night, and we're alone again.

"What do you mean your name isn't Preston?"

"Preston's dead." At my look he adds, "Don't be sad. He's been dead for years. You never met him."

"Huh? I don't understand."

"It's a long story." He opens the driver's side door to the pickup. "You look exhausted. Move over. I'll drive."

I want to hear every piece of this long story. I need to figure out what's happening. But then my eyes catch the clock on the dash. "We have to get to Parvati by midnight." I quickly fill him in about the phone call.

"Did you call the cops?" he asks.

I shake my head as I scoot over the console and into the passenger seat. "I couldn't reach the FBI, and it's not like anyone else would have believed me."

"Yeah. Half the cops are probably on DeWitt's payroll anyway. Let's go get her." He flips off the emergency flashers and guides the truck back onto the road.

"So if Preston has been dead for years, who the hell have I been hanging out with?" I ask.

The boy formerly known as Preston laughs. "My name's Adam. The truth is pretty fucked up. We might not get all the way through it before we get back to the cabin, but rest assured I'm still the same guy that you know." He bumps his fist lightly against his chest. The gesture is so Preston-like that I can't help but smile. I should be furious. He lied to me about hooking up with Parvati and videotaped us having sex. I should seriously kick his ass right here and now. But somehow all I can do is stare, like he's magically risen from the grave. Who cares what he did or what his name is? We can hash out all of that bullshit later. My friend is alive. That's all that matters.

"Adam Lyons," I say.

"Yeah, watch this." Adam punches a couple of buttons on a phone and scrolls through a long list of files. After selecting one, he tosses the phone into my lap. A video of Claudia DeWitt starts playing on the screen.

She's flipping through TV channels in her living room. A phone rings. Claudia mutes the television before answering it.

"What? How is that possible?" she says.

A pause. She turns away from the television. Walks toward the big picture window that looks out onto the lawn.

"You swore all that was in the past. You promised me." A pause. She lifts one hand to her forehead. "Don't tell me not to be dramatic. We covered up a death, Rem."

Rem. As in Remington. She's talking to her husband.

Her voice cracks. She dabs at her eyes with the back of her left hand.

"You know as well as I do that you're guilty of child endangerment . . . perhaps more." A pause. "I'll never forgive myself for the things we did . . . to both of them."

The clip ends. The hamster wheel in my brain starts spinning.

"Play the next one," Adam says.

It's Preston, or who I always thought was Preston, and his dad.

"*I'm tired of pretending to be someone else,*" *Preston says. He paces back and forth in front of the plasma TV.*

"*You agreed,*" *DeWitt says.* "*You agreed to be the son we want you to be until you're twenty-one.*"

"*And what happens then? I just disappear?*"

"*We'll figure something out,*" *DeWitt says.*

Preston turns to face his father. His face is red, his hands clenched into fists. "*Do you regret it?*"

"*Forgetting to secure the gun? Every day of my life.*"

"*I'm not talking about what you did to him,*" *Preston says.* "*I'm talking about what you did to me.*"

"*I like to think Claudia and I gave you a good life. We bought you whatever you wanted, computers, fancy phones, private surfing lessons. We even allowed you to enroll at public school.*"

Preston goes back to his pacing. "*But you told the doctors I was crazy. The shock treatments, the medicine—you screwed up my brain. Sometimes I think about the past and realize I'm remembering something that never even happened.*" *His voice cracks.* "*You tried to erase me.*"

The screen goes dark. Adam reaches over and lifts the phone out of my hand before I can even begin to process what I've seen. Shock treatments? Medicine? What the hell?

"So you know how DeWitt is CEO of DeWitt Firearms, right?" he asks.

I nod. "Yeah."

The truck swerves hard to the left as Adam dodges a pothole I don't even see until we're right on top of it. "So of course he's always been politically aligned with gun nuts, the NRA, etc."

"Yeah?" I don't really get where Pres—er—Adam is going with this.

"When he was nine, the real Preston DeWitt accidentally shot himself with his father's gun."

"Holy shit!" If I were driving I probably would have rammed the truck into a tree. *We covered up a death, Rem.* "Now *that* is some news that never made the *LA Times*."

"Exactly," Adam says. "Daddy's close advisors told him if the news got out his political career would be finished. Not to mention DeWitt Firearms. Not only would he be arrested, the press would destroy him and his company. Pro-gun politician's kid shoots himself with Dad's gun. Can you imagine the headlines?"

"So . . ." Maybe I'm thick, but I still don't get it. "Where do you come in?"

"Apparently the senator covered up Preston's death and then sent his goons looking for a suitable replacement. They found me in a boys' home. I was about the right size and shape, with hair and eyes that could be fixed."

I glance over. Preston had blue eyes, but Adam's are a weird greenish gray. So that's why I never knew "Preston" wore contacts—because they were part of a disguise. And the frequent haircuts I used to mock him for were probably to mask his curly hair. And now the picture in front of the Rosewood Center for Boys makes sense. Because Preston really was there, only he wasn't Preston.

"I didn't know any of that at the time, of course," Adam continues. "The truth leaked out over the past few years. Claudia tends to get chatty when she's drunk." He glances over at me. "At the time, DeWitt's men just told me if I wanted to get out of the boys' home and go live in a big pretty house in the city I would have to change my name and pretend to be someone else. They made it sound fun, like acting. They said they'd buy me whatever I wanted. I'd get my own room, my own *maid*."

"So DeWitt . . . *hired* you? To become Preston?"

"Basically." Adam's mouth twists into something harsh and ugly. "His men helped me run away from the center and brought me to the DeWitts to start my 'great new life.' Only it wasn't great." He bears down on the accelerator, and the pickup's engine grinds in protest. He looks confused for a second.

"You need to slow down or shift up," I say. "The gears are

sensitive on this thing." I watch as he wrestles with the gearshift. How completely bizarre would it be if Adam and I were at Rosewood together? I was only there for about three weeks, but it's still entirely possible. I try to recall the faces of some of the other kids, but they're all blurs. Nameless blank figures who sometimes stared at me but never talked to me. All I remember is Henry.

"For the first two years, they kept me in the house," Adam says. "They told everyone I'd been in an accident and needed plastic surgery. Then they said I went straight from recuperating to boarding school. Only instead of classes I got drilled and redrilled by Claudia about what it meant to be Preston DeWitt. When I screwed up, she locked me in my room for hours until I promised to try harder. Do you know how hard it is to *learn* to be someone else?" he asks. "I ran away once, but they caught me and I ended up in a psych ward. Some shrink decided I had paranoid schizophrenia. He jacked me full of meds and zapped my brain. After that, I didn't run away again, but my memory began to get choppy. I started filming everything I didn't want to forget, just in case."

"That is seriously messed up."

"Tell me about it. And then I started talking to my real mom again—I found her online—and she gave me the great idea to start recording the DeWitts," Adam says.

"Violet?"

He nods. "She raised me by herself because my dad split early. But then the state took me away from her when I was seven because she sometimes left me home alone while she was working. After I found her again, I didn't want to be Preston anymore. Mom said we could get a lot of money from my fake parents. I rigged the house with cameras; getting them to incriminate themselves was child's play. I wanted to save up so me and my mom could disappear and start over somewhere else." He whips the steering wheel to the right to avoid what looks like a dead raccoon. "But those bastards set her house on fire. They tried to kill us both."

"But there was a second body. Who—"

"Some loser frat guy Mom brought home from her job." Adam stares straight through the windshield. "You were right about her being a stripper, by the way."

"But DeWitt—"

"Identified the remains as Preston?" Adam's mouth twists into a scowl.

"Why the hell would he do that?"

We almost fly right past the turnoff to the Colonel's cabin. My eyes flick to the dashboard. 11:51. Adam hits the brakes at the last second, turning off onto a dirt road. Even with the brights on, I can only see a few feet ahead of us.

"I'm surprised he even reported me missing in the first

place. Maybe Claudia did—she seemed to take everything a little harder than dear old Dad. But my guess is that once Langston and his guys got close, they probably wanted to hunt me without any interference from the FBI. DeWitt IDs me as dead, and suddenly everyone stops looking for me. No one would ever expect a distraught father to lie about something like that. And if they did, DeWitt would just pay them off, I'm sure."

"It just all seems so . . . insane."

"Yeah, it does. And now even if I turn up claiming to be Preston, they've probably got real Preston's fingerprints and DNA locked away somewhere. If need be, DeWitt can just pull them out and call me a fraud, perpetrated by political opponents or some shit." Adam squints into the dark. "It's not like he'd let me go back to being Preston after finding out Mom and I were blackmailing him." He glances at the dashboard clock. 11:54. "We need to grab Parvati and then find a safe place to hide out until I can mail my videos to the cops."

"Why not just turn them in yourself?"

Adam shakes his head. "I've got enough money to start over. I don't want to hang out here to testify. I'd rather just let the world think both Preston and Adam are dead."

The road narrows. Tree branches slap against the outside of the pickup like clawing fingers. We're getting close to the cabin. "We should park here and hike in on foot," I say. "If we get much closer they'll know we're coming."

Adam nods. "DeWitt's got a whole group of ex-military thugs doing his dirty work. They'll be ready for you. Hopefully some of them are combing the woods trying to find me. They won't expect me to come back. I can be your secret weapon."

He pulls the truck off the side of the road until it's halfway buried in the trees. We both jump out of the truck and head into the woods. My heart races in my chest. What chance do I have against guys like Langston and Marcus? Almost none. "Wait." I touch Adam's arm as he plunges into the trees in front of us. "Why the hell would they take Parvati from the cemetery? Why would they bring you guys *here*?"

Adam looks back at me. His eyes glow gray in the moonlight. "She knows too much. Not sure why they brought us here. Probably to throw suspicion onto someone else."

"Someone like me." I tell him about the fake eyewitness, the bloody cell phone, my shark's tooth pendant showing up in the fire.

Adam snorts with disgust. "I'm not surprised. DeWitt doesn't care who suffers as long as it's not him."

The Colonel's cabin comes into view, and I pull my hood even lower and drop down into a crouch. My blood roars in my veins, drowning out the symphony of bugs and rustling leaves.

Ducking down below the front window, I put my ear to the wood and listen. I can't hear anything except the slamming of my heart. No voices. No movement. Where is Parvati? Adam and I exchange a glance. He makes a motion like he's suggesting we split up, each of us going around one side of the cabin. I nod. I creep around to the near side and listen below the bedroom window. Still nothing. I do the same in the back, just outside the small kitchen. Silence.

I look to the right, expecting to see Adam's broad form approach. Nothing. Where did he go? Through a window? The back door? Did someone snatch him? My eyes scan the tree line, looking for movement, gun barrels, for the glowing red dots that mean snipers. I don't want to lose my friend right after I got him back.

Suddenly I wish I still had the gun Parvati gave me, or that I was a kickass martial artist like she is, or that I was good at anything besides surfing. *Focus, Max.* Once upon a time I survived on the streets. I was brave. No, screw that. I'm still brave. I don't know if Parvati and I will be together when all this is over with, but I'm not going to let her die.

I wrap my fingers around the doorknob. I turn it just a half inch to see if it's locked. The knob twists freely.

I swear at the moonlight. Unless everyone is tucked away in a bedroom, they'll see the back door open when I try to enter. The best I can do is wait until a cloud passes in front of the moon and be as quick and quiet as possible. I lower myself into a crouch and look up at the sky. My heart rattles in my chest. Every beat feels like a lifetime. It has to be after midnight by now.

Just as a ribbon of gray clouds starts to blot out some of the light, something presses hard against my back. A gun.

Someone clamps a rag over my nose and mouth. It smells sweet, like incense or pipe smoke. I try to pull away, but my body won't obey my brain's commands. My attacker holds the cloth tight over my mouth. My lungs are burning. I gasp for air. My fingers blur on the doorknob. My knees start to buckle and my muscles all go slack. I end up on my back in the gravel, the stars twisting and spinning in the sky above me.

THIRTY-EIGHT

MY STOMACH CONVULSES THE SECOND I open my eyes. I swallow hard and take a deep breath. I'm inside the Colonel's cabin, sitting slumped on the vinyl sofa. My hands and ankles are bound with duct tape. A blurry form sits next to me, dressed in flowing white. Parvati. Her eyes are closed.

"P," I hiss. "Are you okay?"

Her eyelashes flutter, but she doesn't respond.

Adam appears from one of the bedrooms. "Did you know you can actually make chloroform out of stuff just sitting around in chem class?" He twirls a gun around on his finger before pointing it at me.

"Adam, what the hell are you doing?" I glance around, looking for DeWitt's men, looking for anyone else.

But it's just the three of us.

And a gun.

Adam chuckles. "You always were kind of slow."

The haze of drugs begins to fade and the ugly truth becomes clear. "You lying, psychotic son of a bitch. It was *you* who set me up, wasn't it? Not DeWitt."

Adam claps slowly, the gun still aimed at my chest. "Good job, Maximus."

"So all that stuff in the truck was just more lies." I shake my head in disgust. "I can't believe I fell for your bullshit."

He shrugs. "Most of what I told you was true. Well, except for DeWitt's thugs killing my whore of a mother. I set that fire when she told me to go back to California. She didn't want me in her life. She just wanted the money I got from blackmailing the DeWitts. The bitch deserved to die."

"Along with some random guy? He deserved to be burned to death?"

"That guy was so drunk he didn't even wake up the whole time I was switching clothes with him and starting the fire. He probably never even knew what hit him." Adam smiles to himself. "Alcohol is a fabulous accelerant." He glances down at his wrist. "I do miss my watch, though."

"Look," I continue, glancing over at Parvati. "What your mom and the DeWitts did to you is some seriously messed-up shit, but why are *we* here? We're not the ones who abandoned you or tortured you or took away your identity."

Adam's jaw tightens visibly. "No, you're the one who took away my fucking *family*, Max."

Okay. Now I know he's totally lost his mind. I never even met his real mother. And *he* just admitted to killing her. "What are you talking about?" I focus on his gun while I lean against the back of the couch and slip my hands down between the cushions, feeling for the sharp edge of the exposed sofa coil that kept stabbing me and waking me up last time I was here. Got it. Slowly, I saw the tape around my wrists back and forth across the metal, trying not to move my upper body. Now I just have to keep Adam talking for a while.

"You don't remember me, do you?" he asks. "From Rosewood? We didn't really hang out."

So we *were* there at the same time . . . "I didn't really hang out with anyone. I only remember Henry," I say. "And Anna." The tape loosens slightly as I feel individual fibers fray. I pull my ankles apart, twisting my feet slightly, trying to loosen that tape too.

The hard line of Adam's mouth softens for a second and then goes tight. "Anna. She was good to me," he says. "She told me I was going to get adopted. A nice couple named Cantrell. A family."

Shit.

My family.

I stole Adam's family? Darla's favorite story plays in my ear, the one about how they were going to adopt a boy but then she saw me, and she just knew I was the one. Darla and her goddamn savior complex.

I stole Adam's family.

Next to me, Parvati stirs. Her eyes open. Her pupils dilate as she turns to me. "Max," she says softly. "I almost wish you hadn't come."

"I didn't know what had happened at first," Adam continues. "They seemed to like me, but then they disappeared. Later, I saw *you* with them on one of your follow-up visits. You. With *my* family."

"I'm sorry." I try to keep my expression neutral as the tape continues to tear. Getting my hands free is only the first step. I still have to outmaneuver a guy with a gun, probably with my ankles still bound. I scan the entire living room looking for weapons. There has to be something I can use.

But there isn't.

I keep sawing.

"Anna felt terrible for getting my hopes up. She was new. She probably didn't realize people might just change their minds like that. She told me their paperwork hadn't gone through. That it had nothing to do with me." He clenches his jaw again. The muscles in his neck strain against his skin.

"But I knew the truth. After they met you, they didn't want me anymore."

"That's not true," Parvati interjects. "If they had more money, they probably would have taken both—"

"Shut up," Adam snaps. "They were supposed to love *me*. Not him. Not both of us." He slips his finger onto the trigger.

The tape is half torn now. I twist my wrists in opposite directions. I can almost pull one of my hands free. I turn to Parvati. I wish there was a way to alert her to the exposed sofa coil. I'm going to need her mad fighting skills in order for us to have any chance to survive this. I glance over my shoulder and down to where my hands are tucked inside the cushions. Her face remains expressionless, but she scoots toward me. I see her begin to reposition her own hands.

"I've waited so long to get you back. I didn't know if it would ever happen," Adam says. "But then people started asking questions and DeWitt decided to move out of the city."

"How did you end up here?" I ask. "How did you find me?"

"I had already found you online. It was so easy to plant the seeds to come to Vista Palisades." Adam pauses. "Did you know that it's one of the best surfing beaches for miles? Claudia always felt so guilty about everything. She was constantly looking for ways to make it up to me."

"I didn't know anything about you," I say. "I didn't mean to hurt you. And neither did the Cantrells." Only they had.

They had spent time talking to Adam and then decided to adopt me instead. I could see how that might make a kid feel terrible.

And then DeWitt's cronies had shown up and offered Adam the ultimate acting job. Forced to choose between becoming someone else and getting pummeled by Henry the Happy Sociopath for who knows how long, of course he had jumped at the chance to leave Rosewood.

Adam nods. "I know. My mom—Violet—told me I should give you a chance, that it was DeWitt who should pay." His voice wavers. "By that time I had already started watching you and the Cantrells at The Triple S. I never saw you being nice to them. You were always complaining about them—how they made you babysit, like it was such a big fucking chore." Adam bares his teeth. "You took my family and you don't even appreciate them!"

"You're wrong. I do appreciate them." But a tiny pinprick of doubt stabs me in the gut. Would Adam have given Darla a chance to really be his mom? Would she have been better off with him instead of me? My left hand slides free of the duct tape. I separate my wrists slightly, keeping them in the same position so as not to alert Adam.

"Shut up," he says. "Shut up or I will fucking end you."

"Preston!" Parvati sucks in a sharp breath. "Calm down. Let's just talk about this."

Adam backhands her across the face with his gun. Her head snaps forcefully to the side. I grit my teeth, wanting to lunge for him but not wanting Parvati or me to get shot. I have to wait for the right moment.

"I told you my name is *not* Preston."

Even in the dim light, I can see the welt forming on Parvati's cheekbone, but she shakes off the blow like it was nothing. "Right. Adam. That's going to take a little time for me to get used to."

She's talking to him like we're all still friends, like this is a big joke or one of their dare games from Bristol Academy. Just like me, she's trying to keep him going until she can find an opening to make a move. I glance quickly down at her arms. I'm not sure whether she'll be able to free herself too.

"You only *have* a little time, Pervy," Adam says.

She tilts her head to the side. "Come on. You don't mean that. You have no reason to kill me. We're friends. I understand you in ways that most people don't."

Adam turns to me. "Remember that day in the cafeteria when I told you she was a liar and you said she wouldn't lie to *us*? Now do you see? She's full of shit. She'll play any side she needs to." He scoffs. "I bet she'd shoot you herself if I offered to let her go."

"I'm just saying I'm not your enemy and neither is Max," Parvati says. "Let us go, Adam. And we'll help you." She looks pleadingly at him. "Put down the gun."

"How stupid do you think I am? You're trying to manipulate me," Adam says. "The way you manipulated *him*." He pulls the phone with the videos from his pocket. "He doesn't know about that yet, does he?"

Parvati's cool expression falters. "Please don't."

Adam sneers. "Oh, isn't that sweet. She's trying to protect you."

"Protect me from what? What don't I know about?" I ask.

Parvati's lower lip trembles. "Look at us. You won, Pr—Adam. You don't need to do this."

Adam ignores her. "I just wanted to take away something you loved," he tells me. "Things have to be even. I only let you have her so that it would hurt worse when I took her back." He works the touch screen of the phone and then tosses it down on the sofa between Parvati and me. "Watch and learn," he says.

Parvati squeezes her eyes shut. A single tear escapes down her cheek.

The screen comes to life. It's her and "Preston." They're curled up on his bed together. She's got her head tucked beneath his chin, just like she used to do with me.

"I'm bored," Preston says. "You want to do some coke?"

Parvati sighs. "I told you I'm not doing that anymore, Pres. I'll never get into the CIA with a drug history."

Preston cranes his neck to look down at her. "It's not like I'm going to tell them. Besides, that's years from now."

Her forehead wrinkles in concentration as she glances over at the bookshelf. "I swear you want me to be an addict," she says bitterly.

So that's what Adam meant when he said it wasn't his cocaine. Apparently, he's been supplying Parvati. It explains a lot: her mood swings, her impulsive behavior. She was telling me on the phone about why her parents were sending her to Blue Pointe Prep when I cut her off. I wonder if they found some of her stash.

Pres gets cocaine from the hollowed-out book and cuts it into lines with a credit card. They take turns snorting it off the surface of a compact from Parvati's purse.

"Suddenly I miss our dare game," Preston says. "Don't you?"

Parvati shakes her head and her long hair obscures part of her face. "The game that got us expelled? Not really. I promised my parents no more dares. I'm trying to be good."

"Good is boring." Preston tucks a lock of hair behind her right ear. "You miss our dares. I know you do." He kisses the side of her neck. "Let's do just one more, for old time's sake."

Her body folds inward on itself. She turns her head to expose more of her throat. "What did you have in mind?" she asks finally, her voice a shadow of what it had been.

"You know Max, that guy I sometimes go surfing with?"

"The kid from The Triple S?"

"Yeah." Preston's fingertips make their way beneath the hem of her sweater.

My hands are clenched into fists so tight that my fingernails are cutting curved gashes into my palms. I know what's coming, and it's going to be as bad as finding out my two best friends are liars. I twist my wrists one at a time so that I'll be ready to strike when the moment presents itself.

"Why do you always hang out at that place, anyway?" Parvati asks.

"Who cares? I think Max likes you," Preston says.

"Well then, he's got better taste than someone else I know."

Preston smiles his relaxed grin. "I bet you can't make him fall for you."

Real-life Parvati hangs her head. "I'm sorry, Max," she whispers.

"Yeah. Me too," I mutter. If I swing my hip just right I can probably knock the phone to the floor. I won't have to hear that Parvati went out with me as part of a stupid dare. I won't have to learn that my two best friends were never my friends at all. My throat and my eyes start to water.

I can't do it. I need to hear this.

I need to hear the truth.

"Why would you want me to do that?" Parvati asks.

"He needs a little excitement in his life."

"And what about after I succeed? I just dump him? Kind of mean, isn't it?"

Preston snorts. "Right. What was I thinking? You're never mean."

"Not to people who don't deserve it."

"You don't think the CIA is going to expect you to be mean?" he asks. "You're going to have to be able to cultivate assets, you know? Get strangers to trust you."

Parvati doesn't say anything.

"Hey, if you don't think you can do it, I understand," Preston says. "Maybe you're not his type."

"Oh, I can be his type." Parvati reaches down and undoes the button of Preston's jeans. "I'm just not sure why you want to share me."

My turn to squeeze my eyes shut. "I've heard enough. Turn it off."

"Aww. What's the matter, Maximus? Aren't you enjoying these videos of your girlfriend?" Adam's lips twist into a cruel smile. "She only dated you because I *told her* to."

"Fuck you, Adam." She lifts her chin. "Maybe that was true at the start, but it's not true now." She looks over at me. "From our first date, you made me feel things no one else ever had. I need you to believe me."

I barely hear her. Everything is starting to make sense. Adam started out trying to hurt me with Parvati, but somewhere along the way she must have gotten tired of the game. The fake Halloween party at his house—they'd been fighting before I got there. Maybe having sex with me right in front of him was her way of saying she was done blindly obeying him. And Adam didn't like it, so he decided to frame me for "Preston's" murder when he skipped town. He gets free and I get screwed—two-for-one deal.

"I swear I didn't know what he was planning," Parvati continues. "I thought it was just a stupid game."

"For once she's telling the truth. This was all me," Adam gloats. "Once I sold you on the idea of selling alibis at school, everything seemed to fall into place. I knew you'd hook me up with a cover story, especially if it meant getting me away from your girlfriend."

"So you left your bloody phone in my trunk, stole my shark's tooth, and called in a fake tip that we'd been arguing?" As much as what I just learned is killing me inside, I have to keep Adam talking long enough to figure out a way to distract him. I just need him to get sloppy with the gun for a second.

Just one second.

"Basically," he says. "But when I saw that dear old Dad had bailed you out, I figured he might have an attack of conscience and buy you a fancy lawyer who'd get you off on a technicality. I couldn't handle the thought of you going free.

I had to step up the plan one more time."

"So now you're going to kill me instead?"

"I'm going to kill both of you. I just haven't decided who to kill first."

"Me," Parvati blurts out. "Kill me first. I deserve it." She turns to me and mouths something that looks a lot like "you."

Adam aims his gun at her chest and shrugs. "Fair enough."

It takes me a second to realize what Parvati said was "now."

"Good-bye, Pervy." Adam's finger squeezes the trigger.

"No!" With my feet still bound, I lunge for him, just as flame bursts from the barrel.

THIRTY-NINE

THE ROOM EXPLODES WITH SOUND. From the corner of my eye, I see Parvati's body spasm. Blood blooms in the folds of her sari. "No!" I scream again. My arms attempt to circle Adam's waist as my head connects with his stomach. But he's stronger and heavier than me. He resists my tackle and pushes back. We land on the wooden coffee table, which collapses under our weight. My left arm ends up at the bottom of the pile, folded in a way that arms shouldn't fold. I howl in agony. My vision goes white for a second and I lose track of the gun. Then I forget the pain. Fists fly. I push Adam up and away from me. I throw punches in every direction. My arm feels like it's being pulled apart at the joints. I hear a

grunt and a stumble, and then the sound of the gun skitter-
ing across the floor.

Adam's fist connects with the side of my face. Warm liquid
flows. I turn and spit blood onto the cabin's floor. Parvati is
crumpled on the sofa, her skin pale, her sari a mess of blood.
I have no idea if she's alive, but I can't help her. Not until I
deal with Adam.

I flail toward him, lashing out at this face and throat.
"You bastard," I say. "Look what you did!" My ears are still
buzzing from the gunshot and my voice sounds hazy and far
away. "I loved her. And apparently she loved *you*. But all you
did was use her. You've never loved anyone in your whole life,
have you?"

Adam leaps back to his feet, his mouth dripping blood, his
chest caving with each breath. "I loved the Cantrells. But
you ruined that."

"You loved them? After what? A couple of hours together?"
I kick off one of my shoes and manage to free my feet from
the duct tape, which has loosened during our fight. I clamber to a standing position, gasping for breath.

Adam glances over at Parvati. "How long did it take you to
fall for *her*?" he asks. "Five minutes?"

"Fuck off." We stand there for a moment, dancing like
prizefighters and gasping for breath. The front door is

behind me. I could escape, maybe, but then what? Adam took my phone when he tied me up. I can't leave Parvati to die.

Adam doesn't seem interested in running away either. He could make it to the back door of the cabin, but instead he's slowly advancing toward me. And I won't beat him in a fistfight, especially not with what feels like a broken arm. Desperately, I scan the dimly lit room. Where the hell is that gun?

A glint of metal beneath the sofa catches my eye. Adam catches me looking and lunges a split second before I do. He lands on the ground. I land on top of him. We both grapple for the gun and it slides farther under the sofa—all the way against the wall. Screaming in pain, I push Adam away with my bad arm and snake my good arm into the darkness. My fingers close around something, but it's too rough to be the gun. Adam grins wickedly as he pulls his arm back. He's got the gun. I've got a broken coffee table leg.

He hops back to his feet and points the gun at my head. "Wood against bullets. Want to make a wager about how this turns out?" His eyes are gray fire.

"You should get some help for that gambling problem," I say, trying to get in position to attack him with the table leg. I curl my legs around so I'm on my knees. Now at least I can get up without putting weight on my injured arm.

"Your death will devastate poor *Darla*. That's what she gets for changing her mind."

Rage surges through me. My whole body tenses into a coil. "Don't bring her into this. You could've gotten adopted too if you'd stayed at Rosewood. You made the choice to become Preston DeWitt. You made the choice to *stay* Preston DeWitt."

"And now I'm making the choice to kill you. It's perfect, really. No one will suspect a dead man of murder." Adam's finger curls around the trigger once more. "Good-bye, Maximus."

FORTY

I WISH I COULD SAY my life passed before my eyes or that I found enlightenment in the moment when I knew I was going to die. But all I see is my sister Amanda's smile when she gave me the painted mug for my birthday. All I think about is Darla, and how she'll somehow blame herself for this.

And then I see a whirl of white and blood lunge toward Adam.

Parvati.

The side of her hand slams into the back of his knee. He stumbles. Just enough so that the gun barrel angles toward the ground.

It's all the opening I need. I swing my table leg like a

baseball bat. Wood collides with Adam's hand and the gun goes flying. He screams, but before he can even turn on me, I swing the leg again, this time at his head. I hear the sickening crunch of bone. Adam falls to his knees.

I drop the table leg and race to Parvati's side. She's lying atop the remnants of the coffee table, her ankles still bound with tape. There's bits of wood in her hair, and her ripped sari hangs crookedly on her body

Her skin is so pale. Almost gray.

"Hang on." I'm trying not to stare at the great blooming flower in her chest.

"Get the gun," she chokes out. Blood froths between her lips.

I glance wildly around the room. The gun lies next to the TV stand. Adam is sprawled out just inside the front door of the cabin. His phone is half buried in broken coffee table. I reach for it.

"The gun," Parvati repeats. "Not safe."

I get the gun and set it next to me. Then I put the phone on speaker and call 911. Keeping Adam in my sight, I press my palms to the bloody wound in Parvati's chest. Her heart beats in my hands.

The phone rings once. "You're going to be okay," I tell her.

Her lips twitch, almost a smile. "You're lying to me, aren't you?"

The phone rings again. "No," I assure her. "I'm done lying, to everyone."

The call connects. "Nine-one-one. What is your emergency?" the dispatcher asks.

"Someone's been shot," I say. "We need an ambulance."

"What is your location?"

"I. Shit—I'm not sure. A cabin in the Angeles National Forest. Parvati, can you—"

But she can't give me the address. Her eyelashes have feathered shut and her body is still. All I have to cling to are the faintest breaths escaping from her pursed lips.

"Hold while we triangulate your position," the dispatcher says soothingly. "Got it. Help is on the way. Stay on the line."

"Okay. Please hurry." My hands are still sealed to the wound in Parvati's chest. Her pale skin grows paler.

"You are not allowed to die on me," I tell her.

She doesn't answer. I try to imagine what she'd say, a smart-ass Parvati response, but my brain comes up empty. My stomach clenches. I put my ear to her lips to make sure she's still breathing.

She is.

Barely.

A few minutes later, a cavalry of sirens and flashing lights pull up outside the cabin. Ambulances, cops, and feds.

The paramedics take Parvati.

The police take Adam.

The FBI agents take me.

"Sorry I didn't get your message sooner," McGhee says.

I barely hear him. As I duck down to slide into the back of the unmarked sedan, I see the paramedics load Parvati into the ambulance. One of her arms dangles limply over the side of the stretcher.

For only the second time in my life, I pray.

FORTY-ONE

I END UP BACK IN the same bleach-smelling interrogation room. Things have come full circle, except for the fact that Parvati is apparently in surgery and the doctors don't know if she's going to make it.

The first thing I do is hand over the phone with the videos on it. I explain what's going on in the clips Adam showed me, looking away when they get to the one with Parvati. McGhee and Gonzalez excuse themselves to deal with "official business" and promise to return with coffee.

I almost ask them to bring some whiskey too. My arm is swollen at the elbow and pulsing with its own heartbeat. It feels like someone put it in a blender on high speed.

I should have gone to the hospital before being questioned,

but the pain had dulled on the ride back to Vista Palisades—adrenaline maybe—and I just wanted to get it over with. "My arm is killing me," I mumble when they finally return like an hour later.

"Your parents are in the lobby. They'll take you to the hospital once we're done here."

Ben and Darla are probably freaking out, but I'm glad someone called them. I don't want to be alone tonight.

McGhee hands me a cup of coffee. "But you have to stay away from Ms. Amos. There's still a restraining order against you, Max."

"I don't care. You guys can arrest me. I just want to be there in case—" My voice cracks. I can't finish the sentence. As hurt as I am by what Parvati did to me, it doesn't change the fact that my feelings for her were real. They *are* real. When you care about someone, you can't just turn that off because you learn they betrayed you.

"Why don't you begin at the beginning? We need to hear everything." For once there's no judgment or accusation in Gonzalez's voice.

"Okay." I take a deep breath. "So it all started the day I tried to get detention." I remind them about Liars, Inc. and the alibi. Then I tell them about the pictures I found in the trigonometry book, about going to Rosewood, about being adopted when I was ten. At one point, Gonzalez steps out in the hallway to take a phone call and McGhee has me wait until he returns before I continue. I rest my head on the cool metal table until he ducks back into the room. Then I tell them about Adam showing me the video clips and drugging me. As the lies multiply and the story gets more tangled and convoluted, I expect the agents to scoff at me and act all incredulous—well, Gonzalez, anyway. But when I finish my tale about accidental shootings, planted evidence, fake adoptions, and one very psychotic kid named Adam Lyons, all McGhee says is, "Thanks, Max. You should probably get that arm looked at now."

Then his cell phone rings. He answers it, says "I see" a couple of times, and then gets up to leave. "Thanks for coming down," he says. "We'll be in touch."

"Wait. What?" My voice rises in pitch. "What about Parvati and me? Are you going to tell people where you got the videos? Are you going to put us in some kind of witness protection program? Senator DeWitt will kill us if he finds out we handed those over."

"The judge is issuing an arrest warrant for Remington DeWitt as we speak." McGhee fiddles with his tie. "You won't have to worry about him."

"Already? How? I thought hidden videos weren't admissible evidence."

"They're not usually," he says. "But when we confronted

Claudia DeWitt with that footage, she cracked and confessed everything. That's what took us so long to get back to you. We were next door, interrogating her."

I remembered Adam saying Claudia had always been the tortured one, the guilty one. Maybe all this time she had been waiting for a chance to make things right—as right as they could be, anyway. "So then it's over?" I ask. "Just like that?"

"I'm sure DeWitt will make bail, so if you feel threatened at any time you can contact the local police for protection. But we have no immediate plans to tell him you were the one who gave us the phone. As far as he knows, it was Adam that turned it in."

"And what happens to Adam?"

"Two counts of murder, plus kidnapping plus attempted murder? I'd say he's going away for a long time, but I'm sure he'll try to get off on an insanity defense." McGhee yawns. "Either way, he won't be bothering you or your girlfriend for a while."

"Speaking of Ms. Amos," Gonzalez says. "That call I got was an update on her condition. She's out of surgery. Her condition is still critical, but the doctors think she'll pull through."

I exhale deeply, my body slumping back in the chair as the air leaves my lungs. A knot forms in my chest. "That's good,"

I say. "Thanks for telling me."

"Remember. You can go to the ER, but you're not allowed near the ICU where she's staying, okay?" McGhee says. "And technically the nurses can't give you any information about how she's doing."

"I'm just glad she's hanging in there."

"If she's still your girlfriend, maybe her parents will be willing to update you," Gonzalez offers. "Give them a phone call. The restraining order doesn't extend to them." It's probably the nicest thing he's ever said to me.

"I don't even know what she is to me anymore," I admit. "It's complicated."

My whole life went from simple to complicated because of one little lie.

I'm ready for things to be easy again.

EPILOGUE

December 17th

IT'S A WEEK LATER WHEN I finally get my birthday dinner.

The FBI kept their promise, and so far no one has gotten wind of the fact that Parvati and I were involved in Senator DeWitt's arrest. Still, I had to tell Darla who Adam really was. I didn't want her to read about the kid she almost adopted going crazy in the newspaper. She took it like I expected, blaming herself for everything that happened. I reminded her she did what she thought was right for her family at the time, and that a lot of other factors contributed to the person Adam became.

Then I told her I was really glad she made the choice she did. She got a little teary-eyed at that.

The *LA Times* broke the whole story, from the accidental

shooting of Preston DeWitt to the fake adoption to everything Adam Lyons did. The senator resigned from politics and DeWitt Firearms. Claudia DeWitt took a deal from the DA to testify against him. I don't know where Adam ended up. McGhee told me he was transferred to a lockdown psychiatric facility and that Parvati and I would be notified if his status changed.

"Table for four?" The Steak Shack waitress smiles down at Amanda. "Do you want a kids' menu?"

"I'm a vegetarian," my sister informs her.

The waitress laughs. "I'll take that as a no." She seats us at a long table next to a giant plastic Christmas tree covered in fake snow and silver tinsel. Amanda immediately begins to speculate if the wrapped boxes arranged around it have real presents in them. The waitress gives us each a plastic menu shaped like a cow and disappears into the back.

I ball up my straw wrapper and launch it across the red-and-white-checked plastic tablecloth at Amanda. She giggles and takes aim at me with her own wrapper. The crumpled ball pings directly off the center of my chest.

"Nice shot," I say. She flashes me a grin before building a catapult out of a salt shaker and a spoon. The waitress returns with glasses of water and a fake smile. She tries not to stare at the remnants of our wrapper war.

"Settle down, guys," Ben says. "Time to order." We end up

with three steaks and one spinach salad. Ben digs right in, but Darla seems more interested in cutting her prime rib into teensy tiny pieces than in actually eating it.

"If you cut that any smaller it's going to be a liquid," I say. "Are you planning on taking some home for the twins?"

Darla laughs nervously. She blots her mouth with her paper napkin, even though I'm pretty sure she hasn't taken a single bite. "So, Max. We have a couple of things to discuss with you since you're now eighteen."

Uh-oh. Hopefully they just want me to start thinking about what I'm going to do after high school or something. It's a discussion I've been expecting for a while, but, jeez, you'd think it could wait until after my birthday dinner.

"What's up?" I ask.

"Your da—um, Ben and I made some calls. If you're interested in changing your last name back to Keller, we can help you fill out the paperwork."

That's what this is about? I've never even thought about changing my name.

"Don't do it." Amanda kicks me under the table. "I want you to stay my brother."

I see her smile in my head, the one she gave me with my birthday mug, the one I flashed back to when I thought I was going to die. "Mandy, I will always be your brother."

She plucks a slice of tomato out from under a mountain

of spinach and holds it up for closer inspection. "Promise?"

"Fork please," Darla says.

I snatch the tomato out of Amanda's hand and pretend to take a bite out of it. She smiles, but it's a fake smile, mouth only.

"I swear on, uh, this tomato." I make the sign of the cross on it and pitch it back onto the top of her salad. She stabs the tomato with her fork.

I turn back to Ben and Darla. They're both smiling at us, even though Darla's trying to look stern. I feel horrible for the way I've held them at a distance all these years, for the way I never even gave them a chance to be my parents. I could have missed out on so many things because I was afraid to trust them.

You know what, though? I don't think I did. They loved me too much to let me sabotage our relationship. Even though I did my best to keep them locked outside, they found their own ways into my life. When Adam pointed that gun at me, all I thought about was them—my family.

Ben, Darla, and Amanda are my family. And, okay, even the twins, though I can't wait until they outgrow their insane screaming phase. Still, it's a pretty amazing package, and I'm not ever letting anyone—least of all myself—take it away from me.

"Actually, I kind of like being a Cantrell," I say. As I reach out and pat Darla on the hand, I try to squeeze out the word "Mom," but I can't quite make it happen. But just because I can't say it, doesn't mean I don't feel it.

Darla sniffles and I keep talking so that she doesn't break down right here at the Steak Shack. "Well, then," I continue. "If all the boring stuff is out of the way, let's go back to having fun." I launch a packet of sugar at Amanda with her salt shaker catapult. She drops her fork and catches it.

Ben clears his throat. "There is one other order of business."

Oh boy. He sounds very serious. I fiddle with the edge of my cast. Maybe this is the part where I get the lecture. "Yeah?"

Ben hands me a white box with a blue ribbon. "This is for you."

Everyone watches as I untie the ribbon and lift up the top. Inside it are a manila envelope and a birthday card shaped like a drum. The card looks like it's for an eight-year-old, but at least Darla didn't get one of those ones with poetry verses and people holding hands around a lake.

I flip open the card and the keys to Ben's truck fall out. I almost don't recognize them without his ginormous work key chain attached. "I don't understand," I say.

"We didn't know what your plans were regarding college," Darla says. "But we figured that no matter what you were going to need something to drive." Her face brightens into a smile. "The car seats fit better in my car, anyway."

I am, literally, speechless. I broke down and told Ben and Darla the whole story after most of the charges were dropped, including how Langston and Marcus got rid of my car. They were less than thrilled. I never expected them to give me 50 percent of their wheels.

"Thank you," I finally manage to choke out. A lump forms in my throat, but I swallow it down. Now I'm the one in danger of losing it at Vista Palisades's *numero uno* family restaurant. I blink hard as I turn my attention to the manila envelope.

I undo the clasp, figuring my birth certificate or some other legal junk they felt compelled to give me is inside. I peek inside and see a letter and what looks like a bank statement. I can't help it—I look at the bank stuff first. The statement's in my name. My jaw drops. I glance over at Ben. "This can't be right."

"We didn't read that," he says. "Straight from the lawyer. It's not our business what your dad left you."

My fingers shake a little as I read the letter.

Dear Max,

Enclosed you will find information regarding Alexander Keller's assets at the time of death, 100 percent of which was bequeathed to you, Max

Alexander Keller, now Max Alexander Cantrell. This amount is payable in full on or after your eighteenth birthday.

Please contact my office at your convenience for more information.

Sincerely,

Roy Tanner, Attorney at Law

"Holy sh—crap," I say. Darla clucks her tongue. Amanda looks at me curiously. I slide the paperwork back in the envelope and put the envelope back in the box. I never really thought about my real dad's estate. It's going to feel weird having money. "Dinner is on me," I say with a grin.

"Absolutely not." Ben grins back at me. "But we'll let you buy dessert from the Cupcakery if you insist."

"Sounds like a plan," I say, but I'm already plotting one more purchase. If they can give me Ben's truck, I can replace it with a better vehicle for them—a nice one, like my family deserves.

As Darla pulls her car into the driveway, the sun hovers just above the horizon, painting the sky a mix of pinks and oranges. Wind sends a cloud of the neighbor's grass clippings spinning across the lawn. It's a beautiful Southern California evening.

But there is something even more beautiful sitting on the front steps. Parvati. She's dressed in camo pants and an olive-green long-sleeved shirt. Her hair is back in a ponytail so tiny that she must have hacked off a couple more inches at some point. I don't think she's wearing a speck of makeup, but somehow she's never looked more stunning.

Amanda bounces out of the car while I'm still gathering my thoughts. "Hi, Parvati," she bubbles. "I heard you were in the hospital. Are you better now?"

"I just got out today." Parvati pulls the collar of her shirt down slightly to expose the edge of a gauze bandage. "I'm mostly better but I'm going to have a really cool scar."

"No way," Amanda says. "I know this other girl with CF like me and she has a scar—"

"Let's let Parvati and your brother talk, okay?" Darla steers Amanda into the house.

Ben disappears into the garage. I sit next to Parvati on the steps, both of us staring straight ahead, watching the bits of grass dance across the driveway.

Parvati opens her mouth to speak, but then the door squeaks and the twins' babysitter slides out of the house. She bounds down the front steps and heads toward a car parked across the street. Parvati and I watch as she pulls away from the curb.

"I'm glad you're okay," I say finally.

"You too." She turns to me, her eyes lingering on my cast.

"Simple fracture," I say. "No big deal."

She nods. "My parents dropped the restraining order so I could come give you this." She tosses me a rectangle of white fabric, tied closed with a plastic bow. It looks suspiciously like a piece of the sari she wore to Pres's funeral.

I untie the ribbon and fold back the cloth. My shark's tooth pendant spills out onto my palm. The cord is mostly burned away, but my breath catches in my throat as I finger the sharp point of the tooth. "Thank you," I say. "But how?"

"I stole it out of the evidence locker."

"Parvati! You're going to—"

"I'm kidding," she says. "My mom heard that Adam confessed to setting the fire. I knew they wouldn't need it anymore. We went to get my dad's gun back, and I asked her to pull some strings. I think she might have had to sign that she was part of your legal counsel to get it." Her eyes flick up to meet mine. She tugs at the ends of her hair. "I guess I should go so you can be with your family, huh?" The muscles in her jaw strain against her skin. I can feel how scared she is as she waits for my response.

I make her wait longer than I should, but there aren't words for everything I'm feeling. Or if there are, I don't know them. Finally I say, "You don't have to leave."

Her dark eyes grow damp and she immediately turns

away. She counts to five under her breath and turns back, her face a mask of composure. "Do you *want* me to stay? Because if not, I don't need your pity."

"I mean, you got yourself shot and still managed to save my ass," I say lightly. "That's probably worth a cupcake."

The joke falls flat. "You don't owe me anything." Parvati starts to stand. "I know how bad I hurt you."

I reach out and touch her arm. "Hey. I want you to stay."

She exhales a single, shaky breath as she lowers herself back to the porch. "Really? It's just, you didn't come see me in the hospital. You didn't even call."

"Sorry. Once we knew you were going to be okay, Darla started bugging me to catch up on schoolwork, and then I had to deal with all this legal stuff. The awesomeness that is my lawyer helped me get my charges reduced, but what's left still scored me a month of suspended-sentence jail time and about ten million community service hours." I rake a hand through my hair. "I guess I wasn't too eager to get in more trouble by violating a restraining order."

"Oh." Parvati's voice is barely a whisper. "I thought maybe you didn't even want to be my friend anymore."

"Is that what you want?" I ask slowly. "To be friends?"

Her eyes water again, and this time she doesn't fight it. "No, but I don't want to lose you totally, so I can settle for that."

I snort. "Parvati Amos? Settling? I'll believe it when I see it."

A smile plays at her lips. "I still want to be with you, Max. But maybe I don't get to have everything I want. I feel like we broke up. Did we?"

"I sort of stopped thinking of you as my girlfriend when I found out you dated me as a dare."

"I guess I can understand that." Her lower lip trembles and a single rogue tear cuts a slick path down her cheek. "You want to hear the whole story?"

"Probably not," I admit. "But it's okay if you want to tell it."

She nods. "I was going to tell you everything after the funeral, I swear." Her body trembles slightly. She looks down at the porch. "I met Pres, Adam, whoever, freshman year. For some reason I just . . . liked him. He was different from most of the kids at Bristol. More raw. More real." She laughs bitterly. "Or so I thought. We got up to all kinds of trouble, and I told myself we were besties, partners in crime. In reality I was just some girl he screwed when he was bored." Her thick eyelashes glisten with tears. "I never should have listened to him. What I did was thoughtless and cruel." She looks up. "I was so blind. I let him use me to *hurt* you. I know how pathetic that is."

Sometimes I think I'm the worst sheep of all. I remember the tiny flash of vulnerability I saw the night of "Preston's" New

Year's Eve party. Adam played her, just like me. And I can understand what it's like to do dumb things for something that feels like love.

She turns away from me and blots at her eyes again. "I hate being pathetic."

I reach out and touch the back of her arm, squeezing gently. "You're not pathetic," I tell her. "You're just human, that's all."

She shakes her head. "I know I let you down, just like I let down my parents, and everyone else." She turns back to face me, her emotions once again under control. "I'm sorry."

"I thought you didn't believe in apologies."

"I'm beginning to think I was wrong about everything." She sighs. "I have so much to make up for. I can't believe I have to leave in a couple of weeks."

A fist clenches in my stomach. My feelings for Parvati are all tangled up, but I can't imagine surviving the spring semester without her. Still, maybe her parents are right. Maybe she does need to get away for a while. "It'll probably be good for you, you know? Help you with the coke thing."

"I don't have a *coke thing*, Max," she huffs. "I only did it every once in a while, and I quit soon after we started dating. Unfortunately, I had a little left and my mom found it in my room."

"You quit using because of me?"

"You made me realize I didn't need it," she says.

As I try to figure out what she means, she continues, "Remember our first date?"

"Yeah." I took her to this place called Rings Rock that you can only get to at low tide. The ocean rolled in and we had our own private island for the day. We ate sandwiches and went swimming, and when we were in the water together she kissed me in a way that pretty much guaranteed I could have whatever I wanted from her. I feel kind of sick thinking about it, now that I know it was part of a dare.

"You went on and on about how pretty and cool I was, about how much you liked me." The edges of her mouth turn upward.

"Did I? God, what a loser."

Her smile gets bigger. "Of course I thought you were just trying to get in my pants, which was perfect since it's what I had planned from the start. But then you rejected me."

"I wouldn't say I *rejected* you. It just didn't feel like the right time, you know?" Mostly I was scared I'd disappoint her or get caught with my trunks down by the Jacobsen brothers.

"Yeah." She nods. "But then I realized all that stuff you said—you really meant it. You liked plain old me. No coke. No craziness. You didn't want to hear about my future plans.

The person I was at Rings Rock was enough for you."

"More than enough."

"No one else has ever made me feel like that. Especially not Adam. Maybe it doesn't matter, but I never let him touch me after I was with you." She pauses. "I'm going to do whatever it takes to make things up to you. I'm already trying to think of ways I can get kicked out of Blue Pointe."

And even though she's never said it, I finally know for sure how she feels about me. Darla was right about what love is. And there is apparently no end to the stupid stuff Parvati will do for the people she loves.

But do I love her back?

Maybe. I hate seeing her in pain. I want her to be happy.

Is that enough?

I don't know.

Can you ever really know? Trust doesn't come easily to me, and if I stay together with Parvati we'll have to rebuild it almost from scratch. I'm not going to lie, though. There are a lot of things I'd enjoy doing over with her.

I study her expression, trying to memorize what love looks like, just in case things don't work out. Apparently, it looks vulnerable, like a dog that's been hit by a car. Just lying there on the pavement, waiting for you to run into the street and scoop it up in your arms.

I think I would run into the street for her.

I can't help it. I lean in close to brush my lips against her jawbone. She's so warm. She smells so good—no perfume, no cinnamon. Just softness. "Don't get kicked out. It's only a semester. Besides, I recently came into a little money, so if you're nice, I *might* even come visit you."

Parvati bites at her lower lip. "Really?" One word. So much hope.

"Let's take it a day at a time and see what happens," I say.

"Okay." She reaches out for my hand. "Do you know why I love you, Max Cantrell?"

I let her slip her fingers between mine. "Because your dad hates me?"

"No."

"Because I recently came into a little money?"

She laughs her tinkly little laugh. "Because you make me want to be better." Lifting her chin, she stares at me with her dark eyes. Her breath is a whisper against my skin.

I squeeze her hand as I tilt my head low. Our lips brush, just barely, and it feels like something worth saving.

The front door slams. "Eeeew," Amanda says. "You guys are gross." Sighing, I turn toward my sister reluctantly. She's holding a cupcake in each hand. "Mom says it's time for cupcakes and to tell Parvati she's invited."

I arch an eyebrow. "You want to stay?"

"Sure." Parvati lets me pull her to her feet. She keeps hold of my hand as we follow my sister inside. "Cupcake time," she tells Amanda. "My favorite time in the whole world."

I lean close to her. "Liar," I whisper in her ear.

"Sometimes," she admits. "But I'm working on it."

ACKNOWLEDGMENTS

MUCH LOVE TO MY FAMILY and friends for being awesome and putting up with my insane schedule and volatile mood swings throughout the writing and revising of this book. I think the end result was worth it. I hope you agree.

Thanks to Jennifer Laughran, Karen Chaplin, the amazing staff at HarperTeen, the YA Valentines, my street team members, and everyone who takes the time to rate or review my books. Your feedback—the positive and the critical—is invaluable to me.

I had a lot of early readers who helped me take this book to the next level: Cathy Castelli, Marcy Beller Paul, Jessica Fonseca, Ken Howe, Antony John, Heather Anastasiu, Tara Kelly, Howard Price, Ben Oris, Stacee Evans, Sarah Reis, and Surbhi Patel. Thanks to all of you for serving as betas or experts. Other people who rock: All of Team Canada—there are too many of you to name, but you know who you are. Jessica Spotswood and Elizabeth Richards, for email therapy and believing in me. Christina Ahn and Jamie Krakover, for being my St. Louis blogger-reader-writer friends forever. Monica Lopez, for always playing WITWI and teaching Parvati and me how to search by image. And of course Nikki Wang, for ALL CAPS, endless support, and general Nikki Wangishness. None of you are ever allowed to change.

And as always, thanks to the readers. There are so many other things you could be doing, so many other books you could pick up instead. Thank you for making it possible for me to live my dreams.